For Jenni'

Aminah

8/8/09

Dreaming of America

Dreaming of America

Armineh Helen Ohanian

To order additional copies of this book, contact:
Xlibris Corporation
1-888-795-4274
www.Xlibris.com
Orders@Xlibris.com
16711

To my husband, without whose help
and encouragement this book would not have been possible.
Also to all my loved ones.

Contents

CHANGE OF LIFE

On a late August night in Tehran in 1988, a tall, slim woman shrouded in a black silk *chador* walked briskly on the crowded Sadi Avenue. She appeared tense as she nudged her way through a throng of dark-complexioned men and covered-up women. The woman in the black *chador* turned hurriedly into a dark alleyway. She scurried past a few dimly lit, three-story apartment buildings and stopped in front of a small, redbrick house with tightly drawn shutters. She hammered five swift knocks at the gray wooden door and waited, trembling with fear.

"Please do open the door before a patrol car shows up!" Leyla, the black-*chador*—covered lady, told herself as she drew the veil tighter around her delicate face and sculpted figure.

Leyla could hardly wait to get inside the house. She feared that if, by bad luck, Ayatollah Khomeini's police, the *pasdars,* were to suddenly appear in their patrol cars, they would undoubtedly arrest her.

"No," Leyla whispered to herself, as she glanced nervously about. *"It would be fatal if the pasdars find me here!"* Indeed, if she were arrested, her husband, General Farhad Shirazi, who was hiding inside the dark house, would be discovered and executed.

Seconds passed like hours as she stood in front of the door in the dark alley. She could hear her heart drumming loudly in her ears. Every sound coming from the main, well-lit street, made her jittery.

As soon as the door opened, Leyla shot inside like a gust of wind. She breathed a sigh of relief the moment she set foot into the foyer, decorated by a red-and-beige Isfahan carpet and some family pictures on the wall. Leyla now felt safe from the dangers lurking outside in the dark.

"*Salaam*," she greeted Mohsen, a young, slim guy of medium height, wearing a pair of striped black-and-white pajamas and brown leather slippers. "Is Farhad in the basement?" she asked timidly.

"Yes," Mohsen answered with a lopsided smile, "I was just about to let him know that it is safe for him to come upstairs."

"Don't bother please, I'll visit him in the basement," Leyla said and hurried down the concrete steps leading into a cold basement. She could hardly wait to throw herself into the strong arms of Farhad, whom she had not seen for over a month.

After the Shah's downfall in 1979, General Farhad Shirazi, one of the Shah's high-ranking officers, having miraculously escaped execution, had been hiding in the basements of friends and relatives for nine years. All the Shah's officers and ministers, after Khomeini's takeover of the government, were put to death. For some reason, during the turmoil of the revolution, the *pasdars* had not immediately sought to capture General Shirazi, and by the time they had started looking for him, Farhad had already gone underground. From then on, Farhad Shirazi had become one of the most wanted men, with a price on his head. But the general's benefactors had managed to confuse Khomeini's *pasdars* by regularly moving him from one hideaway to another. Presently, however, the situation had changed and Farhad's hideouts were becoming unsafe. It was time for him to escape.

Farhad was opposed to the idea of leaving Iran, where he had spent almost all fifty-five years of his life. What's more, he hated the thought of being away from his family, even though he hardly ever saw them now. Leyla, who was desperate to save the life of her husband, had tried to persuade him to escape whenever she had had a chance to visit him at one of his hiding places.

"The time bomb is ticking away. You've got to save yourself."
Leyla insisted that night at Mohsen's house, the moment she
stepped into the gloomy and cold basement where her adored
husband was hiding. Not only did she love him dearly, but she
also found him to be the most attractive man on earth.

Farhad smiled absently but did not respond to Leyla. He
appeared to be millions of miles away. He did not even seem to
notice the worry lines on his 45-year-old wife's delicate visage.

"That wretched Hooshang won't give up!" she added heatedly.
"I wish he'd drop dead!"

Farhad stared vacantly at the austere cement-paved floor,
still not answering his wife.

"I know what you're thinking about . . . it's hard for me too,
but we've got to make a move. Listen, you have no choice!"

Farhad tucked his hands into his faded blue jeans and began
pacing the length of the musty, cold basement. He tottered back
and forth despairingly, trying to come to terms with the idea of
his escape. He was well aware that the situation was not as it
used to be. Hooshang Afshan, an ex-colleague of Farhad's from
the old days when Farhad was a young officer in the Shah's army,
had recently been appointed as the head of Khomeini's Secret
Police and was out to get him. He had hated Farhad to death
during those days because of a rivalry in their careers, and now
he was in a position to get back at him.

Hooshang had instructed the revolutionary guards to intensify
their search for the capture of the deposed general. He personally
had appeared on national television and urged the noble citizens
to help the revolutionary government capture the enemy of the
nation.

Leyla gazed at her husband and found it heartbreaking to
see her hero turned into such a wreck! He once was a strong and
dynamic man whose presence commanded respect from
subordinates and friends. He was a witty, driven, good-tempered
and humorous person who used to bring joy to his household.

Now, Farhad Shirazi was a different person. He looked aloof and hardly ever smiled. His brow was permanently marked with deep frown lines and his eyes were melancholic. The Shah's downfall and his own sorrowful situation had turned him into a depressed, frustrated and angry man. His fervor for life was lost and his mind was filled with negative thoughts.

"I know that you want to hang on until Khomeini's regime collapses." Leyla said and paused, watching Farhad lower his tall, well-built body onto the sagging cot which had served as his bed for the past two weeks. "But, you know better than I that it won't happen during our lifetime. Besides, now we have Hooshang to worry about."

Farhad stared hopelessly at the low, cement ceiling of the basement and its dark walls. He had had enough of these foul-smelling, tomblike habitats. *"The only good thing about escaping,"* he thought, *"will be that at least I would be able to enjoy some daylight which I haven't seen for years."*

"Are you listening to me?" Leyla demanded, letting the black *chador* slip off her head onto her shoulders, revealing a mass of her dark, shoulder-length, wavy hair. "The situation has become very dangerous, thanks to that monster, and your hideouts are not safe anymore!"

Farhad finally replied, "Yeah, I heard you . . . I know!"

"Then, what do you say? Come on, we don't have all the time in the world!"

Farhad sprang to his feet angrily and glared at Leyla. "Leave me alone!"

"How would that help the situation?"

"I don't know . . . What do you want me to do or say? Do I have any power? Do I have freedom to decide?"

That was absolutely true. There was nothing Farhad could do about his fate. His hands were tied and his power was taken away from him a long time ago. The once-powerful general was now like a wounded bird with a broken soul whose wings had been savagely ripped away from his body. What's more, for a person who had served Iran with utter devotion during the Shah's reign, it was demeaning to be branded as the enemy of the nation. He, who loved his people with all his heart and soul! But, as far as Khomeini was concerned, Farhad had been the Shah's servant and could not be anything but the nation's enemy.

Farhad started pacing the length of the basement again, taking deep breaths to compose himself. He turned to his wife shamefacedly and said, "I'm really sorry to have flared up at you."

Leyla sighed and said softly, "It's okay; don't worry."

Forcing a sad smile at his caring wife, Farhad continued to walk back and forth. Pacing the basement was what he usually did during daytime in his gloomy cells, as this helped him kill time and take his mind off his unbearable situation. This time, however, he was facing the reality of having to abandon his family and beloved country. Farhad knew that Leyla was right. The *pasdars* were apt to capture him any day. Farhad also knew that he had no right to endanger the lives of his benefactors and their family members. If he was caught, everybody involved with him would be in deep trouble.

"Leyla, you, my lovely daughter Jalleh, my caring son Jamshid, as well as all these good people, are entitled to a peaceful and happy life . . . ," Farhad started saying.

"Meaning?" Leyla cut in.

"Meaning I have no right to be selfish. I think you're right. I have to go, whether I like it or not."

"Farhad, it's not about us. It's about you . . . I want you to stay alive, and I'm happy that you have finally decided to leave!"

The general smiled weakly at Leyla and told himself that she was a jewel! Farhad found her very pretty with her thick, dark hair and charming black eyes. He loved her tall and trim figure, which she carried as gracefully as if she were a swan gliding over smooth waters. What's more, he found Leyla compassionate, enterprising, bold and intelligent. Her strength of character was incredible! Indeed, not too many women could have endured the pain that the revolutionary guards had put her through! Leyla was constantly interrogated and tailed. She had had no rest all through the years of Farhad's hiding from the revolutionary officials and guards. Yet, Leyla always remained strong and never showed any signs of weakness. She tirelessly tried to find ways to keep her husband safe from the clutches of the *pasdars*. And now, she was about to meet with the head of the smugglers to arrange the details of the general's escape.

The smugglers were highly recommended by the general's Iranian and American military ex-colleagues in Washington. Several times before, Leyla had tried to hire different smuggling networks, but to no avail. Each time, the bandits had pocketed the initial payment and disappeared.

For Leyla—who ran their livelihood with the income earned from their small, two-story rental apartment building—it was infuriating to see the smugglers pinch their much-needed money. Leyla and Farhad had had the presence of mind to purchase an apartment building as an investment when Farhad was still earning a good salary and had the benefits of being a general during the Shah's reign. The Shirazi family owned another large house with a huge garden, where they still lived.

Before going underground, Farhad had managed to put away his yearly earned bonuses in Saderat Bank for several years, which Leyla had tried not to touch. Their bank savings was equivalent to $60,000 in Iranian currency. Having some money in the bank gave Leyla a sense of security. She believed it would come in handy in case of emergency, or could be spent on wedding expenses when Jamshid, their young handsome son and their sweet and bubbly daughter Jalleh, decided to get married. At the moment, they were both studying at the University of Tehran. Farhad and Leyla were both very proud of their children, who took their studies and responsibilities seriously.

The smugglers and the general's friends from America contacted the Shirazi family through Simin, Leyla's childhood friend. The night before, Simin had called Leyla and asked if they could meet at Café Naderi for ice cream.

Sitting in Café Naderi overlooking Naderi Avenue, Leyla remembered how lively that street had been during the Shah's reign. Young, good-looking, well-dressed rich boys and girls used to parade along its sidewalks eyeing each other. How different the café looked now. Leyla pictured Café Naderi the way it used to be: cozy and pleasant, with a western atmosphere. During the summer nights, its first-class outdoor restaurant served excellent *steak tavehs.* She could still taste those delicious pieces of sizzling filet mignon put on the table in heavy black skillets in which they had been prepared. No other restaurant could match them in preparing such tasty *steak tavehs.* Leyla looked out with nostalgia through the brown glass panelled doors at the large garden that used to be the outdoor café. In those days, it was filled with all kinds of flowers and willow and cherry trees. The raised dance floor and the awninged bandstand had stood at the far end of the garden. It was such a fun place, where lovers and families enjoyed good times and good food.

Leyla recalled sitting with Farhad at a table covered with white, crisp tablecloth, beneath a low-branched cherry tree. Thoughts of the soothing, soft lantern lights, the perfume of the jasmines and roses, and the joyful music of the band brought tears to her eyes. If only she could bring those pleasant days back . . . if only she could feel happy again!

Presently Leyla and Simin sat at a wobbly table among morose—looking, *chador*-covered women and frigid bearded men. Ayatollah Khomeini's picture, which had now replaced the Shah's portrait, stared at the people in the café, with his penetrating dark gaze. The bearded man, who stood behind the dessert counter wearing a small, white, rimless skullcap that covered the crown of his head, looked typically Islamic. Clearly, every person and object in the café made people conscious that the ruler of the time was Ayatollah Khomeini.

Simin whispered through a mouthful of ice cream which tasted like rosewater, as she wiped the sweat off her brow with the back of her hand. "Your friends from the States called last night."

"Did they? About what?" Leyla murmured, fanning herself with her hand. The grimy, humming fan facing them on the counter did nothing to bring relief from the suffocating August heat. At least the cold ice cream helped a bit.

Simin, gazing at her cup of ice cream, shrugged as she answered, "They called about the general!"

Leyla pulled up the top of the *chador* that had almost slipped off her head, curved her black thin eyebrows and asked, "My general?"

"No, my general!" Simin teased her, smiling mischievously as she enveloped her head and half of her face tighter in the black, silk Iranian veil—*chador*.

Leyla giggled softly and gazed at her funny friend. *"Thank God for a loving person like Simin,"* she told herself. Indeed, what could she have done without the support of her devoted and kind friend? True, she had Jamshid and Jalleh living with her, which was a real blessing. They were both thoughtful and loving. However, it was Simin who always helped Leyla to cope with her fears.

"You have a rendezvous with the head of the smugglers to discuss Farhad's escape," Simin hissed in Leyla's ear. "He will be waiting for you at Zafar's jewelry store in the bazaar tomorrow morning at eleven," she pressed on, fixing a pair of worried eyes on Leyla. She was well aware that the Shirazi family was under the constant surveillance of the revolutionary guards. But Simin also knew that Leyla was adept at misleading the guards. The general's wife had learned how to escape a tail.

The following morning, cloaked in a black polyester *chador*, Leyla cautiously stepped through the back door into the bare and treeless blind alley. She then sneaked into the main street, mixing in with the crowd. Leyla was now safe from the hawkish gaze of the *pasdars;* she was now among the sea of *black crows.* All the black *chadori* women looked the same and there was no reason for her to be singled out.

Stopping a battered black-and-white cab, she climbed in

and asked the driver not to take other passengers. Taxi drivers in Tehran often stop and pick up a few more people headed along the same route.

"I'm in a rush. I'll pay you extra," Leyla told the jovial young driver with dishevelled curly black hair and unshaven visage. The driver accepted with a nod and sped away recklessly amid a sea of zigzagging and honking cars.

Once at the bazaar, Leyla trotted through a maze of narrow, winding streets bustling with *chadori* women and men wearing brown felt skullcaps. Their baggy trousers flapped rhythmically about as they trudged behind heavily laden, braying donkeys. She hated the way they heartlessly jabbed at the ribs of the poor, fed-up donkeys with short poking sticks.

The Tehran bazaar was huge, with its labyrinthine streets housed under a multitude of adjoining domes. A few years back, the bazaar roof had caught fire. Although most of it was repaired, some cracks still remained open, letting shafts of sunlight into the dark marketplace.

Leyla found herself in an alley where rows of spice shops were located, displaying large, multi-colored trays of curry, turmeric, black pepper and paprika.

The pleasant aroma of the spice and the delicious odor of simmering basmati rice and charcoal-grilled meat wafting from the nearby Shamshiri Restaurant made Leyla hungry. She wondered what her old mother, who was visiting her that day, was going to make for lunch. Leyla wished she could stop at Shamshiri after her meeting and have a hearty portion of *chello kebab* with grilled tomatoes and mixed pickles on the side.

Leyla crossed a muddy street lined with rows of shops carrying household goods, and then made a turn towards the clothes bazaar. A cool draft swayed the long drab-colored robes hanging on racks outside the stores. The smiling shopkeepers standing by the entrances tried to entice passersby to go inside their stores. Leyla shook her head, refusing them each time, as she hopped over puddles of muddy water in the unpaved lanes of the musty smelling bazaar. Around the corner from the clothes section were the fabric stores that sold bales of colorful cloth stacked all the way to the ceiling along the walls. Next came the jewellers' bazaar, which brightened up the area with its rows of glittering display windows.

A young, dark-complexioned and bearded shopkeeper bowed politely to Leyla from behind a long, L-shaped glass case of gold, rubies, diamonds, sapphires and emeralds. He introduced her to Gholi, the cheerful-looking head of the smugglers. Gholi greeted Leyla warmly and led her through a narrow opening into a small storage area at the rear of the shop. A blue-beige-and-red floral-designed Kashan carpet, serving as door, hung over the opening. Lifting the side of the carpet, they entered the room. The jeweller then sent for tea and in no time a small boy with an egg-shaped, shaved head entered, carrying a round brass tray with black tea, three small tumbler glasses, and a pot of lump sugar. Iranians drink tea out of small glasses instead of cups.

Leyla sank uncomfortably into a low, black vinyl-covered armchair in the small, dim room, amidst piles of cardboard boxes. She looked at the smiling eyes of Gholi staring at her from beneath a pair of bushy eyebrows and said without preamble, "I'm not paying you a single *rial*, not before I see some action with my own eyes."

"Of course, *khanum*, I understand you," the short, friendly smuggler reassured Leyla. Smiling broadly and exposing a row of uneven teeth, he continued, "I swear that you're going to be satisfied with us. We've helped hundreds of people escape from Iran."

"I'll believe it when I see it!" she said curtly. She had been burnt too many times to allow herself to trust any man, good tempered or not.

"I promise you that your husband will be out of Tehran within one week," the smuggler stressed.

RETALIATION

Farhad was the only one of the Shah's high-ranking officials to be hiding in Tehran. A few of the general's colleagues had escaped to America even before Khomeini's return to Iran; right in the beginning stages of the rebellion when Farhad had come home to Tehran from Khouzestan, where he had been serving as the military governor of that state. In those days, no matter how often Leyla had urged her husband to also escape and save himself from possible execution, he always refused.

"How can I turn my back on this sacred land and my family?" he had objected, believing that he could always serve Iran no matter whose rule it was under. "I've got a lot to offer to my country," the general had added. "Besides, Khomeini might need officers of my caliber."

"No way! He doesn't need you," Leyla had argued. "Do you really believe that Khomeini will trust somebody like yourself who has served the Shah faithfully for years?" And then without allowing her husband to respond she had added, "No my dear, he'll have you shot without batting an eye."

The general had nodded with consent as the truth of Leyla's statements made him conscious of the gravity of the situation. Suddenly, his enthusiasm had given way to disappointment and his world had shattered. Farhad had heaved a sigh, fixed Leyla with a poignant gaze and remembered the happy years they had spent together. He had shaken his head with dismay and told himself, *"Everything's gone . . . everything's destroyed, all because of the Shah and Khomeini!"*

"It's not fair, after all the sacrifices we made for the Shah!" Farhad voiced loudly to Leyla one day, before going underground, as he sat in their bright, spacious lounge. "He shouldn't have left us in limbo and saved himself. If he had only ordered us to use force against the troublemakers!"

"Well, what's done is done. Your duty now is to figure out how to stay alive," Leyla smiled sweetly at her bewildered husband. "It's a good thing you returned home from Khouzestan and . . ."

Farhad cut in, "I had to! I needed to find out whether I should put down the rebellion in my region or not."

Leyla was right. As soon as the old mullah came to power, he made it clear that he was in no mood to deal with the Shah's men. Khomeini wanted the arena completely cleared and cleansed of the Shah's crowd before setting up his official rule. And his revolutionary guards and the *Basij*—the fundamentalist hardliners—wiped the arena clean by butchering almost all of the Shah's high-ranking officials. They also killed anybody who appeared progressive-minded, moderate and non-fundamentalist. Blood was shed generously and without pity! Even innocent people were not spared. Neither were the minorities. Elghanaian, a Jewish industrialist, was put to death under the pretext of spying for Israel. Some Iranians, who were converted to Christianity from Islam by American missionaries, had their throats slit open by the *Basij*. Innocent citizens were dragged out of their homes and shot down like rabid dogs merely because their neighbors falsely accused them of being the Shah's sympathizers or American informers. It was a time of retaliation. Anybody who had the slightest grievance against a friend, relative or acquaintance simply went to the revolutionary headquarters and fabricated something about them. In the new Islamic Republic, people didn't feel secure even in the comfort of their own homes, not knowing who would accuse them of some false wrongdoing. All these atrocities were committed in the name of God. In reality, what Khomeini wished to accomplish was to rid Iran of the Shah's influence and create terror among his sympathizers. In the meantime, Khomeini strengthened and nurtured fundamentalist Islamic factions not only in Iran, but also in the Islamic countries. He also created the Hizbollah terrorist movement, which rapidly spread into Middle Eastern Islamic countries, whence terrorist activities emanated.

"I always knew that Khomeini hated the Shah and the Pahlavi dynasty, but never to this extent!" Farhad told Leyla a few days later, after Khomeini's slaughter of the Shah's officials. "You know where his hatred stems from, don't you?"

"No, tell me," Leyla said. She was not really interested in why Khomeini hated the Shah. She was merely concerned about the present. Leyla wanted to know what was going to become of her husband and how they were going to save him from the *Basij* and the *pasdars*.

"No, you tell me . . . what do you think?" Farhad said calmly, leaning back in his armchair, as if he had all the time in the world and as if everybody else but himself would be captured and put to death.

"Well, let me think," she tried to be polite. Deep inside she felt nervous and found that discussion a waste of time. "I know! Because the Shah westernized the country."

"But, darling, don't you think that the real architect of westernization was Reza Shah Pahlavi, the Shah's father?"

"Of course," Leyla agreed nonchalantly.

Indeed if Khomeini had to hate anyone it should be Reza Shah, the archenemy of Islamic fundamentalists. He stripped the mullahs of their power and tried to westernize the country very rapidly by brute force. Reza Shah ordered the policemen to tear the *chadors* off women's heads. Instead, he made them wear hats and western attires. During Islamic mourning days, *Moharam*—the anniversary of the martyrdom of Shiite Imams— Reza Shah ordered musicians to play cheerful music in the main squares of cities, towns and villages. Traditionally, on such days, long processions of black-attired men march all day long in the streets. They beat their chests and shoulders with chains, chanting repetitive sad verses, as wailing *chadori* women sit on rooftops and balconies watching them pass by.

Farhad finally explained, "Yes, Khomeini did hate the Shah's father for trying to westernize Iran, but the main reason for his hatred was because of the Shah's land reform project."

"What land reform are you referring to?" Leyla asked breezily.

Farhad looked annoyed with his wife's lack of interest in the conversation. "There's only one important land reform act. I'm talking about the land reform of the 1950s," he said firmly.

"I see."

Farhad, taking on a serious demeanor, went on, "In the early 1950s, the young Shah introduced the land reform act by breaking up large parcels of land belonging to prosperous village lords and distributing them among the peasants who worked like serfs on those lands."

Leyla looked confused. "Why would Khomeini be upset about that?"

"Very simple! Khomeini, at the time, owned a village called Khomein located near the city of Arak . . ."

Leyla blurted out, "I get it. Under the land reform act, he lost his village to the peasants."

"There you go!"

Farhad left his comfortable armchair and started pacing about with his hands clasped behind his back. "During World War II, the Allies exiled Reza Shah to South Africa and put his son on the throne."

Farhad went on to explain how the young Shah eased the pressure off the religious heads and gave people freedom to decide whether or not they wished to observe Islamic customs.

"If women wanted to wear *chadors*, it was all right with our ruler."

"Yes, but there were millions of women who preferred to be modern and keep up with the latest international fashions," Leyla stressed.

They both remembered how, during the Shah's reign, one could see women wearing miniskirts or western clothing walking alongside black *chadori* figures in the streets.

Farhad said, "Obviously, conservative Islamic women hated their westernized sisters, whom they called *'leg—and bottom-exposing prostitutes'*."

Leyla agreed with him and emphasized that neither did the religious fundamentalist men show any respect for the modern female population.

Farhad grimaced, "Yes, you're right. They pinched, abused and even sometimes raped them. Unfortunately, nobody, including people like myself, did anything to help those poor women."

"Except for the *Shahbanou* . . ."

"Yes, you're right," Farhad cut in. "The Empress did try to help women to some extent; she would have done even more if the Shah's reign hadn't collapsed."

Leyla, who was deeply immersed in her thoughts and had not heard her husband's words, grumbled under her breath, "The Empress established the Iranian Women's Rights Organization. But where is it now? What happened to the women's rights?"

Farhad, noticing his wife's sullen mood, said, "Well, our friend Khomeini took it upon himself to do away with all the good things that the Pahlavi Dynasty did for this land."

He then mulled over Khomeini's hatred toward the Shah and his father Reza Shah. Farhad remembered how, during the primary stages of the Shah's reign, Khomeini had fearlessly criticized the Iranian monarch.

"Do you know how arrogant Ayatollah Khomeini was toward the young Shah?" Farhad snorted and gazed at Leyla, awaiting some sort of reaction from her.

"I'm not exactly sure."

Farhad said, "Well, my dear, he accused our patriotic and devoted ruler of being an *'American Servant'*!"

Leyla appeared aloof and impassive.

The general gazed at the yard through the open window and watched a school of goldfish splattering noisily in the pond, as if they too were having a heated political discussion. Farhad smiled while still staring at the nervous school of fish and carried on, "Our ruler, being a fair person, did not arrest Khomeini. He merely sent word to him saying that if Khomeini continued with his subversive behavior, he would give the Shah no choice but to wear his father's *boots*."

"What exactly did he mean by that?" Leyla interjected.

"Apparently the tips of Reza Shah's boots were saturated with some sort of lethal venom. Rumor has it that when he kicked his opponents or those with whom he was displeased, they immediately died."

"Goodness, that's scary!"

"You think so? I wish the Shah had worn his father's boots. Because if he had, Khomeini wouldn't have come to power and so much blood wouldn't have been shed. Sometimes it pays to be ruthless with dangerous people!"

"So what was Khomeini's answer to the Shah's message?"

"Khomeini sent word back saying, 'Your father's boots are too large for you!'"

"Khomeini was right. The Shah was not as tough as his father," Leyla said, nodding her head.

"Yes, Reza Shah would have eliminated the arrogant mullah without a second's hesitation."

He then concluded, "When the Shah realized that Ayatollah Khomeini was not going to give up his subversive activities, he arrested and exiled him from the country."

"What was the point?" Leyla shook her head desolately. "Khomeini went on with his activities for years against the Shah even in exile, until finally he managed to rally large masses of supporters behind him."

Farhad sighed. "That's right! And it seems like our so-called allies, France, Germany, Britain and the United States backed him up and facilitated his plans for returning to Iran."

"How do you know?"

"Just common sense. Besides, how did he get to Iran?" Farhad asked, arching his eyebrows and went on without giving Leyla a chance to respond. "By an Air France carrier. Not Iran Air."

Farhad believed that the French had returned Khomeini to Iran with the consent of the British and U.S. governments.

"I wonder why they'd do such a thing?" Leyla asked casting her eyes down.

"You wonder why? Yes, so do I! I also wonder why they turned their backs to the Shah."

"God only knows."

"Well, one thing is obvious. They didn't need the Shah anymore."

Leyla pressed, "I think the Shah had become troublesome; he kept raising the price of the oil."

"You're so right! Also, I think the Shah became arrogant and too independent."

Leyla and Farhad continued with their political discussion, and as the hours went by, they got more and more immersed in the subject. They discussed how Khomeini prepared speeches on tapes when he was in exile and sent them to Iran for circulation among religious groups at bazaars. Then the tapes were duplicated and distributed among the people.

"Why at bazaars?" Leyla queried.

"I guess because bazaars in Iran, being centers of businesses, are very important to the Iranian economy. Besides, the merchants in the bazaars are very religious."

"What a smart man! How clever of him to start his activities through the *bazaris!*"

Farhad wondered why the Shah and top officials had never realized the importance of the influence of the *bazari* merchants upon the masses. What's more, he thought that the Iranian monarch should have changed his autocratic rule into a moderate, democratic system as soon as the signs of unrest had emerged. Or, if he did not wish to change his rule, he should have used his powerful army to suppress the rebellion.

"God knows why the Shah didn't react!" he told Leyla the following day. "Was it because he knew he was dying from cancer?"

Leyla shrugged. "Maybe, but even so, wouldn't you think that he would want to prepare the grounds for the smooth succession of his son to the throne?"

"I would think so."

GOING UNDERGROUND

At the time of the unrest, Farhad, a two-star general, was the military governor of the State of Khouzestan. While he worked and lived in the southern region of Iran, his wife and children stayed in Tehran. Schools and universities in the capital were far superior to those in the provinces, and Farhad wanted the best schooling for his two children. The general spent time with his family during holidays and vacations, while Leyla and the children went to live with him during summertime. Life went on happily and uneventfully until the beginning of the revolution, when Farhad returned to Tehran. To his dismay, upon his return, Farhad discovered that the army was falling apart. What's more, the Shah soon abandoned the country, leaving his cabinet members and the officials at the mercy of Khomeini. Then, a few days later, when Farhad's colleagues were arrested and executed, he reluctantly went underground.

The first day of the general's hiding at his second cousin Ardeshir's dungeon-like basement was the toughest day of his life.

Sitting alone on his bunk bed next to a brass table and a white-shaded lamp in the musty smelling cell, he pondered his fall from glory. It felt like he had plunged headfirst from the peak of a high mountain into a dark, nasty pit. He sat there limply for hours and mused over his wounded dignity. Farhad now understood why ancient Japanese warriors committed *hara-kiri* when faced with defeat and humiliation. He was more than humiliated; he was disgusted with himself because he cowardly hid when nearly all his colleagues were executed. Farhad thought of going upstairs and grabbing a kitchen knife. He thought that it would be much easier if he took his own life. He did not want to give the angry revolutionary guards the pleasure of executing him in public.

Farhad climbed the basement steps and struggled in vain with the doorknob. It was locked. It appeared that his cousin had locked the door from outside for safety. Frustrated, Farhad descended again and slumped back into his cot. As he sat there thinking, his mind gradually cleared from negative thoughts, he told himself, *"Maybe it is meant for me to stay alive and suffer humiliation."* Then he thought of Leyla and wondered what she would think of him if he were to commit suicide. *"A coward,"* he thought, *"that's what she would think I am."*

Farhad just sat glumly on his bunk bed and stared at the magazines strewn on the brass table. He reached for one, but immediately withdrew his hand. He was in no mood for anything; the pain within his soul was too intense. But what else could he do than to suffer the tortuous, slow-passing minutes of that never-ending day? Then, many agonizing hours later, the sound of some muffled footsteps was heard from above. Farhad now could tell that Ardeshir, a friendly, gentle young man in his late thirties, and his frail-looking shy wife, Parvin, were home from work. He soon heard the key turning in the basement door and Ardeshir descended the stairs to greet him.

"You can now come upstairs. It is dark outside and safe for you to leave the basement." Ardeshir said with a friendly voice.

Farhad and Ardeshir sat solemnly in the narrow, rectangular dining room with its shutters snugly drawn, waiting for the food to be served. Ardeshir stared pitiably at Farhad and thought that he had never before seen his dynamic cousin in such a melancholic mood. Farhad resembled a pale cadaver, slouched limply in the chair with his shoulders drooping like a weeping willow.

Ardeshir draped his arm around Farhad's shoulder and said

compassionately, "I guess there's no point in me asking you how your day has been, is there?" "

Farhad fixed his gaze bleakly on the opposite wall.

Ardeshir uttered softly, "I know . . . I know. You don't have to say anything."

Suddenly, Farhad burst out crying, with his shoulders convulsing uncontrollably, while Parvin, who was bustling around the table, quietly disappeared into the kitchen. She thought that it would not bring honor to a man of that caliber to have a woman standing by and watching him cry. Moments later she came out of the kitchen carrying the heavenly smelling celery *khoresh* and the rice. Parvin said, as she gazed bashfully at the floor, "I know I can never match Leyla's cooking, but I hope you'll like the *khoresh* and the rice!"

"Oh, I'm sure that you're a great cook," the general forced a sad smile. "I'm just not hungry."

"Come on!" Ardeshir insisted, "You need to store some energy in case you have to escape through rough mountainous routes."

Farhad gaped at Ardeshir glumly. "Who wants to escape?"

At the time when Farhad went underground he was forty-six. He was tall and of strong build. His dark gaze, sleek dark brown hair and strong features gave him a distinguished look. As a free man, Farhad had always carried his body upright. It was amazing how different he looked from one day of confinement, with his grim face and stooped frame.

As time went by, Farhad gradually succumbed to destiny. There was nothing else he could do but to endure dishonor and defeat. It was either to capitulate to solitude in basements, or be captured and die. Therefore, he gave in to his sad fate, living day by day in his dark, solitary cells, awaiting a miracle to change his life. In the meantime, he tried to occupy himself with reading and working out several times a day.

Although the *pasdars* were sure that Farhad was hiding in Tehran, they had no idea about his whereabouts. His benefactors regularly moved him from one household to another, making it impossible for Khomeini's police to find him. Presently though, the *pasdars* had widened their hunt for his capture by carrying out an intensive house-to-house search, and Farhad was running out of safe hiding places. What's more, Farhad and his family knew that they had no chance against their powerful enemy, Hooshang, who had made Farhad's arrest his personal priority.

Hooshang's animosity with Farhad went as far back as the mid-'60s, when they both served in the Shah's army as second lieutenants.

Being a jealous person by nature, Hooshang was in constant competition with Farhad, who happened to be a much more capable and gifted officer. This caused a great deal of frustration for him, and it later developed into hatred when Farhad's star started shining more and more each day.

Once they both participated in a military air show at the Mehrabad airport in the presence of the Iranian monarch and thousands of spectators.

The Shah and the viewers looked up at the bright, sunny skies of Tehran dotted with numerous skydivers, who zoomed down like shooting stars with arms and legs stretched out. Farhad and Hooshang, who were the last two jumpers, tried to resist the pull of gravity like all the others, before pulling the ripcord. At one point they descended side by side, almost colliding. But Farhad was in full control. He skillfully managed to put a safe distance between them. Hooshang landed first, while Farhad managed to continue a few moments longer with the free fall before pulling the ripcord.

There was a loud roar of applause as Farhad sprang to his feet immediately after landing, with his parachute trailing behind him.

That evening, during dinner, Farhad told Leyla, "Next thing I know I'm summoned by the Shah."

Leyla breathed, "How lucky! You saw the Shah?"

"Yes, Ma'am!"

"Tel me about him . . . how did he look? He's so handsome, isn't he?"

"Hey, you . . . watch out! No, really, putting jokes aside, he is very striking and stately looking."

"Were you nervous?"

"No, actually I wasn't. I had no reason to be. He asked me questions about my family and career and I told him everything."

Leyla threw her hands up in the air. "You are amazing! How can you be so cool and confident?"

Farhad laughed. That was true. He was blessed with a charismatic, confident and outgoing character. He had conversed with the Shah with the same ease as he normally would with his fellow officers.

From that day on, Farhad had many other occasions to come face to face with his ruler, and the Shah gradually got to know the young lieutenant in person. The Shah also learned from Farhad's superior officer that Farhad was an ambitious and brave character, willing to take on dangerous missions.

To test his loyalty and leadership qualities, the Iranian monarch instructed Farhad's superior to assign him to head sensitive military operations. Sometimes those assignments were dangerous and top secret; mostly revolving around tribal unrest. Farhad served his country with distinction and succeeded in putting down those rebellions, for which he received medals of honor from the eminent Shah of Iran.

Farhad became captain at a young age and was assigned to head a series of military training programs in the United States and Germany. Hooshang, who was still a second lieutenant, and who happened to be one of the five officers going to Germany in Farhad's group to study counterinsurgency, abhorred the idea of subordination to Farhad. However, he had no choice; Farhad was the superior officer and his commands had to be obeyed. Hooshang, being a scheming person, tried to create discord among the officers in the group, but to no avail. They were all serious and ambitious fellows, like Farhad, who were there to acquire valuable knowledge.

Hooshang had another serious problem: his poor knowledge of English. The study material, being quite complicated, made it practically impossible for him to follow the course. He, therefore, fell behind in his work, which in turn added more to his frustration. Within two months after the start of the course, Hooshang was forced to return to Iran and resign from the army altogether. Nine years after the establishment of the Islamic regime, he applied for a position in the government. Having had a clean record, with no history of loyalty to the Shah and a proof of devotion to Imam Khomeini, he reclaimed an assignment as the head of the secret police.

As soon as Hooshang attained his important position, he decided to reopen the almost dormant dossier of General Shirazi. This, he thought, would give him a great opportunity to try to get even with his previous rival.

"I can't wait to see him kneeling at my feet and begging me for mercy," he sniggered to himself, sitting behind a mahogany desk in his bright office overlooking the broad and crowded Avenue of Revolution.

The next thing Hooshang did was to increase the reward on General Shiraz's head. This, together with the broad house-to-house hunt for Farhad's capture, forced Farhad's family to contact the smugglers and persuade them to rush the plans for the general's escape.

THE TRUTH ABOUT

THE REVOLUTION

All through the nine years of his underground life, Farhad wrote letters to his friends living abroad, but never signed his name. He always closed the letters by the phrase, *"Your friend."*

The letters to Farhad from abroad were sent via Simin, Leyla's friend, without specifying the name of the addressee.

Once, Haro, an Armenian friend living in Paris, sent Farhad an old issue of the *International Herald Tribune*. Fortunately the postal clerks did not become suspicious of the manila envelope containing the newspaper. Western papers and journals were, and still are, not allowed into the country. If they had opened the envelope, not only would the newspaper have been confiscated, but the addressee would also have been summoned to the nearest police station for interrogation. The result would have been a whole series of complications for poor Simin and her husband. If that had happened in the early years of the Islamic Republic, the envelope would not have escaped the curious eyes of the clerks.

Farhad read the paper from the first page to the last, like a thirsty traveller in a desert stumbling upon a source of water.

The front-page article of the newspaper was about the Iranian revolution. Farhad was flabbergasted by what he read. In Iran nobody could ever accept that their revolution was engineered by the great powers from abroad! *Hadn't the will and the solidarity of the Iranian people caused the Shah's downfall,* as claimed by everybody?

At this time, Farhad was hiding at the house of Payman, a forty-year-old bachelor friend.

When Payman returned from work, Farhad greeted him with enthusiasm. They sat in the sitting room and had some vodka before dinner.

Payman obtained his bottles of vodka and wine from his Armenian friends who brewed their own alcoholic beverages secretly at home.

"What's up? Contrary to usual, you seem bubbly today," Payman smiled, arching an eyebrow inquisitively.

Farhad blurted out, "I have something important to tell you."

"What, good news?"

"No, nothing of the sort."

"What is it then?" Payman looked perplexed. He was well aware that nobody would dare to contact Farhad during the day. It was too dangerous.

Farhad smiled. "I couldn't wait all day to share with you the contents of an interesting article that I read in the 1980 issue of the *International Herald Tribune.*"

"Nineteen eighty? That's ancient!" Payman smiled, putting a friendly hand on Farhad's shoulder. "Anyway, how did you get it?"

"Yes, you're right. It is ancient. Haro had kept the newspaper all these years to send it to me at the proper time."

Farhad then lit a cigarette and carried on, "Last time Leyla visited me, she brought the newspaper along. But I couldn't read it immediately, because I was busy reading the *daijan Napoleon.* I only had a chance to read the old paper today . . ." Farhad shook his head and continued, "Man, wait till you hear what I read!"

Payman slumped into the living room armchair and kicked his shoes off. He took a deep, contented breath and said, "I'm all ears."

Farhad sipped his drink and started recounting the contents of the article as he fixed his eyes on Payman through a thick cloud of cigarette smoke.

"According to the *International Herald Tribune*, during the last days of the Shah's reign, Mr. Zbigniew Brzezinski, President Carter's National Security Adviser, suggested the U.S. stand by the Shah to the bitter end. However, Carter's other advisers in the State Department, as well as his Secretary of State, Cyrus Vance, advised him against it.

"They were convinced that the United States should support the political forces—including even Ayatollah Khomeini—who were trying to dispose of the '*Peacock Throne*'," Farhad said with a sigh.

"You're joking!" Payman jumped out of his armchair, almost spilling his vodka.

"No, I'm not." Farhad took on a serious demeanor. It had been a while since he had had the urge to discuss past political matters. He had never shown any interest in articles written in the Iranian papers concerning the Shah and the past politics. He knew that they were never written from an objective point of view.

"Okay. Go on. This sounds interesting." Payman sat back in his seat, looking eager.

Farhad added that, against the adamant opposition of Brzezinski, in December 1978 official U.S. contact was initiated with Ibrahim Yazdi, a member of Ayatollah Khomeini's coterie. Then, upon Mr. Vance's insistence, Carter consented to send an emissary to Ayatollah Khomeini for direct talks. As mentioned in the article, Farhad stressed, there was only one matter that everybody in the U.S. government agreed upon and that was the importance of being in touch with the Iranian military high command, no matter whom they supported.

"The irony is that the Iranian army was left in limbo without any instructions from their superiors on how to react." Farhad sighed and continued sullenly, "So, the troops refused to use force against the demonstrators, who greeted them with bouquets of flowers."

Payman laughed. "Yes, there was no real army for anybody, including the United States government, to rely upon during the time of the unrest!"

Farhad nodded with consent, "Exactly! During the upheavals I waited to receive orders from Tehran to do something in my region about the unrest." He shook his head and added, "Nothing . . . there was no news whatsoever from Tehran. I called the headquarters several times. Nobody would answer the telephones."

"That's when you came back to Tehran."

"Exactly."

The same was true with other commanding officers. Their hands were tied and they felt useless without the existence of strong leadership. It was a daunting situation.

Farhad sighed, "What good were the officers when they did not have any power to bring about stability?"

Payman agreed. Indeed, the sudden change of political situation in 1978-'79 had been mind-boggling for him too.

They reminded each other of all the signs of unrest and destruction in Iran. There was violence everywhere. Military trucks, police cars, liquor stores, cinemas and banks were being burned. People carried arms and became a danger to one another. They were no longer afraid of speaking their minds against the Shah.

This reminded Farhad of an interview with the Shah by an aggressive young female reporter on national television. The general was stunned to hear the bold questions addressed to His Majesty. This took place a few days before the Shah's downfall, when Farhad had returned to Tehran. He could not believe how subdued his ruler looked and how patiently and meekly he responded to each of the reporter's questions. Such a thing had never happened before.

That day Farhad became disheartened in everything he had believed in and started worrying about the future of his country. Millions of troubling thoughts circled in his head. He was afraid that Iran was headed toward destruction. Indeed, that was the beginning of the revolution, when the Iranians started cursing the Shah and praising Khomeini who was still in exile in France.

A few days later, the Shah and Empress Farah left Iran. For Farhad it was such a heartbreaking event to see the Shah on TV, at the airport, ready to board the aircraft. Farhad couldn't help but cry when a soldier knelt and kissed the Shah's shoes as he was about to board the aircraft. The fleeing monarch appeared gloomy and teary eyed, with *Shahbanoo*—the king's lady—at his side.

"No," Farhad had hollered, holding his head in both hands. "This is not a dream. My king is really leaving. What good am I anymore?"

The general suddenly felt like a rag doll. A nobody! He told his wife, "It feels so strange! Is this situation real or am I dreaming?"

"Yes, my dear, it sure is real. Things are rapidly changing and you are not a general anymore!" Then she smiled sweetly and carried on, "But you'll always be my general!"

Yes, he knew that. But the truth was that he was devastated. What had become of all his might and importance? How could things have changed so fast from one day to the next?

After the Shah's departure, Farhad still wanted to be optimistic. He had shaken his head and said decisively to Leyla, "I don't think this situation will last long. I'm sure that things will calm down and the Shah will return. He's done it before."

"Let's hope so." Leyla sounded dubious.

"Yes," Farhad stressed, "Islam's roots have been weakened in Iran for good. The people will not tolerate a mullah ruling the country."

"Do you think so?"

"Absolutely! Don't you remember what happened when the Shah was married to Soraya?"

"Yes, during the days when Prime Minister Mosadegh stirred nationalistic feelings in people and wanted to rid the country of foreign influence?"

"Exactly. Do you remember how the Shah left the country then?"

"I do, clearly."

"Mosadegh didn't last long. The Americans crushed his followers, put him under house arrest, and brought the Shah back."

Leyla pressed, "I was a girl of ten then. I remember that day so vividly when bullets were flying in the air, landing in peoples' backyards during the clashes between the Shah and Mosadegh's followers. I also remember how, towards the end of the afternoon, the Shah's supporters drove around in cars honking their horns and turning their headlights on, announcing the defeat of Mosadegh's forces."

Farhad nodded. "I also remember that day."

"Who led the rebellion against Mosadegh's forces?"

"General Zahedi, the chief of staff of the Shah's army." Farhad smiled and added, "So, you see, somebody will bring the Shah back again."

It seemed like Farhad had lost touch with reality. He had been immersed in his own world and had not noticed that more and more Iranians were turning to religion. It was different this time. Besides, President Carter's administration was not supporting the Iranian monarch as what the United States had done before. Farhad had no idea what was in store for Iran as well as for the world at large. Ayatollah Khomeini's rule was to create a new monster that would threaten the future of the world even more dangerously than communism did with all its evils. Khomeini's regime was to strengthen fundamentalism and anti-western sentiment, as well as creating the *Hizbollah* terrorist movement in the Islamic world.

In the Shah's absence, a ruling council headed by Prime Minister Bakhtiar was formed, but it was obvious that his government would not last long.

On January 31, 1979, Farhad watched the television with dismay as Ayatollah Khomeini triumphantly arrived in Tehran, greeted by tumultuous demonstrations. Ayatollah Khomeini appeared happy and smiling as he stood atop the steps of Air

France's carrier, waving at the cheering crowd. As he descended, some of the people standing closest to him, wishing to touch His Holiness, knocked Ayatollah's turban off his head in their excitement. Nobody, before that incident, could have ever guessed that the good-looking Ayatollah was completely bald.

The jubilant Ayatollah's bodyguards then quickly whisked him away for fear of his safety.

A few days later, Farhad watched the television with disbelief as his colleagues who were executed were named. He also watched as the Shah's Prime Minister, Hoveyda, was handcuffed and taken on his way to prison.

Farhad remembered what a good-tempered person the Prime Minister was. He used to smile at people as he walked with a slight limp, leaning on his walking stick, with a pipe in his mouth, and being dressed smartly in checkered vests with a white carnation on the lapel of his designer blazer. He looked like an inspector from the old French detective films.

Hoveyda was put to death after being judged speedily in a kangaroo court. When asked questions during the trial, he responded boldly, "I'm not going to answer your questions. What's the point of this false trial? I know that you've already made up your minds to execute me. So why waste time?"

Truly, there was no point in his defending himself. Hoveyda was doomed one way or the other. What was his crime? Like Farhad, he had lost touch with reality. He believed that all the Iranians were well-to-do and that they all owned houses. That was exactly what he claimed in an interview with a foreign journalist a few weeks before the revolution.

SOLITUDE AND

EMPTINESS

For nine years Farhad had not seen a single ray of sunshine. Days and nights were one and the same to him. Every day he awakened to pitch-dark surroundings and he had to turn the light on. At night, when his hosts returned from work, he joined them upstairs in curtain-drawn rooms lit by electricity. He lived entirely in a dark, empty world illuminated only by electric bulbs. His moves from one residence to another were carried out in the wee hours of the morning, when it was still dark. Sometimes, like a prisoner who is allowed into open air, he would be driven by his hosts to the outskirts of Tehran, into the wilderness. They let him walk a while under the towering Alborz chain of mountains that encircled Tehran like a ring. In the darkness of the pre-dawn, Damavand, the highest mountain in the range perpetually covered with white glittering snow, peered gracefully at the amber moon.

Farhad would slump back on the pebbly and dusty ground and gaze at the dark sky, glittering with thousands of stars that looked so close. Then he would get up and stare at the sea of lights engulfing Tehran in the distance, where free men and fugitives lived side by side. Somewhere out there, his beloved wife and children lived without him. How he wished he could be with them! Alas, it was not possible. Ayatollah Khomeini's men had taken that pleasure away from him for good.

Those rare pre-dawn jaunts were the only occasions when Farhad could inhale the real earthy smell of the barren land and the fresh elixir of mountain air. Otherwise, he lived like a perpetually hibernating animal in a cave where seasons never changed.

Autumns, winters, springs and summers had come and gone. For nine years Farhad had not cast an eye on the pink blossoms of almond trees, or the white petals of cherry blossoms dancing merrily in the air with the skin-caressing spring breeze. He had forgotten how fresh and mild the sunny Tehran spring days felt. Neither could he remember anymore the mystifying effect of the aroma of jasmine flowers on his lungs and spirit. Farhad and Leyla once took great pleasure in their garden, filled with aromatic Persian flowers and towering old sycamores and arching elms. The branches of their jasmine bush, covered with small dark green leaves and hundreds of white, tiny flowers, hung over the brick garden wall into the street. Its aroma was so pungent that it felt as if hundreds of bottles of Calvin Klein's *Obsession* had been pumped into the air.

Before becoming the military governor of the southern province of Khouzestan, Farhad, when he was still living in Tehran with his family, would water the flowerbeds every evening after work. Leyla would bustle over carrying a tray with two tumblers of strong tea and some lump sugar. They would lean back in the green wooden bench by the little pool, enjoying the mild evening air filled with the damp smell of the wet soil and the flowers. They would sit side by side on the bench, sipping the aromatic tea and enjoying the cool of the evening, filled with the mesmerizing perfume of the flowers.

Nine gloomy years of hiding in dark basements had caused Farhad's pleasant memories to evaporate into a hazy, shapeless dream. Farhad's world was different now. It was a world made up of solitude and emptiness. He was a different person too. Farhad was now very humble, as well as fragile. The general had lost every grain of arrogance and pride that he used to possess when he was free and powerful.

Solitude had taught him to accept life the way it was. He had learned to occupy himself with things that he would never have considered doing before. Farhad now cooked all sorts of tasty Iranian food. Every day he went upstairs at dusk and quickly drew the curtains and the blinds. Next, turning on the lights, he started cooking. When his hosts returned home from work, the table was nicely set and the food ready. The general's friends tried to hide him at households without children as much as they could. Such childless couples normally both worked. Life had become very expensive, with one income not being enough to pay for all the expenses.

The general had also learned to knit. He loved knitting and had produced loads of sweaters for his wife, daughter and the hostesses. Who would have ever believed that the military governor of Khouzestan would one day turn into a perfect *"househusband"*!

Farhad, who had always been fit, routinely worked out each day. This helped him to take his mind off his sorry condition. So did knitting and cooking. He looked forward to the evening hours when he could come out of his *"coffins"*, as he jokingly called his daytime cells, and cook delicious dishes like *estanbolli polo,* served with pickles, raw onion, scallions and radishes and varied kinds of tasty *khoreshes* served with rice.

The mouth-watering aroma of Farhad's cooking, with its keenly spiced odors mixed with the smell of meat and herbs, as well as the delicious odor of the basmati rice, would make even those with no appetite hungry. From the moment his hosts would set the key into the keyhole and enter, they could not wait to sit down at the dinner table.

Farhad was so content to have his wife and family mem visit him occasionally under extreme caution. They would come to see him at late hours in the night and only short time. Those visits meant the world to him, although they occurred only briefly and seldom. After they left, he would try to guard the sweet memory of their presence in his mind. Then, in no time, the dark world would engulf his whole being and mind.

At night when his hosts returned with newspapers and stories from the outside world, Farhad would listen to them eagerly. He would read the papers, close his eyes and imagine himself as being free and living among people. But when he would open his eyes, he would suddenly be jolted back to reality. His real world was that of an underground, sheltered existence where he lived under the shadow of his benefactors. Now, suddenly his secluded life was going to come to an end. Farhad was scared of coming out into the open! One should think that he would be happy to be released from his different *"coffins"*, but Farhad had come to be scared of the outside world. The situation had not been the same in the beginning. He had always tried to figure out how he could sneak out into the streets when dusk settled in.

Two years into his hiding, on a cold, winter night Farhad decided to venture out. He was bored and had enough of leading a hermit's life. He desperately yearned to see some signs of life, walk the streets and inhale a bit of fresh air.

Having found a set of spare keys, he locked up the house, put his hand into his black overcoat's pockets to keep warm, and stepped outside. Fear gave way to a certain ungovernable ecstasy as he walked along the sidewalks. For a short while he was oblivious of the dangers lurking about him. Then suddenly he became apprehensive. The thought of the *pasdars,* the *Zeinab Sisters* and the *Basij* sent a shiver down his spine. *"What have I done?"* he asked himself. But experiencing the fresh air and the outside world was wonderful. He could not bring himself to return and hide in his dark world.

It felt strange to Farhad to be walking alongside people. Two years of confinement in basements had turned him into a recluse. Farhad had forgotten what fresh air and outdoor life was like!

Although the general was scared, he did not care that he was the most wanted person in Iran. At that point, what mattered to him was that he had managed to escape his suffocating cage. Farhad wished that he could keep on walking forever and ever. He yearned to fly to his house like a bird and be with his lovely daughter, Jalleh and loving son, Jamshid. He desperately longed to hold his wife in his arms and never let go.

"Will I ever live with them like before?" Farhad sighed. *"Will the present government ever change? Will the young Shah reclaim his father's throne one day?"*

No, it did not seem likely to the general that such a miracle could ever take place during his lifetime. So what was he supposed to do? Where was his life leading him? Was he destined to hide in dark basements the rest of his life? Nobody could tell. The main thing at that moment was that he could walk outside freely. *"Thank God that his friends were late,"* he thought. If they had come at the usual hour, they would not have allowed him to leave the house.

There were piles of snow on both sides of the wide street, and the sidewalks were solidly frozen like shining glass. Farhad took small, careful steps to avoid slipping while he inhaled the biting cold air into his shrunken lungs. They hurt badly, not being used to cold, fresh air. It felt like somebody was puncturing his lungs with a sharp dagger.

He walked on and on alongside the scurrying men wrapped in their overcoats. Some gift shops and green grocery stores were still open with their merchandise displayed outside. The smell of *kebab, khoresh* and aromatic rice wafted from a basement restaurant that had narrow stairs leading down to it. A young fellow with greased hair, who was wearing a thick brown sweater, stood in front of the entrance, rubbing his hands together and stamping his feet to keep warm. "Come on . . . come on, you nice folks. Come in and taste the delicious *ghormesabzi, khoresh badenjoon and shirin polo* of Agha Mahmood," the young man advertised. Farhad smiled at him, wishing he could go in and have a feast. Further on, he came up to a well-lit butchery with lamb carcasses hanging on hooks on the four-tiled walls of the shop. Shiny apples and oranges were placed in the round carved rectums of the carcasses to make them appear more appealing.

Farhad was filled with fear at the sight of a patrol car parked right by the butchery, and the two *pasdars* leaning against it and chatting away merrily. He cast a wary eye towards the revolutionary guards, not knowing what to expect. *"Would they recognize me?"* he wondered. *"Should I run? Should I turn back?"* On second thought, Farhad decided to ignore them completely. He told himself that if he acted like an ordinary passerby, they might not suspect anything. However, the more he tried to control his composure, the more distressed he became. Suddenly his legs felt like each weighed a ton. His body temperature skyrocketed despite the cold weather, and he heard his heart clacking in his ears like an old loom. The *pasdars* cut their conversation short and cast an intense glance toward Farhad's direction.

"That's it, they're coming to get me!" Farhad muttered under his breath, cursing himself for having come out into the open. And sure enough, the guards suddenly left their position and headed towards the general. Farhad, feeling completely helpless, stood frozen in place like a bedazzled deer facing the headlights of an oncoming car. The guards trotted onwards, getting closer and closer. As Farhad prepared himself to surrender, he noticed that the *pasdars'* gaze was fixed not on him, but rather straight ahead. The guards marched on, brushed against Farhad hurriedly and came to a sudden halt in front of a pretty, slender young woman a few steps away. The woman wore a long, black, fashionable skirt and a half-length purple overcoat. A purple silk scarf tied loosely around her head exposed a bit of her highlighted fringe. She fixed the young officers with her bold gaze and inquired aloofly, "What's wrong?"

"Cover your head properly, *khanoum*," the stocky, green-uniformed *pasdar* ordered harshly, and the young woman pulled her scarf over her bangs reluctantly.

Farhad, regaining his composure, breathed a sigh of relief and slowly edged into the chattering crowd. He pressed on nervously, zigzagging and nudging his way. The general had to hastily return to the safety of his refuge. Unfortunately, in his great hurry, when he had hardly gone a few yards, he slipped on the icy sidewalk, falling on his back and hitting his head against the frozen ground. The *pasdars*, having instructed the woman to cover her head properly, rushed to Farhad's rescue. "Are you all right?" they asked as they helped him to his feet.

Farhad was shocked! He had expected to be handcuffed instead of being fussed over.

"Oh, yes . . . yes. I'm fine," he lied. He felt a sharp pain in the back of his head. "P . . . please, don't bother yourselves for me, officers," Farhad stammered, feeling scared. "It's very cold; do get back to your car."

The general then turned on his heels and scurried away to avoid giving the *pasdars* a chance to recognize him. He took slight comfort in the knowledge that he looked different with his moustache and beard. *"Maybe, after all, I do look like the normal Islamic guys walking on the sidewalks,"* Farhad thought.

Farhad had walked not even half a block on the frozen sidewalk when he realized that he had lost the house keys. He thought that the keys might have flown out of his hand into the pile of snow when he fell. He was forced to go back and search frantically in the snow with his bare hands. The streetlights were not strong enough to help him locate the keys. The general wished he had worn his gloves. His fingertips were numb.

Suddenly, strong headlights illuminated the snow. He looked up and noticed that the guards had reversed the patrol car a couple of feet to brighten up the spot where he was looking for the keys.

When Farhad finally arrived home, his hosts had already returned.

"Where were you?" Nasrin, Nader's wife, demanded, furrowing her brow. "We were sick with worry."

Nader, as tall as Farhad, draped his arm around the general's shoulders and smiled at him, "Thank God you're safe! We were so worried about you!"

Nasrin, straightening her brown headgear, stared at Farhad with cold eyes and barked, "It's so stupid of you to endanger yourself and us."

"Lay off it!" Nader snapped at his wife. "He's not a child and doesn't need you lecturing him."

Nasrin stormed out of the room with a flushed, angry face, slamming the door hard behind her.

"I'm really sorry, Nader. Nasrin's right. It was really stupid of me to do what I did."

Farhad understood Nasrin's anger. If the *pasdars* had recognized and arrested him, his benefactors could be in deep trouble. He realized that he had acted mindlessly. He had no right to be selfish.

THE DOCTRINE

OF THE *GREEN BELT*

That evening, after his return from the forbidden outing, the general and Nader reclined comfortably on the sofa, and held a political discussion over a few precious glasses of illegally obtained wine. A thick cloud of cigarette smoke filled the semi-dark living room with its curtains and shutters tightly drawn. Both men were heavy smokers and the more they drank, the more they smoked.

Nasrin stuck her head in to ask the men if they wanted some tea. She immediately withdrew, slamming the door shut as she coughed, and hollered from behind the closed door, "How can you breathe such foul air?"

The two men ignored her as they shook their heads, "These women!" Nader complained.

Farhad smiled at his friend sympathetically, thinking that if he had a nagging wife like Nasrin, he would run millions of miles away from her. "*Thank God for Leyla,*" he told himself. "*Not only is she good-tempered, but she is also an understanding and compassionate person.*"

Farhad really missed her. Through all the years of their marriage, she had been like a rock on which he had leaned for strength and support. Leyla had been a friend as well as a lover. Moreover, she had been a good mother who had brought up proper children. He could not remember a day when Jalleh and

Jamshid had ever given them cause for any misgivings or pain. They were both studious. They cared about their mother and took care of her in his absence. Farhad knew that they were always there for her in case she needed their help.

"What are you thinking about, Farhad?" Nader interrupted the general's thoughts.

"Oh, nothing special," Farhad muttered breezily. He could not tell him that he was comparing Leyla with his unfriendly wife. "I was just thinking about my family."

"I see. You must be missing them," Nader said compassionately, putting a firm, friendly hand on his shoulder. "Now, back to our discussion. Before Nasrin interrupted us, we were talking about the U.S. support of the Islamic regime."

"Yes, the United States government thought that their strategy of support for the Islamic government would enforce the doctrine of the *Green Belt*—"the Islamic belt"—on the southern border of the Soviet Union," Farhad mentioned, looking angry. This subject always enraged him. It was immeasurably painful for him to think how the *Green Belt Doctrine* destroyed his world.

"They were convinced that the establishment of the *Green Belt* would prevent the spread of communism to the Middle East, denying the Soviet Union access to the warm waters of the Indian Ocean, which Russia had always coveted. Not to mention the vast deposits of Middle Eastern oil which constitutes one-third of the world's oil reserve," Nader concluded, staring thoughtfully at the brown, closed shutters behind the windows. He too was unhappy with the Islamic Republic. He had been much happier under the Shah's rule.

"And of course the U.S. government officials mistakenly thought that the Islamic government would be their ally!" Farhad sniggered, feeling quite tipsy by now.

"Yes, everything backfired and the U.S. government got itself into a jam!" Nader, too, slurred his words.

Farhad and Nader both agreed that whatever incentives the U.S. might have had concerning Iran and the Middle East, nothing could have justified all the bloodshed and the misery that followed. Thousands upon thousands were executed. Millions of people were forced to leave all their belongings and escape to foreign lands.

Farhad had learned, through letters from his friends residing abroad, that the Iranians were living under extreme hardship and humiliation in foreign lands. Wherever they went, they were looked down upon just because they held Iranian passports. The fact that millions of these Iranian passport holders were liberal, anti-Khomeini people, or that they were Jews, Armenians and *Bahais* escaping a repressive Islamic regime, did not matter to anybody. Farhad wondered if it were not merely a few years back when Iranians traveling abroad were treated with respect and dignity. *"And, why not?"* he thought. *"They were the ideal tourists."* It was true; Iranians in those days had money and were welcome everywhere. The Shah was also an important figure. He was highly regarded all over the world. There was hardly a soul in the universe that was not interested in the glamorous lifestyle of the Iranian royal family.

"Some might claim that the Iranian Revolution was beneficial for the mass of the population," Farhad's host said, raking his fingers through his thick hair.

The general smiled wryly, placed his empty glass on the coffee table and retorted sarcastically, "Well, probably the well-being of the masses is more important than the misery of a few million others like you, me and the Iranian refugees living abroad!"

ENTERTAINING THE SHAH

One of Farhad's best memories of his days as military governor of Khouzestan was when he played host to the *Shahanshah*—"king of kings"—just a few years before his downfall.

The governor's mansion had large rooms, high, plastered ceilings, and shimmering crystal chandeliers. The floors were covered with large, fine Persian carpets. Walnut wood-framed French windows opened up onto a well-manicured, shady garden. Once Farhad entered his stately mansion with its enclosed green garden, he would forget that he lived in a hot, dry land with scant vegetation and a few palm trees.

The Shah and the general dined alone in the spacious, guest dining room, sitting at opposing ends of the long, oval table. That was the arrangement the Shah had asked for. Farhad believed that he must have had enough with protocol and formality.

Professional, tuxedoed waiters served caviar, champagne and *foie gras,* followed with roasted turkey, leg of lamb, glazed potatoes, vegetables and salad.

Having tasted a bit of everything, the Shah sat back comfortably in his high-backed chair, holding his head upright graciously. He accepted a cigar offered by the waiter and lit it, sipped his brandy contentedly, and started a warm conversation with Farhad. He wanted to know the details of the projects that were in progress in the governor's region. Ever since Farhad had taken charge of the area, new roads had been built, historical buildings and mosques had been renovated and the water system had been improved.

Farhad proudly reported the progress of his projects to His Majesty, with whom by that time, he felt completely at ease. The Shah seemed very satisfied with the general's accomplishments. Farhad expected him to be a bit more curious and show interest in visiting some of the sites and buildings that had been renovated. It appeared that the Shah simply trusted his general. Farhad felt honored and flattered, but also concerned. He knew that most of the Shah's officials painted rosy pictures to please the king and the Shah believed them, just as he seemed to believe him now.

The general leaned forward on the table and gazed at the Shah's dark, keen eyes and inquired, "Is there anything special Your Majesty would like to do tomorrow after breakfast?"

He thought that the monarch might want to meet the troops or some of the officials, and perhaps tour the city.

"No, thank you. I'd like to rest a while before returning to Tehran in the afternoon." He responded good-temperedly and then added, "By the way, no breakfast for me. And for lunch I would simply like some soup."

"Yes, Your Majesty," the general nodded. He was relieved that the Shah just wanted to have a light meal. *"Less pressure and headache!"* he thought.

To Farhad, the Shah appeared simultaneously elegant, poised, down to earth and amicable. He also found the *Shahanshah*— "king of kings"—impeccably well mannered, sophisticated and distinguished looking. His friendly smile and relaxed disposition made him feel comfortable, but Farhad was still concerned about the Shah's lack of interest in seeing the accomplishments in his region.

"Well, that's because he knows I won't pull the wool over his eyes," he reassured himself. But then he asked himself, *"How about the others? I know so many dishonest high-ranking officials."* But then he told himself that he was sure that the Shah knew what he was doing. To the general, blinded by patriotism and total devotion to his ruler, the *Shahanshah* represented a symbol of goodness and perfection. So one can only imagine his devastation and disappointment when the Shah's reign came to

such an abrupt end. What's more, it is not surprising that with his fall, Farhad also fell not only from power, but in spirit as well.

That night after dinner, as the Shah headed towards his bedroom, he made sure that the dining room lights were turned off. The general was amazed to see the Shah of Iran occupying himself with such trivial matters as saving electricity. However, that made Farhad admire his king even more.

After turning the lights off, the Shah thanked Farhad for his hospitality, and demanded, "I'd like Fred to sleep in a bedroom next to mine."

"Of course, Your Majesty!" Farhad uttered, without even knowing who Fred was. He thought once the Shah went to bed, he could inquire about "*Fred*" from his bodyguards.

When they came out into the well-lit foyer, with its walls decorated with ancient Persian paintings and the floors with navy blue Nain carpets, Farhad noticed a guard standing behind the massive carved dining room door, holding onto the leash of a black Great Dane.

The guard stiffened his body like a stone carved statue and clicked his heels as soon as the Shah came into the foyer. He stared straight ahead at the opposite wall. The moment the huge beast saw His Majesty, he pounced up on his tall hind legs, placing his paws on the Shah's shoulders, and started licking his face.

"Okay . . . okay, enough already, Fred!" he ordered, pushing the huge, affectionate dog down to a sitting position.

"So this is who 'Fred' is!" Farhad sighed with great relief, gazing bemusedly at the beast.

As promised, the general let the lucky dog stay in one of the best bedrooms next to the Shah's.

"Was it out of love or because of security that the Shah had wanted Fred to sleep next door?" Farhad wondered.

THE NEIGHBOR'S

DAUGHTER

Farhad, who had lost his parents as an infant, was brought up by his eldest sister, Nazilla and his brother-in-law, Javad.

Life for Farhad as a little boy had been happy. Nazilla, who had no children of her own, had dedicated her life to making her little brother the happiest boy in the neighborhood. Javad had also treated Farhad as if he were his natural son and enjoyed coming home from work to play with the boy. Farhad remembered Javad, who had passed away, with great affection. As a small boy he could hardly wait for Javad to come home from work and spoil him. Javad used to carry Farhad on his shoulders, then he neighed like a horse and trotted around the small pool which had lain in the center of their cobblestoned bare yard.

One day, when Farhad was nine years old, the next-door neighbor, who also happened to be his sister's best friend, was in labor. In those days midwives, called *mama,* delivered babies at people's homes. Women did not give birth at hospitals. What's more, a telephone was a luxury. Almost nobody owned one, except the very rich. Farhad's sister, Nazilla, who was at the neighbor's house helping her, ran back home and called him, "Farhad, I want you to go to Mrs. Kazemi's house and bring her to our next-door neighbor's place, okay?"

"What for?" Farhad complained. "Can't you see I'm playing?"

Nazilla, who was a tall woman with a delicate frame, walked over to her brother and almost sat down to be at the same level as the little boy. She pressed him against her chest, gave him a kiss and said, "Look, my dear, if you go right away and fetch the *mama*, I'll buy you an ice cream, okay? Run along now, good boy!"

The midwife's house was only two blocks away and it would take Farhad' s little feet between five and seven minutes to get there.

The moment he set foot into the unpaved street with its brick built huts, he saw Hooshy kicking his soccer ball. Hooshy was a year younger than Farhad. Like Farhad, he had a shaved head and was wearing a pair of white baggy pants.

"Hey, Farhad, do you want to see my new bicycle?" Hooshy's big black eyes shone with enthusiasm like diamonds.

"Oh, yes! Will you let me ride it?"

"Of course, you're my best friend."

Off they went to play with Hooshy's shiny bicycle on narrow, winding dirt roads. Farhad sped along like a maniac, screaming wildly with joy. He zoomed by Hooshy, giggling playfully as Hooshy tried to stop him and get his bicycle back. Then it was Hooshy's turn to ride with Farhad in pursuit.

When Farhad returned home two hours later, it was late in the afternoon. A shabbily dressed beggar was sitting by their door stretching his cupped palm to the passersby, begging for alms. Farhad smiled at him and entered their courtyard. The moment he set foot into the yard, he remembered that he was supposed to fetch the *mama*. It was too late; the neighbor had given birth to a baby girl whom they had named Leyla. When Farhad had not returned in time, his sister had sent the next-door neighbor's husband to fetch the midwife. Unfortunately, Farhad's behavior had not only been a cause for laughter and jokes in the neighborhood, it had also cost him his freedom. Nazilla and Parvin, Leyla's mother, had decided between themselves that because of the funny nature of that incident, Farhad had to marry Leyla when they grew up. As simple as that!

At the age of nineteen, when Farhad was about to leave his sister's house to study at the military academy, Leyla had turned into a cute ten-year-old girl. Farhad could tell that she was gradually developing into a little woman with her curvy body and lemon-sized breasts. He also caught her stealing shy and interested glances at him. Farhad looked handsome and strong with his tall muscular frame, strong jaw, dark brown eyes that had an aloof gaze, and the same color of straight hair. Farhad and Leyla hardly ever spoke to one another. It was not customary for young people from decent families to talk or spend time together without a chaperon. Not that Farhad cared to do so. To him, Leyla represented nothing but a cute ten-year-old child. He did not even take the question of their betrothal seriously. For some reason, he believed that during his long absence, they would marry her off to another person. At least that's what he hoped. Farhad did not believe in arranged marriages and found it a primitive custom. Of course, he did not dare to confront his sister about it. In Iran, especially in those days, people never stood up to their parents or older siblings. They were to be respected and their word was the law.

The military academy was known for graduating well-educated officers. The military cadets were each given a small room with a few amenities in a large, spread out, ranch-style building. The cadets lived under strict rules and had no time for anything but study, military drills and exercise.

The academy's huge garden, dotted with old, large chestnuts, spruce trees and flowerbeds, served as the study area. Even at night, the studious pupils would sit outside and study on benches under the old round lanterns with metallic, black posts. During the day they would walk about, reciting and reading their lessons aloud as they prepared themselves for their exams. Somehow, this manner of studying seemed to be a more effective way of learning than being cooped up in a small room.

Outside the academy the streets of Tehran were bustling with life. Peddlers were singing out praises of their merchandise, veiled women were scurrying about from one vendor's cart to the other, and children were screaming and playing on the sidewalks. The cacophonous noises of the horns of cars and horse-drawn carriages, the neigh of the horses, the braying of the fed-up donkeys, and the clamor of the crowd tempted Farhad to go out and enjoy the real life. He longed with all his heart to visit a *chello kebab* restaurant and regale a portion of charcoal-grilled meat or chicken served with rice. He thought of how he could melt a tablespoonful of butter in the steaming rice, mix a raw egg yolk with it, cut up some grilled tomatoes and put them on the rice. Then he could place the grilled meat or chicken pieces on top, sprinkle them with *somagh*—a sour dry powder—and gobble the whole thing up. They did not serve such tasty food at the academy's mess hall, but Farhad had plenty of time to enjoy his favorite foods later on in life. What mattered at the moment was his education. He took his studies very seriously. Each year Farhad passed his exams with top grades and finally graduated from the academy as a first lieutenant at the age of twenty-three. It was wonderful! Farhad felt proud and accomplished. He thought he was ready for life and service to his country. Then he met Ellaheh.

ELLAHEH

After graduating from the academy, First Lieutenant Farhad Shirazi was assigned as adjutant to General Vakili. General Vakili's department was responsible for security on roads between cities and villages. There had been some cases of tribal attacks and robbery on travelers traversing precipitous mountain routes. The general was in his early forties. Although appearing very relaxed and laid back for an army officer, he was a demanding person who would not accept anything but perfection from his subordinates. He liked Farhad for his presence of mind, boldness and leadership potential.

The first weekend after taking up his new career, Farhad went to visit his Aunt Masumeh, who was the younger sister of his deceased mother. He remembered his cousin Feri from childhood days, when Aunt Masumeh would come over to visit Nazilla with little Feri. Farhad had not met her since then, neither had he seen his Aunt Masumeh recently.

It was lunchtime as Farhad stepped out of his second-floor, one-bedroom apartment, and stepped into Manuchehri Avenue. Manuchehri, which was a narrow street with nice stores of food and delicatessens, connected two busy main avenues. *Chello Kebabi Khatam* stood on the right-hand side, at the end of Manuchehri.

Farhad walked through a massive wooden, creaky door into a large, dimly lit restaurant. Its whitewashed walls were embellished by miniatures illustrating Omar Khayam's poetry. One painting depicted a turbaned man—maybe Omar Khayam himself—sitting comfortably under a willow tree. A young girl with joined arrow-shaped eyebrows and large, dark eyes stood by him wearing a pair of sheer baggy pants and a short, flared skirt over it. In her delicate, almost transparent hand she held a pitcher of wine, while the thirsty man lifting his glass waited for it to be filled with the *"wine of love"*.

The restaurant air was permeated with the aroma of mouth-watering *kebab* marinated in onion and lemon juice. The sound of traditional Iranian music poured out of the loudspeaker over the din of the crowded restaurant. Being Friday—the Iranian weekend—the restaurant was full of hungry men, women and children. Large families were seated around big round tables, helping themselves to drained yoghurt, all sorts of herbs, white cheese, mixed pickles, flat Persian bread and of course, *chello kebab*. A few other couples sat around small tables. One could tell that they were lovers or engaged couples from the way they whispered softly and stared at one another.

After lunch Farhad walked to Ferdosi Avenue and passed by the wooded British Embassy compound. Two Pakistani guards in their national military uniforms and feathered turbans stood guard at the embassy's grated iron gate.

A few blocks down he turned into Lalezar Avenue and elbowed his way through a throng of well-dressed men and women. In those days the lower-class and fundamentalist Iranians lived and worked in the southern part of Tehran. One could very rarely see *chadoris* or mullahs in the downtown shopping area. Farhad had to hold his breath as he passed by the well-known fish store on Lalezar with its doors thrust wide open, exhibiting large trays of sturgeon piled on crushed ice.

Farhad entered Naderi Avenue lined with rows of gift and souvenir stores, where his aunt lived, and came to a stop in front of a two-story building marked number 45. As soon as he rang the bell, a young, brunette girl, whom Farhad assumed to be his cousin Feri, stuck her head out of the second-floor window.

"Who is it?" she called out, looking down.

"It's me, Farhad."

Farhad could hear Feri's quick footsteps clacking sonorously against the concrete steps as she hurried downstairs to open the door.

"Hello there, dear cousin!" Feri grinned.

Farhad instantly liked Feri, who appeared to be friendly and warm. She was a modern-looking young girl, dressed very tastefully. Feri wore a black short skirt and a pink satin shirt. She wore a soft makeup and had long, straight brown hair. Farhad looked with admiration at his cousin's trim, well-shaped figure and smiling, hazel eyes which were prominent on her fine, oval face.

Feri arched an eyebrow as she sized Farhad up. "Finally *we* have the honor of meeting *our famous* cousin!" she commented flirtatiously.

Aunt Masumeh rushed out of the kitchen to meet her nephew, with a cigarette in her mouth. She was heavy built, with tinted yellow hair and friendly brown eyes. She hugged Farhad and uttered with a shrill voice, "My God, what a handsome guy you've turned into!"

As Feri was busy preparing tea, the doorbell rang. She looked down the window and cried out with joy, "Oh, how nice Ellaheh's come to visit us."

When Ellaheh walked through the door into the bright sitting room that had off-white curtains, navy-blue-and-white Nain carpet and comfortable beige armchairs, Farhad felt like he had been struck by lightning. He was mesmerized by Ellaheh's sapphire blue eyes, long, wavy, blonde hair and delicate and curvy medium-height figure. *"Could it be love at first sight?"* he wondered.

Farhad scrambled politely to his feet, bowed and shook hands with Ellaheh, who in turn greeted him warmly. "So, you're the *famous* cousin," Ellaheh smiled boldly at Farhad.

"I guess I am!" Farhad asserted with a crooked smile.

They had tea, talked about every subject they could think of and laughed a lot. They all liked Farhad and he loved them all.

They were very special and modern people. Even his Aunt Masumeh was different! She was nothing like the women living in the south of Tehran, where Nazilla and Leyla's family lived. Aunt Masumeh did not cover her hair and she wore western-style clothes.

As Farhad got up to leave, he asked Feri, looking at Ellaheh through the corner of his eyes, "Can I, one of these days, invite you and Ellaheh to a movie?"

"With pleasure!" Feri answered for them both as she winked at her cousin with a grin. She could tell that Farhad liked her friend.

From that day on, Farhad started courting Ellaheh and they fell in love. The two lovers saw each other every evening and became almost inseparable. They spent their days doing things together, and had so much fun. They rode horse-drawn carriages, with decorated horses and thick-mustached coach drivers. They crossed all over Tehran in those coaches on warm summer afternoons just for fun, passing by national parks, blue-domed mosques and the *Majlis*, the Iranian parliament. They also walked hand in hand through quiet, shady streets with treetops arching from both sides, almost touching.

Farhad was in seventh heaven! To him it felt like he had always known that warm and pretty girl, in whom he saw no faults. This was exactly the kind of a girl he approved of: fun, open minded and westernized.

They saw each other for a year and Ellaheh's parents did not mind their daughter spending time with Farhad. They trusted her, and for some reason, Farhad too. They knew that Ellaheh would never do anything silly. They also knew that she was in love and were happy to see her so vivacious and full of life.

Farhad and Ellaheh spent hours walking and talking about their dreams, until one day Farhad realized that he would love to have her as his wife. So he decided to ask Ellaheh's parents for her hand without consulting Nazilla, his eldest sister. Farhad knew that he was being bold, but he chose to do what he thought was right for him. He believed that Nazilla would have no choice but to go along with his decision once things were formal between Ellaheh and himself.

Ellaheh's father was a medical doctor and had his private practice. He was very kind to Farhad and looked upon him as the son that he did not have. Ellaheh was his only child and he cherished her dearly. To him, Ellaheh's happiness was very important and when Farhad asked for his daughter's hand, he consented with a nod. "If my daughter's willing, I've got no objections."

Ellaheh's mother, who was a professor at Tehran University in the Department of Foreign Languages, smiled at them joyously and said, "Congratulations!"

"As simple as that!" Farhad thought. He couldn't have asked for any better! Now he had to inform his sister out of respect.

"No, it's impossible," Nazilla yelled over the phone when Farhad announced the news of his engagement. By then telephones had become quite common in Tehran.

"Why not?" Farhad protested.

"What do you mean, *'Why not?'*" she repeated his sentence mockingly. "Have you forgotten that you have been engaged to Leyla since you were a little boy?"

Cold sweat covered Farhad's forehead. His heart nearly froze with disappointment. "Do I have a say in this or not?" Farhad demanded.

"No!" she barked.

"But I thought the question of my engagement to Leyla was only a joke."

Nazilla snapped, "It is most serious!"

Silence. The line went clink . . . clink . . . and then Nazilla's harsh voice startled Farhad. "You know what, brother? You can't go back on your word."

"My word?" Farhad asked sarcastically.

"Your word . . . my word. What's the difference?"

"There's a big difference," Farhad almost told his sister.

"Actually, Leyla's parents are expecting you to offer her a ring and make it official," Nazilla said, still sounding angry. "Don't forget that she is now of official age for marriage. Besides, if you don't marry her, nobody else will, because she has been engaged to you all her life."

There was no point in arguing, although Farhad wished to tell her that he loved Ellaheh, not Leyla. But in those days in Iran it was not proper to do so. One could never oppose one's parents, or elder siblings, in Farhad's case. Most of the time they were the ones who would decide whom one married. There were not many progressive families like his Aunt Masumeh's or Ellaheh's parents who had had their education abroad.

Farhad had to explain his situation to a teary-eyed and understanding Ellaheh, who agreed to the annulment of their unofficial engagement. Farhad had not yet offered a ring to Ellaheh.

"Of course I understand," Ellaheh told Farhad. "You can't go against tradition, but you should've told me that you were already engaged before asking me to be your wife."

He wished for the ground to open up and swallow him alive, or to melt like snow in the sun.

"I honestly thought that the idea of my engagement to Leyla was nothing but a joke between my sister and her friend," Farhad pleaded. "Please believe me and do forgive me," he added shamefacedly, dodging Ellaheh's gaze.

"You should've at least checked with your sister and prevented such a situation," Ellaheh cried softly.

"I don't know what to say. I'm really sorry!" Farhad smiled sadly at Ellaheh and went on, "It's your fault . . . you shouldn't be so pretty. I couldn't resist falling in love with you."

She wiped her eyes and smiled back sweetly.

Farhad's misery was immeasurable! He felt humiliated and debased. Besides, it was not easy for him to break a relationship with a sweet girl who had opened up such a special place in his heart. He cursed tradition. He cursed lack of freedom and himself for having broken an innocent girl's heart. Farhad wondered why he hadn't thought about that silly business of engagement before allowing himself to fall in love with Ellaheh. He wanted to know why he sometimes acted so mindlessly.

GETTING ENGAGED

Farhad isolated himself from his friends for months by working longer hours to take his mind off Ellaheh. His small windowless office felt like a cage to the young heartbroken officer who also felt embarrassed for his irresponsible behavior. He thought he could never again face his cousin, Feri. He probably had put her to shame in front of her best friend and her family. He did not even dare to call her. Then, one day Feri herself telephoned Farhad and said that Ellaheh had another suitor. This made him feel both jealous and relieved. *"At least Ellaheh was not sad,"* he thought. The matter was now definitely over between them. Ellaheh was officially engaged to a young doctor.

Farhad reluctantly went to the bazaar and bought a one-carat emerald ring encircled with a cluster of diamonds set in white eighteen-carat gold. He also bought a box of assorted chocolates and decided to fulfill his duty by going to Leyla's parents and settling the matter of his engagement with their daughter.

The following day Farhad, accompanied by his sister, took the ring and the box of chocolates to Leyla's house. That meant that he was officially asking for Leyla's hand from her parents. In Iran, contrary to the American and European tradition, a young man has to ask the girl's parents for their daughter's hand, and not the girl herself. Of course, the young fellow has to be accompanied by his parents.

Nazilla was bubbling with joy. She got up and kissed them both, congratulating them as well as Leyla's parents.

64

"Well done, brother," she whispered happily in Farhad's ear, as they sat side by side on the sofa after he slipped the ring onto Leyla's alabaster white finger. "Thank you for not putting me to shame in front of my friends."

"Putting you to shame? So this is all about you!" he imagined himself telling her. Farhad believed his sister to be extremely selfish, but in the meantime he knew how much she loved him. He was sure that, by arranging that marriage, Nazilla indeed had his best interests in mind. At this thought, his anger toward her thawed.

He winked at his jubilant sister and whispered half jokingly, "Hey, I did it for you!"

Suddenly Farhad's heart filled with affection for his sister, who had made so many sacrifices in life to bring him up. He realized how much he loved her. Where would he have been without Nazilla? Who would have raised him? And who would have paid for his tuition at the academy?

Nazilla gave Farhad a broad smile and boxed him affectionately in the ribs, making sure nobody was looking on.

Farhad noticed that the neighbor's daughter had turned into a real Persian beauty. What made her even more attractive, he thought, were her timid smile and jet-black, thick-eyelashed, drowsy eyes. Her eyebrows were joined in the middle, like the ancient girls in the Omar Khayam's miniatures. Moreover, she appeared to be a warmhearted, friendly person. Leyla was polite, but very shy.

Leyla's gray-haired and friendly middle-aged father congratulated his future son-in-law, looking approvingly at his serious demeanor. He probably thought that Farhad would make a good husband for his eldest daughter, who was then sixteen. Farhad, filled with apathy, believed that the man should be very happy to have one girl off his hands. Leyla's mother, though, did not show any emotion. It seemed that she took her daughter's engagement as a natural happening. Farhad thought, *"After all, hadn't it been she and Nazilla who had decided that the baby and the little boy should get married when they grew up?"* To him, Leyla's mother seemed like a nonchalant and cold individual. His fiancée's sister, however, a thirteen-year-old girl with shiny black eyes and long, straight, black hair, appeared to be a nice and fun girl. Like her sister, she was wearing a long-sleeved, cotton floral dress, but no scarf. Leyla's mother, on the other hand, had wrapped herself in a cotton black-and-white-patterned *chador*. Nazilla had a white silk scarf covering her brown hair, which she wore in a bun behind her head. She also had on a long-sleeved black robe that covered her tall, slim and upright figure down to her feet. The black color nicely contrasted with her pale face and honey eyes.

On the day of their official engagement party in the presence of friends and relatives at the residence of Leyla's parents, Farhad felt like a stranger.

Leaning against the wall all by himself, he observed the guests who were sitting on rented metallic chairs in the two large, adjoining rooms. The door between the two rooms had been thrown open that day, allowing people to circulate from one room to the other.

On a long table, Leyla's family had spread a buffet of delicious Persian *polo khoreshes*, roast chicken, stuffed wine leaves, grilled fish and different salads and greens. The guests were helping themselves to the delicious food, chattering happily and laughing. A group of men were standing on one side of the room smoking cigarettes and telling jokes. Most of the women had *chadors* on, but underneath they were wearing their party dresses. Others were attired in long robes and scarves. They looked somewhat funny, almost like Barbie dolls, with their heavy makeup. Men and women sat separately and stared at one another between their group conversations. Certain well-to-do women showed off their two middle front gold-capped teeth by laughing constantly. In those days, gold-capped teeth were very fashionable among women and were considered a sign of wealth and beauty.

Farhad lit a cigarette out of boredom and turned his head towards the direction of the women's room, where Leyla was busy entertaining her friends and guests. She looked quite cheerful, despite her shyness. Farhad stared disapprovingly at her unbecoming conservative, long robe and wished she were different. *"Why couldn't she dress like Ellaheh?"* he wondered.

Under the curious glances of the guests, Farhad approached Leyla in the women's sitting area, where other men did not enter. But Farhad, being a daring person, did not care what people thought, or what was proper and not proper. He decided that since he was forced into marrying the neighbor's daughter, he had better get to know her.

Leyla turned crimson red as Farhad stood next to her and gazed intently into her charming, black eyes. He liked her eyes, that was for certain!

"Are you still going to school?" Farhad tried to make conversation.

Leyla swallowed hard to moisten her dry throat and took a deep breath to calm her rapid heartbeat. Farhad was standing too closely. It was too much for her! His body heat and the masculine smell of his aftershave were making her heart go haywire. Leyla loved him very much, unlike Farhad, who had no feelings for her. She had always been in love with him, even when she was a ten-year-old girl.

"No, I got my high school diploma in June," Leyla finally answered sheepishly with her eyes cast down.

Farhad moved even closer and whispered, "Hey, look up. I won't eat you."

Leyla giggled, still dodging his gaze. "I know you won't eat me," she said sweetly and burst into uncontrollable laughter. So did Farhad, and this broke the ice between them.

As they went on talking, Farhad realized what a sweet person his fiancée was and how well read and informed she was about different subjects, even their government and the king.

"Not bad!" he told himself. *"At least I can talk with her. If only she would dress like Ellaheh!"* he repeated to himself.

"Leyla," Farhad told her, "since we are going to get married soon, you better learn certain things about my career."

"Yes, what sort of things?" she asked with rounded, red lips. Leyla had made herself up for their engagement party and was wearing a shocking bright red lipstick. Other women had now taken their headgear off, revealing their disheveled hair and heavy makeup. Although Leyla's face did not appear as ridiculously painted as theirs, it was clumsily and unskillfully made up. Farhad remembered what an expert Ellaheh was in the art of makeup.

"I have to stop comparing her to Ellaheh all the time," Farhad reprimanded himself.

"Well," Farhad went on, "I'm an officer and my job sometimes will require me to be absent from home for long periods of time."

Leyla suddenly took on a confident demeanor and said curtly, "No problem. I can handle that."

"What a sudden change of personality! This shy girl's character seems to be made up of some fine fiber," Farhad thought contently. That was good news for a person with great expectations from a wife-to-be.

AMERICA

A week after Farhad's official engagement to Leyla in 1956, when he was still a second lieutenant, the government of the time sent him to the United States for a year's training as a paratrooper in Fort Monmouth. There, Farhad not only learned everything about parachuting from aircraft and military tactics, but he also learned to love the United States and its people. What he liked the most about the Americans was their openness and geniality. He found that unlike the Europeans he had met in Iran, Americans were unpretentious, informal and straightforward. Unfortunately, this was not the case with Iranians. Farhad found most of his countrymen to be *tarofi*. He liked to speak his mind and wanted to know where he really stood with others. The *tarofis* did and said things without any sincerity. They said *yes* sometimes when they really meant *no*, and they did things out of politeness when in reality they had no desire to do so.

Farhad was amazed to see that the Americans practically never walked in the streets. He realized that almost every member of a family over the age of sixteen had a car. The distances between their homes and work, schools, and stores were simply too far for walking. In Iran, although there were some who owned cars, people mostly rode buses, taxis and horse-drawn buggies, or simply went about doing their business on foot. Iranian women, contrary to the Americans, walked to the stores and carried their heavy bags of groceries home.

The other aspect of life that he found to be different was that

American men helped their wives in the kitchen. In Iran, the kitchen was considered to be feminine territory.

Farhad had developed friendly ties with a few of his fellow officers, one of whom happened to be a sad-faced, big, beefy fellow named Jeffrey. Jeffrey helped Farhad familiarize himself with the region when he first arrived at Fort Monmouth by showing him around.

"I really appreciate your kindness," Farhad told Jeffrey one Saturday afternoon as they picnicked under the shady trees of the military compound, encircled by a vast velvety green land.

Jeffrey answered, "I feel comfortable with you. That's why I don't mind driving you around."

"Thank you. But how come? You don't even know me well," Farhad said bluntly.

"Well, you're a friendly guy and you put me into a good mood. Besides, you're the first Iranian I've ever met and I'd like to know you better."

"Am I really the first one?"

"Yes. Tell me, what makes you such a happy person?"

Farhad laughed heartily. "I, happy? Well, I don't know!"

"I wish I could be like you!" Jeffrey sighed, gazing solemnly at Farhad.

Taking on a serious demeanor, Farhad scrambled to his feet and started pacing the lawn.

Jeffrey, noticing Farhad's sudden change of mood, inquired anxiously, "Have I said something to offend you?"

"Oh, no. On the contrary, you have done nothing but to praise me."

"Then what is it? Tell me."

"Well, you don't know the real *me*."

"Who is the real *you*?"

"As the Iranian saying goes: *'If you were to put someone under a microscope, you would come across different characters'.*"

"Really? How's that?"

"Well, if you were to put me under a microscope, you would probably come across three opposing personalities."

"Interesting! Go on."

Farhad explained pensively, "The first and the main character would be the military man in me with bold and ambitious traits. He would be fearless and cruel and would kill without batting an eye for the good of the country and the king. For him humanity has no meaning when dealing with the enemies of the system in which he operates."

Jeffrey looked at Farhad quizzically. "Are you sure you're not exaggerating a bit?"

"I wish I were! No, Jeffrey, I'm painting the real picture of me," Farhad said earnestly.

"Okay, now paint the other two pictures of you."

Farhad sat back on the bench, gazed at the three-story L-shaped, brick-built military complex and beamed, "The second Farhad is the one who could be a loving father and husband. He is the one who loves to laugh and have fun. He also likes pretty girls!"

Jeffrey cut in, "That's nice. What about the third one?"

"Oh, let me see, this one is more difficult to explain," Farhad said, looking over the sloping lawn at the highway passing below. There was a short period of silence as Farhad endeavored to depict his third self. "This is the character that I don't like. He is fragile, childish, nagging, weak and, strangely enough, poetic."

Jeffrey gave Farhad one of his rare smiles and said caringly, "I must say that I like all three Farhads, and most of all I like your frankness."

Jeffrey always appeared depressed. He told Farhad that his wife, Gladys, had recently left him, because in his previous occupation as a bank clerk he had not been able to give her the sort of a life that she had expected. Gladys had left him for another man, leaving Jeffrey alone to cope with loads of debts and emotional turmoil. Jeffrey had turned to the army thinking it would help him overcome both his emotional and financial difficulties. However, not much had changed, especially because the poor fellow could not stop blaming himself for his failed marriage. What's more, he still loved his ex-wife and could not get over her.

"I'm really sorry about your wife leaving you and your tough situation. But I promise you things will work out for you." Farhad tried to cheer him up. "You'll see, I'm sure that you'll find another nice woman."

"Women don't interest me anymore. They're all the same," Jeffrey panted angrily.

A few days later, after dinner in the noisy mess hall, Jeffrey invited Farhad to come to his room for a drink. Farhad first went to his quarters, located at the opposite wing from Jeffrey's, to pick up a bottle of wine which had been sitting for a while on his old, oak desk and then he headed to visit his friend. Farhad had bought the wine during one of his shopping trips with Jeffrey to the nearby small town; a town with one long main street, one movie house, one diner, one liquor store, one hairdressing salon and one of everything.

The narrow, labyrinthine corridors were deserted. The officers were either in their rooms or at the officers' club having fun.

As Farhad approached Jeffrey's room, a sharp ping of gunfire froze him in place. *"What was that,"* he wondered. *"Was it really a gunshot?"*

Fear overcame Farhad's whole being as he stood in the narrow, neon-lit corridor. He was afraid that something was terribly wrong. However, he did not allow himself to think that the sound of the shot had come from his friend's room.

Cautiously he approached Jeffrey's door and tapped a timid knock at it. There was no answer. The air was static and he could hear a buzzing sound in his ears and the rhythmic thumping of his heart. He knocked at the door again. There was still no answer. *"How strange,"* he told himself with apprehension. *"Jeffrey said he would be in his room!"*

Gently, Farhad pushed the door open and peeped in with uncertainty.

"Oh my God!" Farhad hollered, "Have mercy!"

Farhad's head started spinning and he felt nauseated. He

leaned against the cold, whitewashed wall from fear of passing out and closed his burning eyes.

"No this is impossible!" he moaned loudly, as cold sweat covered him all over.

A throng of officers, having heard Farhad's cries and groans, rushed out of their rooms and surrounded him.

"What's the matter . . . what's happened?" they all persisted as Farhad pointed with a shaky finger toward Jeffrey's room and made them rush inside.

A cacophony of confused voices poured out of Jeffrey's room, as the bewildered officers expressed their emotions.

Jeffrey had shot himself in the head. His body was leaning back on the chair with his brain and blood splattered all over the back wall and the black-and-white poster of Manhattan skyscrapers.

"What a shame . . . what a waste of life!" Farhad whispered with melancholy, and turned on his heels and walked toward his room, still dazed.

Feeling terribly depressed, Farhad decided to take a shower and go to bed. He stripped down to his white flannel and long johns, while letting the shower run and waiting for the water to heat, but to no avail. What bad luck; he could not even take refuge into the warmth of the shower. Farhad thought that there could be something wrong with the boiler. Turning the shower off, he headed toward the basement just the way he was dressed to see if he could fix the problem.

The hallway was dimly lit and luckily there was nobody to see him in his undergarments.

He stepped into the cold, musty boiler room that was covered with cobwebs, and tried to fidget with some wires without any success. There was definitely something much more complicated than he could handle. Farhad decided to go back and call the office and ask them to send a technician.

As he came out into the dimly lit hallway, a soldier was coming towards him from the opposite direction. Upon seeing Farhad, the soldier faltered a second, looking frightened. He then scratched his shaved blond head and looked back to see if there were other people in sight. But the narrow hallway was completely deserted. Fixing his bewildered eyes on Farhad, he approached him with an unsteady gait. Farhad, who was embarrassed to be seen in his undergarments, tried to dodge the soldier's gaze.

"Ghost . . . son of a gun!" the soldier yelled as he closed in on Farhad. The horrified fellow socked him with a harsh blow and took off like a gazelle.

Farhad, who had not expected such a move from the soldier, rubbed his burning face in bewilderment and uttered to himself, "Wow! What a strong soldier!" Then he laughed and went on, "The poor fellow mistook me for a ghost and it isn't even Halloween yet."

Suddenly it dawned on him that the soldier, having seen him in his white long johns and flannel, in the dimly lit hallway, must have imagined him to be Jeffrey's ghost.

A KIND OF LOVE

Returning to Tehran upon the completion of his military training, Farhad went to visit his fiancée. Strangely enough, he could not wait to see her. By that time, Farhad had completely pushed Ellaheh out of his mind. During the last few months of his stay in America, he had often thought of Leyla with affection. It seemed like the memories of his short encounter with her during their engagement party had gradually brewed into a form of love.

Leyla was glowing with joy when her fiancée stepped into their bright, sunny living room. Her mother was sitting cross-legged on the floor with her *chador* flaps wrapped around her waist and tied behind her back. She was busy folding her laundry that she had just collected from the clothesline in their sunny yard. Farhad greeted her politely and she responded to him with a nod of her *chador*-covered head.

Farhad stared at Leyla in whose gaze and body language he could detect signs of passion. This excited him tremendously and made him want to cuddle her tightly and kiss her. Alas it was not possible. Leyla's mother would not leave them alone.

"*What's happening to me?*" he asked himself. "*I never felt like this towards Leyla before!*"

Farhad noticed that Leyla had become prettier. She also appeared less shy than the year before and he liked it!

The moment Leyla's mother left the room to put away the laundry, Farhad crept closer to her and whispered in her ear, "Have you missed me?"

Leyla chuckled and pulled away from him. It was dangerous; her mother could walk in at any moment.

Farhad was fed up with all those unnecessary inhibitions. *"Why can't we be like the Americans?"* he wondered. *"Why can't her bitter-faced, bad-tempered mother go out of the house and let us kiss like two lovers should?"* Farhad concluded that the only thing he could do to be with Leyla was to get married as soon as possible.

On their wedding day, Farhad's bride looked lovely in her long, flared, white bridal gown and simple, short veil.

A ripple of passion filled his whole being as he looked at her thick eyelashes, shimmering black eyes and sensuous full mouth. Farhad's heart fluttered with excitement thinking that soon, after the religious ceremony and the reception, Leyla would be his forever.

The groom leaned against the wall in the large hall of Park Hotel under the bright light of the huge chandelier, and looked at his beautiful bride and new wife talking to the guests. Farhad himself was dressed in a black tuxedo, white evening shirt and a white bow tie. His brown hair was greased back, making his forehead and brown eyes more prominent on his strong-featured face. He looked handsome and happy.

Leyla, as if feeling Farhad's gaze on her, turned back and smiled admiringly at her husband. It was obvious that she found him handsome.

Farhad and his wife began a happy life together in a two-bedroom second-floor apartment. Their dining room overlooked a busy square with a medium-sized pond in its center, encircled by a red-and-white geranium flowerbed. The bedroom windows opened onto an austere, walled-in narrow backyard. The neighbors used it as storage for their bicycles and extra objects. The apartment itself was a pleasant one and was conveniently located within good shopping facilities.

To please Farhad, Leyla tried to dress according to his taste. She was no longer wearing a headscarf for modesty, but she still felt very uncomfortable putting on sleeveless dresses or a swimming suit. Nevertheless, she allowed Farhad to choose her dresses for her and even let him buy her some sleeveless ones and a swimming suit too. She was indeed turning out to be the kind of a wife that Farhad approved of. What he liked the most about Leyla was that she was good-natured and loved to laugh. When she laughed, her black eyes shimmered like two brilliant stars. Moreover, she was an extremely good housewife and prepared delicious Persian food. Farhad loved her *aashes*, the mouth-watering, thick soups of vegetable, noodle and legumes, and the *polo khoreshes*—those delicious thick stews served with basmati rice! Also her fish, chicken and vegetable dishes tasted equally heavenly. Not only did Farhad like Leyla for all those good qualities, he was also falling deeply in love with her.

A year after their marriage, Leyla gave birth to Jamshid, who was a miniature version of Farhad. Jamshid was a quiet baby, with black, drowsy eyes like his mother's. Then two years later Jalleh, their skinny baby girl, was born.

"Thank God the baby has your lips and not mine," Farhad told his wife, rocking his little girl in his sinewy arms.

"But her eyes are a carbon copy of yours: brown, inquisitive and mischievous," Leyla uttered through rounded lips.

Farhad replied, allowing himself a faint smile of satisfaction, "Yeah. You're right. It shows that she's mine!"

Leyla giggled and answered proudly, "Yes, also nobody can go wrong about your son!"

Farhad winked at Leyla and nodded in agreement. He then started singing a lullaby for his sweet baby and rocked her gently to sleep.

Farhad's happiness was complete, so was Leyla's, who found her husband good tempered and loving. Farhad was also doing very well in his career.

Every evening he could hardly wait to get home, to shower his wife with kisses and to play with the little ones. When he had reluctantly taken the engagement ring to ask for Leyla's hand four years earlier, Farhad had never envisaged that one day he would adore the *"neighbor's daughter"* so intensely. Neither had he dreamed that the same person would provide him with such perfect bliss, for which he blessed his sister, Nazilla.

When Farhad became a major, he was once again sent to the United States for six months' training with the Special Forces at Fort Bennington. Farhad's supervisors wanted him to specialize in American warfare tactics, which would enable him to train Iranian soldiers and officers upon his return to Tehran.

The training with the Special Forces proved to be very harsh. The trainees had to spend weeks in a hot, scorching desert learning methods of survival under severe living conditions. The struggling officers had no access to food or water and it was up to them to figure out how to stay alive. Therefore, they had no choice but to hunt down for food any moving creature that they could lay their hands upon. Farhad could have never even dreamed that one day he would gladly eat barbecued snakes and rats. They also had to find alternatives to water, such as sucking on the cactus plants to draw out some moisture.

The training with the U.S. Special Forces later served to be valuable in Farhad's harsh assignments and clashes with the rebellious tribes in the barren regions of Iran.

Two years later, Farhad and a small group of officers went to Munich to take a course in counterinsurgency with the U.S. forces stationed in Germany. This was the time when Hooshang was one of the participants.

Farhad was allowed to take his wife along that time, because the training was civilized and they could live at the officers' quarters, where wives were allowed. They left their two children with Leyla's parents.

For Leyla, coming from an Islamic family, German culture appeared quite shocking, especially when she saw how free and uninhibited young men and women were. She could not understand how they could cuddle up together and kiss romantically in public. Leyla had never seen anything of the sort happen in Iran. Husbands and wives never even kissed or showed any affection to one another in front of others. Loving and kissing were reserved for bedrooms. But those things did not bother Farhad. He had a more open mind to western ways. In fact, he liked it. He did not find anything wrong with two young people in love kissing each other in public. This annoyed Leyla very much. She would sometimes sulk for days, brooding over the fact that her husband should approve of such behavior.

"What's the matter?" Farhad asked Leyla one day, draping his arm around her shoulders. "Why don't you talk to me? Have I done something wrong?"

Leyla pushed her husband away from her grudgingly and uttered, "You know what's wrong? It's your attitude which is wrong!"

"What about my attitude?" he inquired innocently.

"Tell me, since when have you become a European?" she yelled at him with her ringing voice. "I can't understand how you can approve of this public kissing and hugging!"

"Oh, so that's your problem!" Farhad uttered. "Whether I approve of it or not, we can't change a culture."

Leyla looked at her husband forbiddingly and said with an angry, trembling voice, "Well, then I guess you wouldn't mind kissing one of those no-good blond girls yourself."

Farhad laughed, hugged her lovingly and replied, "No, my dear! Don't you worry. I have a beautiful wife whom I adore and don't need to kiss one of those '*blond girls*'." He then looked intently into her charcoal black eyes and continued, "But I don't think you should call them '*no-good*'."

Leyla complained with a frown on her brow, "Why not? I don't understand why you should be sticking up for them!"

"You know what, my darling?" Farhad shook his head with disappointment. "You don't need to be so jealous. Besides, I'm sticking up for nobody. All I want you to know is that people of different countries have different customs and ways of life. That does not make them *bad* and us *good*."

Leyla smiled sweetly and cuddled up against her husband like a cat. Farhad knew that she would eventually come round and understand what he meant.

Three years after their return from Germany Farhad came home one evening glowing with joy. He walked into the house singing and dancing with his arms waving in the air. Leyla, hearing him singing, rushed out of the kitchen, wiping her hands on her flower-patterned red apron.

Farhad kissed his wife on the tip of her carved nose and said, "Guess what?"

"What . . . what? Tell me quick!" she squealed. From her husband's contented, smiling face, Leyla could tell that something extremely important had happened.

Farhad announced gleefully while pointing with a finger at his epaulette, "Congratulate me. I'm a colonel now!"

He then lifted Leyla in his arms, turning her round and round as the children ran around them and screamed happily.

Words cannot explain the extent of jubilee that followed in their household after his announcement of the good news! The children were bouncing on their parents' bed, using it as a trampoline and chanting in unison, "*Baba* is a colonel . . . *Baba* is a colonel . . ."

Leyla, who normally would forbid them this game, left them alone. She looked at her husband proudly and roared with laughter.

Life went on smoothly and happily until 1978. By then, Farhad was already a two-star general, enjoying power and all the comforts of life that one could ask for.

GOING HOME

FOR THE LAST TIME

Farhad got fed up with knitting and threw the half-finished sweater on the brass table. He started pacing up and down the basement floor nervously. A mouse shot like a dart from one corner of the cell to the other, dragging along its long, disgusting tail. The darkness, the stale air, the loneliness and the austere cement walls of the basement were getting to him again. What's more, the thought of separation from his family and the ambiguity of the upcoming trip were driving him crazy. He did not know whether he could trust the smugglers, who had sent word via Simin that all the preparations for his escape were now complete.

Against all odds, Farhad decided to go home and spend some quality time with his wife and children before his departure. Who knew when he would see them again, if ever!

A week before his escape, early in the morning when the full moon and the stars were still illuminating the dark sky and the surroundings, Farhad went home. Luckily his hiding place was only four blocks away from his house. For safety, his host drove him home at two in the morning when the *pasdars* were normally asleep, either at home or in their cars while still on duty. The early-morning rides through dark and deserted back streets had become common for Farhad. In the beginning, he was very anxious about the safety of their operation each time his relatives would transport him from one location to the other. As time went by, he became more relaxed and developed a tremendous trust in the judgment of his hosts, who knew exactly which back streets were not patrolled.

Leyla had stayed up to greet her husband when he arrived home, but Jalleh and Jamshid were fast asleep. They both had early classes at the university.

Farhad felt happy to be at home, lying in his own bed with Leyla by his side. After all those years of separation, holding her soft and warm body against his felt like a sweet dream. How he had missed sleeping in their comfortable bed, rather than on the squeaky and wobbly cots in the humid basements! He had also missed breathing fresh air pouring into the bedroom from the open windows, permeating the room with the heavenly perfume of the jasmine, roses and lilies.

Lying awake, he stared at his wife as the warm moonlight glowed at her face through the window in their dark bedroom. Farhad found Leyla to be special and desirable. What's more, she looked as graceful as ever, even in bed, with the way she held her head and gazed at her husband's face. Farhad wondered whether his wife was thinking about his looks and if she still found him handsome. He knew that he looked good, having worked out rigorously all through his hiding years, despite his graying hair and lines of age. Working out had not only kept him from going insane, but it had also helped maintain his strong, muscular frame.

The following morning, the general went down to the basement where Jamshid had put a *long chaise* for him; Jamshid did this as soon as he had heard that his father was going home. For some reason, this basement seemed friendlier to him than all the others he had lived in so far. Maybe the reason for it was because it belonged to him, or maybe it was because of his being in a good mood. At last he was with his beloved wife. Farhad told himself that even if this were the final day of his life, he wouldn't regret this visit. Every minute of his time spent there was worth all the dangers! He hadn't felt so happy in years.

Farhad lay down on the beach chair and read his newspaper under the bright, bare ceiling bulb of the basement. Leyla kept him company by bringing down fruit, tea and snacks.

Pulling out a plastic chair from a pile stashed in the corner, she sat down facing Farhad, with her elbows resting on her knees and her hands under her chin. Leyla sat there fixing her dark gaze at Farhad, as if it were the first time she was setting her eyes on him. They looked at each other for a while in silence, feeling strange. It was the first time, after so many years, that they were completely by themselves in their own house. From time to time the couple had been alone in other basements. Also, the night before, the couple had just been content to lie side by side and there had been practically no exchange of words. Their contact had been merely physical.

Presently, they just sat there, not knowing how to start a conversation, even though they had so much to talk about. Nine years of separation had put some distance between them. They had each lived in their different worlds and developed separate interests and realities of life. Solitude and depressing thoughts had turned Farhad into an unsociable and taciturn person. He had led a hermit's life and learned to talk to himself. Socially, he was no longer an outgoing and talkative character, as he had been in the old days.

Finally Leyla broke the silence, "You look good."

"Thank you, so do you."

Farhad turned back to his newspaper and tried to read without being able to concentrate.

"Have you prepared yourself for the trip?" Leyla tried again to make conversation.

"You mean the escape?" he asked frigidly.

"Yes, I mean the escape," Leyla snapped and got to her feet.

Farhad, detecting the tone of annoyance in Leyla's voice, said, "Sit down . . . sit down, I'm sorry, just ignore my stupid moods." He smiled at his lovely wife and added, "Let's talk. Who knows when we'll get the chance to be together again?"

They carried on with more small talk until suddenly the ice broke between them and they began chattering hungrily. Farhad noticed how much wiser Leyla had become. Being independent and the sole decision-maker around the house had further strengthened her intelligence, confidence and strength of spirit. The general could not comprehend how his wife could be so enduring and courageous. During their conversation she had not once complained nor shown any signs of discontent. He remembered how understanding she always had been during his long absences from home. Farhad's thoughts went back to their engagement party when he warned Leyla about his long absences from home because of his military career. Leyla had more than lived up to her reply of being able to handle it.

Farhad looked at Leyla admiringly and said, "I'm amazed at how strong you are! Where do you get . . ."

Leyla interrupted him, "Where do I get what?"

"I mean, where do you get your strength from? Do you ever complain? Does anything bother you at all? Look what you've gone through because of me all these years!"

She glared at her husband, looking quite annoyed. "What would you have me do? Cry? Moan and groan constantly? How would that help?"

"I don't know!"

"Well, one has to be pragmatic and face life with its problems and realities," Leyla said, brushing her hair off her face.

Later in the afternoon, Leyla went upstairs to prepare dinner. Then at dusk, Farhad joined his family in their welcoming dining room where all sorts of tasty food awaited him.

For a second Farhad stood by the dining room door, not knowing how to react. He was no longer used to this kind of a life and did not very well remember how to act like a father. Suddenly, overwhelmed by extreme emotion, he broke down and cried. Jalleh and Jamshid rushed forward and embraced their father warmly, as Leyla stood by the dining table gracefully, keeping her cool.

Farhad wiped his tears, took a deep breath and muttered timidly, "Goodness, what has become of me! I have turned into such a soft-hearted person!" and then laughed and looked at Jalleh and Jamshid shamefacedly.

Jamshid smiled, draped a hand around his father's shoulders and said, "It's perfectly all right, *Baba*, to get emotional. We haven't been together for ages." Then, to put his father at ease, he changed the subject as he rubbed the palms of his hands together, and said, "Come on everybody, let's eat and have a feast. *Maman* has prepared delicious dishes for us."

Jamshid led Farhad and Jalleh into the large dining room, separated from the sitting area by white double doors fitted with panes of glass. In the center of the dining room, a rectangular cherry wood table, able to accommodate twelve or more people, stood with its matching chairs. Leyla had filled the table with delicious-smelling Iranian food, enough to feed more than twenty people.

"Oh, how I've missed your cooking!" Farhad exclaimed, pressing Leyla against his chest, when she bustled over with another dish of *khoresh*. He was starting to feel like his old self again. Farhad was opening up and feeling relaxed.

After dinner, Farhad roamed around the house, checking out every nook and cranny and finally ending up in his study, which had an entire wall of shelves filled with Persian poetry books and English novels. Next, he looked at his walnut wood desk placed in the middle of the room with its brown leather swivel armchair. He had loved sitting in that chair in the quiet of his study for hours, reading his favorite poems.

The general then pulled out a volume of Sadi's poetry, pressed it against his chest and sank into the desk armchair. He just remained there motionless, as if he were trying to capture the lost time. A time that had elapsed without him living it. A time during which his study had remained unoccupied, while he was wasting away in dark basements. Tears blurred Farhad's vision as he gaped through a haze at the thick beige curtain that hung over the window on the opposite wall, and the old chiming clock on the mantelpiece next to the window. He noticed that nothing had changed; it was the same old curtain and the same old clock.

By the time the general returned to the sitting room, Leyla and Jalleh had cleared the table and done the dishes, while Jamshid sat in the living room waiting for his father to join him there. He was in seventh heaven to have his father at home.

Jamshid, smiling contentedly, said, "I had forgotten how nice it is to have *Baba* around."

Farhad gazed admiringly at his tall, handsome son and responded, "The same here, I had also forgotten how nice it is to be with my warm and caring family."

Jamshid threw his head back, thrust his shiny, dark hair off his wide forehead, turned to Jalleh and asked, "Hey sis, when are you going to tell *Baba* about the good news?"

Jalleh smiled timidly. Dodging Farhad's gaze, she said, "I think I'll give my big brother the honor of breaking the news to *Baba*."

Farhad's inquisitive eyes opened wide and his eyebrows arched as he inquired, "What news?"

Jamshid's face glowed. Staring lovingly at his sister and then at his proud, smiling mother, he sat down and took a deep breath. His black eyes shimmered with tears as he looked at his father, from whom he would soon be separated.

Jamshid gazed at Farhad intently, took on a serious demeanor, and said, "Jalleh is going to get married and wants to ask for your blessing and permission."

Farhad's heart leapt with joy! He sprang to his feet and dashed towards Jalleh. "My little girl is going to get married?" He blurted out, pressing Jalleh hard against his chest. "Of course you have my permission and blessing! But first you have to give a big kiss to your old 'Baba'." Farhad, then turning his cheek to Jalleh, pointed to it with his finger and said, "Hurry up, place the kiss right here."

Jalleh stood on the tips of her toes and kissed her father's cheek breezily, as her long, wavy, dark hair thrust back and touched her narrow waist.

"Oh, *Baba,* why do you have to be so tall?" she complained jokingly. "I'll have a stiff neck from stretching it to kiss your cheek!"

"*Khubeh . . . khube,* you delicate creature!" Jamshid teased his sister, twisting her arm behind her back.

"You leave me alone!" Jalleh pushed her brother away.

Turning to his father, Jamshid said, "Sir, you haven't asked about the groom."

"Oh, yes, that was going to be my next question. Tell me Jalleh, who's the lucky guy?"

Jamshid did not give his sister a chance to answer and cut in eagerly, "Sir, he is one of Jalleh's classmates. Remember General Farokhzad who was executed right in the beginning of the revolution?"

"Do I remember him?" Farhad uttered, looking sad at hearing General Farokhzad's name.

"*Baba,* he is the late general's nephew."

"My, I'm happy to hear about that!" Farhad said as his face suddenly brightened up.

Jalleh looked at her mother and smiled proudly, and Jamshid's dark, gleaming eyes blinked with joy.

The Farokhzads were one of the most prominent families of Iran. Farhad thought that it was an honor to have his daughter marrying into their respected clan. General Farokhzad, whom Farhad used to know quite well during the Shah's days, was a respectful person and, unlike certain high-ranking officials, did not flee when Ayatollah Khomeini came to power.

Farhad looked at his good-looking children proudly and admired their dedication and unity towards one another. He was overjoyed to see such a loving relationship between a brother and sister.

Jalleh was more like Farhad in character. She was bold, charismatic and was a bit spoiled as a child by Farhad. Jamshid, on the other hand, was more like Leyla. Even though he was outgoing and a warm person, he was also quite formal in his relationship with his parents, especially with his father, whom he mostly addressed as "Sir."

Farhad felt very lucky to have such a "perfect" family, as he liked to call them. He knew that his two children, under Leyla's guidance, were headed for success and prosperity. He was also aware that they would be able to stand on their feet and that his absence was not going to affect them adversely in life.

The general's heart filled with sorrow, thinking about his separation from them all. He especially felt saddened at the idea of not being able to attend his baby daughter's wedding. He enviously wished that he could be free and a part of them for good. Alas, it was not possible. He had to go!

Leyla, detecting her husband's sorrowful mood, cast her eyes down to hide her own tears, but Farhad instantly noticed her weepy eyes.

"No, I just can't go through this painful separation!" he uttered without preamble.

Leyla immediately regained her composure. Looking at Farhad sternly, she found it hard to keep from exploding. "Nonsense! I thought this question was already settled!" She shook her head with disappointment at her husband's defiance. "Listen, Farhad, I want you alive!" Leyla stressed, studying her husband's sullen face lined with the sufferings of the past nine unhappy years, as the hard lines on her own face gradually melted into a smile. "You know what?"

"What?" Farhad said curtly.

"I've decided to accompany you to Tabriz," Leyla announced, gaping at her husband decisively.

Tabriz was going to be the first station of his trip leading to the Turkish border, where he was supposed to meet the first contact man. The smugglers had told Simin to let Farhad know that Keyvan, the contact person in Tabriz, would be wearing a white carnation in the lapel of his jacket. Farhad, in turn, was asked to wear dark sunglasses and wait at the lobby of the Intercontinental Hotel at eleven A.M. on the 23rd of September.

"No way!" Farhad voiced firmly. "I don't understand. Why would you want to accompany me to Tabriz?"

"Well, you know . . ."

"No, I don't," he cut in flatly. "Supposing I agree and you go with me, what are you going to do all by yourself when I leave Tabriz? How will you return to Tehran?"

She laughed, throwing her head back as her sinewy neck muscles bulged. "Have you forgotten that my cousin, Halleh and her husband live in Tabriz?"

Farhad groped in his jacket's pocket for his cigarettes and then got up looking for a match, as Leyla observed him anxiously.

He lit his cigarette, slumped back in his chair and finally said, "That's right. Your cousin does live in Tabriz."

Leyla pressed on, smiling triumphantly, "I might spend a week or two with Halleh and her family," she sighed sorrowfully, looking away, and went on with a trembling voice. "Busying myself with my relatives will help make the separation less painful."

Farhad nodded with consent, "You're right. That's a good idea."

Then staring at his wife's sullen visage he thought, *"If that would alleviate her pain, I would be willing to go along with her wish."*

All of a sudden, in the middle of their conversation, the intercom buzzer exploded in the air, startling everybody out of their wits.

Leyla jumped to her feet with pounding heart, looking helplessly to Jamshid for comfort.

"Who can it be?" Jamshid said anxiously as Jalleh shrugged and commented, "Maybe Simin *Khanoom.*"

Leyla finally made her way to the intercom and demanded over the speaker, "Who is it at this time of the night?"

A harsh voice answered from the other end, "Open up! It's the *pasdars.*"

Suddenly the whole family became panic-stricken. They appeared like scared, cornered animals that turn round and round in circles. The women were running about trying to find headscarves, while Jamshid was hurriedly putting away the ashtray and the drink glasses.

"They should by no means find me here," Farhad told himself. *"It could be extremely dangerous for my family."*

The buzzer sounded loudly again. Leyla rushed back to it and yelled out, "Wait!"

"What's keeping you? Hurry up and open the door before we break it down."

"Yes, yes," Leyla snapped. "You have to wait until the women of the house have covered themselves properly."

That was the best excuse for buying time and the revolutionary guards could say nothing against that. It was the Islamic law and no strange man was allowed to see an uncovered woman. In the meantime, Jamshid rushed Farhad down the stairs to the safety of the pitch-dark basement, where Farhad waited fearfully. A few minutes later, he heard the muffled voices of his family members and a guard arguing about something. Farhad wondered how the *pasdars* knew that he was spending time with his wife and children. Nobody except his second cousin and his wife, who had been hosting him for the past ten days, knew about his visit with the family. Farhad was absolutely certain that his hosts would never betray him unless they were captured and tortured. He hoped with all his heart that he was wrong. Farhad thought that he would never forgive himself if any harm came to his benefactors.

Ten agonizing minutes passed by without Farhad knowing what was going on upstairs. He hoped that his family members were not in trouble. *"What if they decide to take my son to their headquarters for questioning?"* he asked himself. *"Please God, don't let that happen."*

Within a few minutes the general heard the front door slam. He was dying to know what was happening. *"Had the pasdar left, or had another one entered the house?"* Then he heard the sound of footsteps on the basement stairs and imagined a guard holding a gun at his son's head and forcing him down into the basement. He held his breath and begged God for help.

"*Baba*, it's me," the general heard Jamshid say.

"Oh!" he exclaimed with great relief as his heartbeat slowed down.

"Thank God, they had the wrong house. They were looking for a guy called Kazem Moosavi," his son announced gleefully.

"Were they easily convinced that this wasn't the Moosavi house?"

"Not really. They looked into every room and corner."

"Doing what?"

"Checking pictures . . ."

Farhad threw in, "Why pictures?"

"They kept looking at the guy's photo on the flyer and comparing it with our framed pictures on the mantelpiece."

"Oh, I see. If this were his place, his photo would be somewhere in the house."

"Exactly. Then the guards asked us each for our birth certificates."

"Didn't they make a fuss over our family name?"

"No, they were on a different mission and only interested in Mr. Moosavi."

Farhad said, "Poor fellow, I hope they never catch him!"

FAREWELL

Seven days later, at past midnight, a white Vauxhall was awaiting Farhad and Leyla in the dark, dead-end alley behind their house.

It felt so odd and unreal for Farhad to be going away after so many years of confinement. All that while the idea of his escape had felt like nothing but mere talk. He had never wanted to believe that the day of his escape would really arrive!

As they descended the stairs leading to the back door, Farhad began breathing with difficulty. It felt like a ton of cement was pressing against his chest. He was overwhelmed with sorrow and could not bear the thought of separation from his beloved ones for life. Farhad's sole consolation was having Leyla with him, albeit for a short while.

The general pressed Jalleh and Jamshid hard against his chest in the dark street and said with a trembling voice, "I'm sure that God will bring us together again."

That's all he said to them. He tried to make their farewell session as short as possible. Farhad found it less painful that way. Besides, he did not want to break down a second time in front of his children.

After Leyla and Farhad crept into the back seat of the car, the driver slowly pulled away from the curb. A painful lump formed in Farhad's throat. He could not take it anymore; the moment was unbearably painful!

Before the car turned onto the main street, the general turned back to have a last glimpse of his children. In the pitch-dark alley illuminated only by the taillights of the Vauxhall, he could barely make out Jalleh's delicate silhouette and Jamshid's tall and strong outline standing motionless like two dark statues.

The general turned to his wife and complained, "I feel like a chunk of my life has been snatched away from me. I wish I didn't have to ever say goodbye to my *nooreh cheshms.*"

Leyla teased Farhad to lift up his spirit, "How come they are your *'souls'* and not I?"

"Come on, you know very well that you are more than *nooreh cheshm* to me!"

The driver, who knew exactly what his duty was, accelerated nervously, giving a sudden jolt to his passengers.

"He doesn't have good bedside manners, does he?" Leyla muttered.

Farhad smiled and whispered back, "No, not at all! He didn't even answer us when we greeted him."

"He didn't even turn back to see who we were. I wonder how he looks?" Leyla jeered, letting the *chador* slip off her head and rest loosely over her shoulders.

The driver turned into a side street and carried on for a few blocks before entering another lifeless lane. He was trying to go through deserted back streets to avoid coming up against a patrol car.

The dark street resembled a ghost town with its sleeping inhabitants and somber, one-story houses. The shadowy sycamores stretching in a line on both sides of the street resembled a blurred impressionist painting when the car's dimmed lights splashed briefly on them.

Forgetting all about their fears and the dangers, Leyla and Farhad began chitchatting happily. How strange it felt for the general to be sitting next to his wife in a car after all those years of separation! He looked at her almost like a stranger might. She looked good! Even after a whole week of spending time with her, he could not get enough of looking at her face. He loved to have her sitting so close to him. Most of all, he loved her warmth and fresh smell.

The general looked at the driver in the dark car. From time to time, a weak flash of light from the cross streets would reveal some of his features, such as the back of his balding head, his long neck, or round ears sticking out like fish fins.

The back streets seemed as unattractive as they had been before. The one-story, yellow brick houses all had narrow, covered porches. The corrugated aluminium shutters, which served as doors of the closed shops, reflected some light back into their eyes as the car's headlights shone upon them. Farhad remembered how the shopkeepers would roll those shutters all the way down to the ground every night at closing time and secure them with large iron locks. At opening time, they would let the shutters roll back up above the shop entrances with a sudden thrust of the hand.

About fifteen minutes into their drive, the dazzling headlights of an oncoming car lit up the dark street like daytime and jolted them with fear. The driver bellowed nervously, "Hey, you, Mister, down . . . down. Hurry up. Drop down on the floor. It's the *pasdars!*"

For a second Farhad felt upset to be addressed as "Hey, you," but then he reminded himself that nobody cared anymore whether he once had been a respected general or not. These were now Khomeini's days and he was a wanted fugitive with a price on his head.

Farhad immediately obeyed the driver and lay low on the car floor. He rested his shoulders and head against one door and the soles of his shoes against the opposite one, while his knees dug into his chin. Leyla, in the meantime, gathered her legs in towards the seat to give Farhad more room. She then quickly thrust the flared skirts of her *chador* over her husband's head and body, concealing him completely. Next she pulled the top of the black Islamic veil snugly over her head and face, clasping the two sides of the cloth together from inside with one hand and leaving only one eye staring out.

The patrol car started blinking its lights, beckoning them to stop. The driver pulled the car aside and brought it to an abrupt stop.

There was total silence in the car. The only noise that Farhad could hear was the sound of his wild heartbeat. The driver rolled his window down and waited for the revolutionary guard to approach.

"Help us dear God," Farhad prayed quietly. *"Please don't let any harm come to Leyla!"*

A green-uniformed *pasdar* of medium height with a thick moustache approached the car. A machine gun, slung carelessly over his shoulder, swayed from side to side with every lazy step he took.

Silence! *"What's happening?"* Farhad wondered as he was overwhelmed by fear. *"Is he staring at Leyla? Can he see that she is hiding someone under her chador?"* Luckily, the front seat of the Vauxhall had a high back and it concealed Leyla's body. One looking at her from the front window could see only her *chador*-covered head.

"Who's this woman?" Farhad heard the deep voice of the *pasdar* asking the driver, as he stayed completely motionless, afraid even to breathe.

The driver responded nonchalantly, "How do I know who she is? I'm merely a telephone taxi driver. Why don't you ask her yourself?"

The guard then addressed Leyla, "Hey woman, what are you doing out in the streets at this time of the night?"

"Oh my God! How is she going to handle him?" the general wondered, racked with fear. He felt ashamed of himself and humiliated to be hiding under his wife's *chador*. But there was no other choice. Not only would he be in danger if he were caught, he was sure that Leyla would also be imprisoned and tortured. Maybe even shot. He had heard too many horror stories about such incidents. A friend had told him once that late one night, an Armenian couple was returning home from a wedding. A *pasdar* stopped them and asked the husband who the woman was. The fellow said that she was his wife. The *pasdar* did not believe him, thinking she was a prostitute. He detained the wife and asked the husband to go home and bring their wedding

certificate. The poor man, not being able to find the wedding document that night, waited for daytime to call the Armenian Church for help. By the time he brought the re-issued certificate to the prison where his wife was being held, it was too late. The guards had shot her, thinking she was a prostitute.

The general waited fearfully to see what Leyla's reaction to the *pasdar's* question would be. In the meantime, being aware of his wife's boldness and problem-solving skills, Farhad felt somewhat relaxed.

Leyla shifted in her seat nervously and answered with a muffled voice through her *chador*-covered mouth, "Officer, I was fast asleep when the telephone rang. It was my sister urging me to call a taxi and go to my mother's bedside. You see, officer, she's very old and quite ill."

Farhad was afraid that his wife would not easily get away with that story, even though it was true that her mother was old and not so well.

The general was very anxious. His heart was thumping madly. Farhad was not so much worried for himself as he was for Leyla. The thought of her being sent to prison was torturing him. The Evin Prison, which was notorious for being a center of atrocious crimes and torture by the *SAVAK*—the Shah's secret police—was now in the hands of Ayatollah Khomeini's guards. They were using the same methods of torture. One such method was the "human soccer game," in which *SAVAK* agents, now replaced by revolutionary guards, kicked prisoners back and forth like a soccer ball until their bones were completely crushed. Farhad knew that recently the *pasdars* had used this method of torture with a Protestant minister before shooting him in the head. His crime was preaching Christianity to the Muslims.

The general waited nervously to hear the *pasdar's* reaction to Leyla's story. He was angry and fed up with everything, including the late Shah, Ayatollah Khomeini, the revolutionary guards, and the whole world. He thought that if that guy ever dared to harm Leyla, he would kill him with his bare hands.

The guard barked hoarsely, "Hey, who do you take me for?

Don't you think I know what sort of a woman you are?" He then laughed maliciously and carried on, "Of course, you also know what happens to such women when they're caught!"

Suddenly blood rushed to Farhad's head with rage. He pressed the palms of his hands against the car floor to help himself jump to his feet and punch the stupid guard in the mouth, when Leyla's voice stopped him. "Shame on you. How dare you insult me?"

The general could tell that Leyla was now turning her covered face away from the guard as a sign of annoyance, from the movement of the *chador* over his head.

"I'm a respectable, religious woman and one of the Imam Khomeini's followers." Leyla's trembling voice filled the quiet air.

The guard answered sarcastically, "Oh yes? And I'm the Imam Himself!"

One thing Farhad knew was that his wife was not lying, and that she really was a devout Muslim and that she respected Imam Khomeini as a religious head.

"Well, I don't know how else to convince you." She complained hopelessly.

The guard retorted, "I'm all ears. Convince me!"

"All right," she said firmly. "You want proof of my claim, I'll give it to you!"

"Fine."

Farhad wondered what Leyla was going to do. Was she about to ask him for his cellular phone to call her mother's house?

Leyla's voice interrupted Farhad's fearful thoughts. "All you have to do is to get in your car and follow us to my mother's house. It's as simple as that!" she bluffed.

"Leyla . . . Leyla, what are you doing?" Farhad whispered under his breath.

The guard roared with laughter. Then he suddenly stopped. Farhad assumed that he was wagging a finger at his wife, as he growled at her furiously, "Don't you tell me what to do."

"Fine, officer, I'm sorry!" Leyla uttered timidly.

Farhad could imagine how stressed Leyla must feel. He

thought that she must be getting anxious, because she had used up all her resources in dealing with the officer, and now the rest was in God's hands.

Entrapped under Leyla's *chador*, trying hard to endure the hot and smothering air, Farhad found himself utterly useless! He also felt terrible, thinking about all the pain and agony his poor wife had to suffer because of him. The general thought he should have given himself up right in the beginning of the revolution. *"Who knows,"* he pondered, *"Khomeini might have pardoned me! 'Pardoned?'"* Just the way other high-ranking officers were pardoned!

The guard now addressed the driver, "I don't like what I'm about to do, but I'll let this woman go this time." Then turning to Leyla, he added, "When you know that you have a sick mother, why don't you stay with her? This way you won't have to come out late at night."

"Yes, officer, you're right," said Leyla docilely. "But you see, I have two children that need looking after."

The guard pressed on, "How about your husband? Let him take care of them while you're looking after your mother."

Leyla sighed and said softly, "My husband's dead."

"Oh, I'm sorry," the guard said sympathetically. "Then who's taking care of your children right now?"

"I've got a live-in maid who can prepare their breakfast for tomorrow morning and send them off to school."

"I see," the guard said.

"Thank God!" Farhad breathed a sigh of relief. It looked like the guard had believed Leyla.

The officer commanded the driver sternly, "Driver, get going before I change my mind." Then he laughed and told Leyla, "You're one lucky lady to have met me and not another guard."

"Yes, officer." Leyla replied appreciatively, holding on tightly to the *chador*.

Just as they thought that they were off the hook, and the driver prepared to drive away, Farhad heard the guard yell, "Stop . . . stop!"

The driver complained, "What now? Aren't you done yet?"

"*Oh, dear! What next?*" Farhad asked himself.

The guard called out to the driver, "Come out and open the trunk."

"*Oh,*" the general felt relieved. There was nothing to worry about. Luckily they had no luggage with them. Farhad had only a small bag containing his shaving kit and a few pair of underwear. The contact man had insisted that he should not bring along any suitcases or large bags. Leyla also was traveling lightly. She had just a small tote bag.

It seemed to Farhad that the guard must be shining his flashlight into the trunk. Seeing the two bags, the *pasdar* asked the driver, "What are these?"

Farhad heard the driver say breezily, "Oh, these? The little one's mine and the other one's the lady's. I guess she has her overnight stuff in it."

"Very well, you can go, but why don't you pull out into the main street? There is another patrol car a few blocks away and you don't want to be stopped again."

It was definitely a miracle! God had been kind to them!

The driver immediately rolled the window up and sped away with indifference.

Leyla uncovered Farhad and said, "It's okay, now you can get up."

Farhad sat up in his place, wiped his sweaty brow and said, "I'm sorry that you had to go through such an ordeal!"

"The main thing is that it's over," Leyla uttered. "Thank God he didn't suspect that I was hiding you under my *chador*!"

Farhad rubbed the palms of his hands on his knees and nodded. "Yes, thank God!"

PAINFUL SEPARATION

The main street was well lit. Its wide sidewalks were lined with old lanterns and lush leafy oak trees. The multicolored red, green and white dancing lights above the shop entrances livened up the quiet, sleepy street. On hot summer evenings, during the time when Farhad was a free, normal human being, Leyla and he used to stroll leisurely along the pavement of that street.

The car sped along for about four miles until they reached the city limits and turned onto a narrow dirt road. There were no more lights illuminating their way, but for the moon which peeked briefly through patches of cloud. Farhad stretched his stiff body and felt relaxed and temporarily safe.

Leyla fell asleep with her head leaning against Farhad's shoulder. The saga with the guard had sapped her energy. Farhad tilted his head to touch hers and also fell asleep.

The pleasant early-morning sun woke them up. For a moment Farhad was confused and could not comprehend where he was. Then he came to his senses and remembered everything. He looked outside and saw the road snaking through brown, arid land dotted with low hills here and there.

"*Sunshine . . . daylight!*" he told himself. Seeing the sunshine after nine years was a real luxury for Farhad! He could not believe that it was real. He had to shade his eyes with his hand; his eyes were not used to such brightness.

Leyla yawned, stretched her arms and whispered, "Farhad, I wonder if this man is deaf and mute!"

Farhad smiled at her pretty, well-rested face as she continued. "He hasn't opened his mouth to talk to us even once!"

Farhad thought that the poor man must be exhausted and very sleepy. Tapping gently on his shoulder, he said, "Good morning, *Agha*, how are you?"

The driver glanced at Farhad through the mirror with bloodshot eyes and said aloofly, "We're nearly there."

Leyla whispered, "We're nearly where?"

"He means that we're nearly in Tabriz," Farhad said sullenly, as a shooting pain stabbed his heart like a dagger. He shifted uncomfortably in his seat and thought that he was having a heart attack. Then he realized that the pain was the result of stress and sorrow. He was soon going to be separated from his wife for good.

Farhad held Leyla's soft, warm and frail hand in his and pressed it hard. She lowered her sad eyes and tilted her head. He felt like soothing her, but what was the point? Words could not express the deep hurt they were both feeling. The best thing to do, he thought, was to remain silent. So he simply held her hand against his lips and kissed it fervently. This would be their final goodbye. They would not be able to hug or kiss in public later that day when separating for good. The *Zeinab Sisters* would be watching. Besides, in Iran you never did that, not even during the Shah's reign.

They arrived in Tabriz at around 9:00 A.M. Farhad sat rigidly in his seat and looked out as they drove through a wide street with spire-looking poplar trees lining its sidewalks. Water flowed through wide *joobs*, carrying scraps of paper and cardboard. About one mile down the road, they came up to a circle. In the middle of the circle, a turbaned statue of Molavi, the ancient Persian poet, stood on a pedestal. A fountain in the pond at the foot of the statue sprayed water at Molavi's long-robed figure. Farhad looked intensely at the statue and then at his wife. He wanted to make a mental note of their faces forever in the depths of his mind.

As the car sped away, the general looked back and observed the poet's statue with reverence. Molavi peered back at him from behind a rainbow arching through the misty water particles of the fountain in the early-morning sun. The white, red, and green colors of the rainbow reminded Farhad of the previous Iranian flag, stirring feelings of patriotism in him.

Suddenly, in his mind, Molavi came to life. Farhad heard him reciting the heavenly verses, which he and his friends used to take turns in reading at their evening gatherings. Farhad's heart filled with sorrow. *"Oh God,"* he said to himself, *"how can I leave all this behind? This is my culture. It is my language and my life! Am I supposed to forget the past and start a new life?"*

The car turned into an unpaved side street lined with two-story terraced houses. On some of the terraces, sagging clotheslines displayed people's colorful laundry. Boys with shaved heads chased one another, playing hide and seek on the sidewalks. The driver had his fist pressed on the horn, trying to keep the children from running in front of the car.

From there they came out into another main street with towering, old trees and deep *joobs* running on each side of the wide road. The tight-lipped driver slowed down as they approached the ten-story Intercontinental Hotel.

"My mission ends here," he finally said without looking back, and dropped Farhad and Leyla off at the entrance of the hotel.

A navy blue-uniformed doorman greeted the couple humbly with a bow and held the glass door open to let them in. Farhad and Leyla stepped gingerly into the dimly lit hotel lobby and sat discretely on a sofa far away from the semicircular reception desk. The two large burgundy-and-white floral Kashan carpets and the elaborate chandeliers reminded Farhad of the Shah's palace. It brought back memories of *Norooz*, the Iranian New Year receptions at the palace on the first day of spring, when the ministers and high-ranking army officers went to wish the Shah a happy *Norooz*.

At 10:45 A. M., the contact man arrived. As specified, he was wearing a white carnation in his lapel. The general looked with trepidation at his handsome face, coal-black, greased hair and tall, trim frame. He was the last person on earth Farhad wished to see.

"Here he comes," Farhad grunted. Somehow, he was hoping that the man would not show up and he would be forced to return to Tehran with his wife.

The young man approached them, knowing quite well who they were. Leyla had told him about Farhad's appearance when she had talked to him over the phone two weeks earlier. He was to look for a tall man with graying hair, wearing dark sunglasses. Farhad had shaved his moustache and beard when he had gone home the week before.

The young fellow smiled faintly and whispered, "Are you the traveler?"

"Yes I am," Farhad muttered. "And this is my wife."

He shook hands with the general and bowed to Leyla saying, "I'm Keyvan, your contact man."

Keyvan beckoned to a dark brown door at the end of the hall and said, "Let's go there and have something before leaving."

The restaurant was empty. It was not lunchtime yet, but the waiter let them sit at a small table with a red-and-white-checkered tablecloth and a small lamp in the middle. He filled their glasses with water and handed them three menus. They served only western food in that restaurant.

The general and Leyla ate very little. They were not hungry. Who could eat at such a despairing time when they knew that in a few minutes they were going to go through a painful separation, maybe for life! However, Keyvan not only ate well; he ordered the most costly dishes on the menu.

After lunch, the general paid the expensive bill and then they stepped into the noisy street. Drivers drove recklessly, honking at men and women who were jaywalking the busy street.

Keyvan, turning to Farhad, said hastily, "There's no time to waste. We have to leave right away."

Farhad's heart sank. That was it. He was leaving his sweet wife, the companion of his life! The general stared at Leyla's *chador*-covered, stooped figure. He knew she was hurting badly. He had never seen Leyla carry her body any other way but upright. How useless he felt!

He stood there limply, hoping for a sign from her to discourage him from leaving. Alas, no such luck! She just stood like a lifeless statue and waited for him to depart.

"We've got to go," Keyvan pulled at his sleeve.

Leyla, upon hearing this, quickly turned and walked away without saying a word. Farhad stared after her until the bustling crowd swallowed her up like a leaf in a whirlpool.

Keyvan elbowed him, "Let me have your money and let's make a move."

The general handed him the envelope containing all the money for his trip and followed Keyvan listlessly. Farhad's knees felt weak and his head dizzy. He felt devastated and shattered for being so heartlessly torn apart from his wife and children. He hated that moment and Keyvan, who was trying to help him get away, but he hated himself even more!

As they walked through the busy street under a hot, burning sun, a jovial-looking, short man with a round belly joined them. He introduced himself as Gholi. Gholi was the same person who had met Leyla at the jewellers' bazaar.

Smiling warmly, Gholi looked at Farhad with kind eyes overshadowed by thick eyebrows, and gave him an envelope.

Farhad took the envelope nonchalantly without bothering to ask any questions. He simply stuffed it into his jacket's pocket. Then he fumbled nervously in the other pocket for his pack of cigarettes.

Everything he loved had been taken away from him and soon he would be leaving his beloved country behind. The only things that he could hang onto were his cigarettes. Farhad pulled one out of the pack and cupped it in his palm for comfort before lighting it.

Gholi, taking the envelope back from Farhad, said, "This envelope contains an official letter from the Department of Housing of the city of Shapoor." The head of the smugglers then stepped closer to Farhad and whispered, "In this letter you are introduced as Ali Bagheri, an employee of the Department of Housing, who's supposed to release some goods from the Customs in Salmas."

The general felt perplexed and scared. Everything seemed so risky! He wondered if that scheme presented a credible story. If he were a *pasdar* going through those papers, would he be convinced? *"I'm not sure,"* he told himself. But there was nothing he could do about it; he had no choice but to go along with the smuggler's decisions. Besides, it looked as though those men knew what they were doing. It appeared that they had connections with some corrupt, high-ranking government civil servants.

Gholi went on whispering, "At the next crossroad, the guards inspect all vehicles thoroughly. But don't worry, you'll be okay."

"Really? I hope so!"

"We'll be riding in a car with official government license plates. The guards never bother people in government cars."

"Oh, I don't know. Everything seems so risky to me!" Farhad grimaced.

Gholi reassured him, "Don't worry. Even if they do ask some questions, your name's Ali Bagheri, and all your documents are in order." He smiled wryly as he squinted in the hot sun, wiping the sweat off his forehead with the back of his hand. "You see this *sejel*? There's no way anybody can ever detect that it's fake!"

Gholi opened the *sejel* and showed it to Farhad. The general was impressed with how real it looked! The fake ID carried his most recent picture taken at home during the past few days of his stay there. Like any other ID photo, it did not look good. But who cared! All that mattered was the official government stamp in the ID.

"All right, Mr. *'Bagheri'*, let's hurry now. Our car is waiting for us a block away from here."

As soon as he spoke those words, Gholi turned on his heels and disappeared among the crowd, leaving Farhad with Keyvan.

Keyvan and the general walked side by side without saying a word to one another. As they elbowed their way along the sidewalk, Keyvan kept looking admiringly at his reflection in the shop windows, drawing his palm over his sleek, gelled black hair. For Farhad, it was so interesting to observe this young man, especially when he made eye contact with the young girls who, in turn, returned his suggestive glances with smiling eyes. Young girls did not wear *chadors* like married women; they simply wore long brown or gray robes and white scarves.

"*People never change,*" Farhad told himself. "*Take the youth. They always have the same needs and feelings, no matter how much they're controlled.*"

The Islamic Republic's rules forbid young girls and boys from showing attention to one another or being together in public. And of course, women should cover themselves completely in order not to tempt men. "*How come men don't have to cover themselves from women?*" he thought. "*What if good-looking men appear tempting to women, the way Keyvan did to those young girls? People have eyes and feelings. How do you deal with that? How do you control what people should and should not look at, or what they should or should not desire?*" Farhad believed that was something that no regime or law could restrain. Despite all the strict rules of Khomeini's regime, everything happened the way it used to, albeit under cover. Not only that, but women now complained that men made unwelcome advances to them in public, even more than before. Farhad was convinced that it was because of all the restrictions imposed on people.

"*What about prostitution?*" the general asked himself. "*Did it stop because of the stoning and killings?*"

Not at all! It was as rampant as before.

It was now noon and prayer time. Dark-complexioned men in their gloomy-looking Islamic garb, and women shrouded in black *chadors* scurried about on the sidewalks like busy ants. Some of the men seemed to be headed towards the nearby mosque, which had a gilded dome and a tall, blue-tiled minaret.

The sound of the *azan*—chanting call of prayer—bellowed powerfully over the loudspeakers on the blue minaret. The muezzin's ringing voice pierced the air, penetrating every surrounding nook and cranny. The noontime *azan* summoned all the faithful to drop whatever they were doing and worship Allah. *"Allaho Akbar . . . Allaho Akbar"*—"God is great . . . God is great"—streamed from the loudspeaker atop the minaret.

Farhad and Keyvan walked at an easy pace on the cobbled pavement of the busy Molavi Avenue. Then they turned into a side street dotted with young birch trees and some green grocery stores. Soon they arrived at another narrow street, where a brand-new Range Rover was awaiting them. Gholi was also there, busy chatting with the driver. Farhad, Keyvan and Gholi instantly got into the Range Rover, escaping the noontime heat in its air-conditioned interior.

The road to the city of Khoy coiled through a dry valley with its heavy traffic. From time to time, impatient drivers would swerve onto the unpaved shoulder of the road, overtake cars from the right, and create thick clouds of dust. Reckless driving in Iran was and is considered macho and cool. For such irresponsible drivers, running through a red light is an everyday event and driving against the traffic in one-way streets happens to be as common as drinking water. Somehow if another car speeds head-on, one of them swerves and avoids an accident. And sometimes they simply collide. So what if somebody gets injured or killed! *That is what you call destiny.* "Eh, *it was their time, they had to go . . .*" says the fatalist.

After two hours, Farhad and the smugglers arrived at the crossroad mentioned by Gholi. The guards were carefully checking all the cars. The reason for that thorough inspection was to stop young Iranian men and boys from escaping to Turkey. The Iran-Iraq war was going on and those who did not want to become soldiers attempted to escape to Turkey.

It took a good hour for the line of cars to advance and for Farhad and his company to arrive at the checkpoint for inspection. While in line, waiting impatiently, millions of thoughts were brewing in Farhad's mind: *Would he be recognized? Could Gholi pull some strings in case Farhad was arrested? Would they return him to Tehran for execution . . . ?*

The guard at the checkpoint examined the general's face quizzically. It was obvious that he had certain questions on his mind about him. He probably found his face familiar. The general thought that the guard might recognize him from the constant broadcasting of his picture on TV. Strangely enough, Farhad was no longer scared of being detected. A feeling of apathy had overcome his whole being since leaving Leyla behind. That cruel separation had numbed his senses, making him indifferent to the question of life and death.

The guard stepped closer. Balancing the weight of the rifle on his shoulder, he carefully inspected the car's license plate.

The general turned his face away toward the opposite window and tried to dodge the guard's dissecting glances. Suddenly he noticed a poster with an old picture of him in military uniform posted on the wall, together with five other wanted fugitives.

Gholi, realizing the problem, rolled down the window and tried to distract the guard. "Hi, officer, how are you?"

"Fine," he replied indifferently.

"I hope you're not feeling too hot standing in the sun," Gholi asked again.

"Not too bad." The officer said absently, having his mind on something else—something that could possibly be decisive to Farhad's fate.

The *pasdar* fixed his curious gaze on Farhad again, squinting in concentration, but before he could ask him any questions, Gholi interjected, "We're all government officials, as you can see from the car's license plate."

The *pasdar* checked the car's plate again and demanded, "May I ask what brings you here?"

Gholi fumbled in his worn-out blue jeans' pocket, pulled out an envelope and handed it over to the guard.

"As you can see from the text of this letter," Gholi told the guard boldly, "we're on an important assignment."

The almost illiterate *pasdar* was having difficulty reading the text of the letter. To save him from embarrassment Gholi quickly pointed at the official government seal at the bottom of the letter. "Do you recognize this seal?"

The guard immediately stood at attention, clicked his heels and gave a military salute. "Yes, sir. I'm sorry . . . please excuse me!"

Gholi smiled mischievously, "Don't worry son, these things sometimes happen." And then, he uttered briskly, "Thank you, officer, have a good day."

He snatched the letter from his hand, rolled up the window and ordered the middle-aged driver to press on the gas pedal.

Turning back, Farhad noticed the perplexed guard standing by the pictures posted on the wall and rubbing his chin pensively. He then turned around, pointed a hand toward their speeding car and yelled, "Stop . . . stop."

Gholi, leaning one arm comfortably against the back of the driver's seat, instructed him to ignore the guard as if they had not heard his yells. The *pasdar*, giving up on them, left the waiting line of cars and ran into the guard post. A chorus of honking horns and cries of nervous drivers filled the air.

Gholi, smiling broadly, turned to the general and said, "Didn't I tell you that everything would be all right?"

"But the guy ran in to probably inform . . ."

Gholi cut Farhad short, "Don't worry. He can't do anything to harm us. Our official license plate is a real one. He'll call his headquarters," Gholi gave Farhad a broad smile. "And they'll tell him that we're okay."

Farhad had a nagging feeling that something was very wrong, but he also knew that he had to trust the head smuggler. He was sure that this was not the first time Gholi passed through that checkpoint.

"If you say so, then I bet you're right!" the general exclaimed, deciding to lean comfortably back in his seat and observe the barren landscape with its odd trees scattered about.

At around four in the afternoon, they arrived at the city of Khoy. Khoy looked somewhat like Tabriz with its wide streets, thick, tall, old trees and wide, deep *joobs* flowing with murky waters.

Seeing the *joobs*, Farhad smiled, remembering an incident that had happened to Leyla and Jalleh.

One day Leyla was driving on a busy street with Jalleh sitting next to her. On the outside lane, a young driver and his friend in a blue Volkswagen were trying to attract Jalleh's attention by shouting silly remarks.

"Shall I teach them a lesson?" Leyla looked at Jalleh mischievously.

"Oh, yes, please *maman*."

Leyla moved her car closer to the Volkswagen and forced it into the *joob*. Then, mother and daughter sped away, laughing their heads off.

"Now let them beg people to help them take the wheel out of the *joob* and put the car back on the road!" Leyla told Jalleh.

At Khoy, Gholi and Keyvan said goodbye, turning Farhad over to another smuggler who spoke in a soft, soothing voice and looked at him with a friendly, reassuring gaze. Like Gholi, this fellow seemed kind and good-natured. For a devastated fugitive like Farhad, with little hope for anything at all, it helped to have nice people around.

Farhad followed the new fellow through a maze of narrow side streets, nudging his way amongst throngs of *chador*-covered women and their children.

As they passed rows of grocery stores with displays of multicolored trays of spices and some butcheries, bakeries and houses in the narrow, unpaved side street, a short young man approached his guide. He whispered something to him in *Azari* Turkish and disappeared in the crowd. Then, within ten minutes, Farhad and his companion came to a square with wooden electric poles and small one-story houses. A black-and-white taxi was waiting for them in front of a garage filled with old, battered cars. The same short man, who had approached the guide earlier, was standing next to the taxi. As soon as Farhad and his guide slid into the back seat, the short fellow handed some money to the taxi driver and walked quickly away without saying a word.

The driver turned back and gazed at the general's sullen face. "Hello, sir. Don't worry, you're in good hands. I'm sure you're going to have a safe journey to Turkey. My taxi and I always bring good luck to the travelers."

"I hope so!" the general exclaimed, looking at his bulging eyes and gaunt face. He was missing one of his front teeth and he looked quite unhealthy, with his protruding cheekbones and blue-black lips. Farhad wondered if the fellow was an opium junkie. He had that distinct opium addict's look, especially with those bluish lips!

"From my bad luck, I have to fall on a driver who is a junkie!" the general complained to himself. *"I hope he'll get me to my destination in one piece and not fall asleep at the wheel!"*

The taxi driver's middle-aged assistant, sitting in the front seat, turned to face Farhad and grinned. From the way he sized the general up with his piercing eyes, Farhad could tell that the man did not like him. Neither did the general care much for him. His unfriendly face and cocky attitude left him cold. However, Farhad was in no mood to be bothered with such pompous fools. He just sat back aloofly, rested his head on the headrest and closed his eyes.

When the city limits ended, the taxi stopped and the friendly guide departed, leaving Farhad with a feeling of solitude and wariness. *"Could I trust those two strange men?"* he asked himself.

CONFRONTATION

The taxi turned onto a deserted, dirt road leading west. The bumpy road traversed through a valley that was encircled by a range of rocky mountains. Farhad gazed at the gigantic mountains reaching high up and staring down at them from the faraway, hazy horizon. This scenery was not foreign to him. He had led a number of military operations in arid, mountainous terrains during his military career. And now, after nine years of confinement, Farhad was once again out in the wilderness, feeling nostalgic about those memories.

Gradually the day started approaching its end and the sun began losing its radiance. Farhad rolled down the window to breathe some crisp, fresh evening air. Instead, the dust raised by the car got into his throat and nostrils, making him cough and sneeze. He quickly rolled up the window and decided to sit back and enjoy the majestic and awe-inspiring mountainous landscape.

The driver's assistant, whose job was to help the driver with general chores, turned back, arching an eyebrow. "Oh dear, our precious city boy has been exposed to dust!" he said and roared with a wheezing laughter.

Farhad felt aggravated by the fellow's behavior and thought that he would never have dared to talk to him in that tone in the old days. But then he reminded himself that these were the days of the Islamic Republic and that now it was the turn of people like this wretch to feel important and superior to the *"city boys"* like him. Anyway, he indeed was a nobody. Who cared whether or not he had once been a mighty general? That was all in the past. Farhad had to once and for all come down from his high horse. He had to learn to forget about the past glorious days.

When they arrived at the first village, the car pulled next to a small mud hut. A young man wearing a small, brown rimless felt hat, black, collarless shirt and black pants was waiting for them.

The driver's assistant got out and left them abruptly. *"Good!"* Farhad told himself, *"Let him go. This is one person I'm not going to miss!"* Then he immediately shook his head, feeling quite disappointed with himself. Farhad was sorry to admit that he had become a petty and vengeful person. *"What have all these years done to me? What has Ayatollah Khomeini turned me into?"*

A stupid child, that's what he felt he had regressed to. The same ten-year-old boy who used to fight over a bicycle with his friends. The same little guy who was spoiled by his sister and always got his way.

The man in black got in the taxi and guided them to an apple orchard through a bumpy village road flanked by half-grown birch trees.

The way the metallic green leaves of those trees shook and danced with the cool, late-afternoon breeze made Farhad reflect about a little village with similar trees where his sister and her husband used to take him on picnics in the summertime. Its pleasant, cool air and sweet spring water felt divine compared to the scorching heat and warm tap water of Tehran.

At the apple orchard, another person awaited the travelers. Farhad was about to greet him as he got out of the taxi, but the man's reticent and cold disposition prevented him. The drowsy taxi driver and his passenger said a hasty goodbye and drove away, as Farhad strolled grudgingly toward the young man. Farhad wished he could ignore idiots like the taxi driver's assistant and this unfriendly fellow, but he couldn't help it! He realized that the new world and its people were not to his liking at all. It was a world shaped during the nine years of his absence. It was a world where people appeared arrogant. They did not respect him and Farhad did not like it. Unfortunately, he was in no position to have any expectations from the new breed of men who had revolted to get rid of people like him. He had no place in their world. His era was over and he had to go.

"I assume you know who I am," the general said, not knowing what name to give. The real name?

"Of course!" smirked the bearded guide and gave him the cold shoulder.

Farhad tried to hide his anger and asked aloofly, "And who are you?"

"Mahmood," he replied callously.

Farhad turned his back to Mahmood and started kicking some pebbles angrily. He thought that he did not have to take it. If the fellow wished to snob Farhad because he was a fugitive, then Farhad did not see the need to be nice to the guy.

They had been waiting for barely ten minutes when a shabbily dressed, jolly-looking teenager approached them with a grimy rag bundle dangling in his hand. The boy smiled at Farhad scrunching his nose. "Here, this is your dinner," he said, handing the dirty bundle over to Mahmood, who snatched it from the boy.

"The savage seems to be very hungry and looks like he can't wait to open the soiled bundle," Farhad pondered, as he observed Mahmood with disgust.

"Let's go somewhere where we can sit down and eat." He beckoned Farhad to follow him.

The general slogged behind Mahmood feeling terribly upset. As if the driver's assistant were not enough, now he had to suffer this one! Farhad wished that the smuggling network would make a better selection of their guides.

They made their way through the shabby village lanes lined with mud huts and a few food stores. The village sat in a basin surrounded by mounds of dirt and pebbles. This region of Azarbayjan province was very dry and barren with scant vegetation. As usual, the boys playing on the roads had shaved heads and the girls, matted uncombed hair. Some had round dark eyes and plump red cheeks. Others were pale and skinny with runny noses that attracted hordes of flies to their faces.

Mahmood kept ordering Farhad around with an attitude, as if he were his hired hand or slave. He sometimes demanded that Farhad walk faster, while other times he instructed him to lag behind and not to look at other passersby. Farhad obeyed him halfheartedly. He thought that the man might be concerned about his safety and that he did not want Farhad to be noticed by the villagers.

As they left the dingy village and started walking into the wilderness, the powder-like soil and the pebbles scrunched under their feet, raising heavy dust behind them. After about twenty minutes, they reached an open area strewn with a myriad of scattered small and large rocks.

Mahmood commanded firmly, "Sit down on this rock and let's have our dinner."

"Oh, what a disgusting dinner!" Farhad turned his face away to avoid smelling the terrible stink of the stale, yellowish feta cheese when Mahmood opened the dirty rag bundle. Some flat Persian bread and different sorts of green herbs lay beneath the cheese in the rag—Iranians like to make a wrap of white cheese and herbs in the flat bread. It is a staple food of the poor.

"Come on, have some. This is all we're going to have till we reach our next destination," said Mahmood grumpily.

"No, thank you. I'm not hungry."

"Well, suit yourself. Unfortunately, I can't get you a five-star restaurant meal!" he snapped.

The general, with his arms wrapped around his knees, stared angrily into Mahmood's cold, expressionless eyes. He felt lonely and homeless in the cold and barren land. He dreaded the approach of the night, unprotected and out in the open. At least in the basements he felt sheltered and out of the sight of the revolutionary guards. *"What if we ran into a patrol car?"* he thought with fear. *"Wouldn't the pasdars be suspicious of two people idling around in the wide-open desert?*

"Well, whatever. Since I have started this escapade, I must accept that there is no return from it," Farhad admitted to himself, looking up at the fast-moving clouds in the sky. *"Is there a storm in store?"* he wondered.

Soon a cold wind chilled the air and in no time dusk fell upon them. The vast and barren landscape and the towering mountains surrounding the valley were no longer visible. The world seemed like a black rimless ocean, about to swallow them. Farhad shivered with awe and cold.

They had been sitting idly in the dark for approximately two hours, when suddenly the echoing clatter of hooves broke the deadly silence of the night. Startled, Farhad sprang to his feet and anxiously inquired, "What was that? What's happening?"

"Calm down," Mahmood barked harshly. "These are our people who've come to take us away."

"Hey, take it easy, man. You don't need to be so unfriendly," the general said scornfully. He'd had enough of that fellow. A bitter anger had been brewing in him since meeting Mahmood. And now he was about to explode.

"Look, Mister, we're not here to please you. We're here to do our job," Mahmood retorted sharply.

Farhad turned away from him and muttered, "I wonder who taught you your manners!"

"The same person who taught you yours," he snapped back at Farhad.

Flames of anger rushed to Farhad's face. He leapt like a panther at Mahmood's shadowy figure, knocked him down and sat on him. His years of martial arts training came in handy.

The general was enraged beyond control and his heart was thumping madly.

"I'm going to break your bones if you don't shut up!" Farhad yelled.

Mahmood, who was about a head shorter than the general, felt completely trapped under Farhad's weight and decided that he was no match for him. He did not even struggle to free himself from Farhad's grip and merely pleaded, "All right . . . all right, let me go please. I'm sorry!"

"You better be! You arrogant *pedar sag*," the general cussed. "Also don't you forget that you're being paid for doing your job."

"I told you that I was sorry, didn't I?" Mahmood beseeched Farhad.

The general grabbed the guy's hand and helped him up. He thought Mahmood's body must be hurting badly from its hard impact against the rough, pebbly ground.

"Good! That'll teach him a lesson," Farhad told himself, his rage gradually ebbing away.

In no time the silhouette of two horses took shape in the pitch-dark night. Farhad saw the shadow of a man perched on one of the horses and the blurry figures of three other men on foot.

As the men and the horses approached, Mahmood softly asked Farhad to mount the free horse. Then Farhad heard a merry voice echoing in the dark. "Hello, gentlemen. I'm your head guide and I'll be helping you cross a high mountain tonight."

Mahmood and the general greeted him, happy to distract themselves from what had just happened between them a short while back.

"Gentlemen," the guide's voice echoed. "We have a long and steep climb ahead of us, but when we start to descend please make sure that your horses don't go down fast."

The head guide, as Farhad learned during the trip, knew his way through valleys and mountains blindly, even in darkness.

"If you allow your horses to go fast, we could lose one another in the darkness. Besides, we don't want to make too much noise, do we? You never know who else might be traveling on the mountain." The head guide chuckled good-naturedly and went on, "No, I'm joking. The villagers and the *pasdars* use the roads. They don't need to climb the mountain to get to the next village.

"It's just dangerous to let the horses go down fast. You might topple over the edge of the mountain into the ravine."

"That's all I need," the general muttered under his breath. "To escape from Khomeini's firing squad only to die falling off the cliff!"

They set off on the obscure journey with the first rider in front of Farhad, while the head guide led the way on foot and the two others and Mahmood followed behind.

The rhythmic clatter of the hooves against the rough terrain seemed like a lullaby to Farhad in spite of the forbidding, ambiguous wilderness. The swaying of the horse rocked his body, making him very sleepy. It had been a long day and he was still tired from the previous night's trip, but Farhad endeavored to concentrate on the ride in order to keep awake. He figured that the other rider must also be a fugitive, trying to escape Khomeini's regime. Farhad was dying to find out who the fugitive was. There was no way he could approach him because the head guide wanted them to move in a file. Besides, they were instructed to keep silent.

They rode for an hour on the flat, hard surface and then moved onto a rugged path. In the pitch-dark night, Farhad could hear the rippling sound of a river flowing close by. The melodious flow of the water soothed his weary soul and shattered nerves. After a short while, they left the river behind and the road took on an uphill slant. They were now starting to climb the mountain. The guides told them that in about an hour they would reach a paved road, running like a belt through the belly of the mountain. That road served to connect one village to the other and was used even at nighttime.

The horses heaved as they struggled uphill. Farhad thought that if he were a horse, he would want a light female rider, especially when climbing uphill. Farhad found it very hard to keep from falling backward because of the steep upward climb. He had to hold on firmly to his horse's neck to keep his body forward and to avoid falling off its back. This sitting position gave him a terrible backache.

He was relieved for all of them, including the poor animals, when they finally hit the paved road. Farhad thought that the horses could breathe more comfortably, now that they were going to ride on level ground for a while until they started their climb again. Unfortunately, it did not prove to be so. They had hardly set foot on the road, when suddenly a bright projector-like light split the darkness of the sky.

"Oh, damn, it's the patrol car of the revolutionary guards!" cried out the friendly head guide. "We've got to rush back down. Hurry up, you two, and get off your horses," he urged them hastily, grabbing their hands and pulling them down.

The two fugitives trotted down the mountain holding on to the harnesses of their horses, with Mahmood and the guides following behind.

"For goodness' sake, run faster! Do you know what they'll do to us if we're caught?" the head guide said, gasping heavily.

"Yes," the other traveler replied sullenly.

"Yes, gentlemen, they'll shoot us without blinking an eye!" added the head guide.

"Thank you very much for the *heartening* information!" Farhad said sarcastically.

The young voice of another guide rang in the mountain, "No, really, it's true. It's happened several times before. They've got no mercy."

Farhad's stomach twisted with fear, thinking how many skeletons must be scattered around. He had heard that many people who had attempted to escape to Turkey and from there to Germany were never heard from again. God knows what had become of them!

Nobody could see where they were headed as they ran in the total darkness. The general fell down several times, but he got up instantly and continued running. The smugglers preferred not to use any flashlights. It was much safer that way. Farhad felt like a helpless blind person wandering in an unfamiliar place, not knowing if he was going to crash into something.

Just before coming to a full stop on a flatter spot on the mountain, Farhad fell again, but this time on a sharp piece of rock.

A sudden excruciating pain paralyzed him, making it impossible for him to move on.

"What do you think you're doing, my friend? Why are you taking your time?" urged the head guide. "Don't you see that we're in danger?"

"The *pasdars'* car is equipped with revolving projector lights," hissed the second guide. "If they ever decide to use these lights they'll immediately spot us and start shooting," he added.

"I know . . . I know!" Farhad snapped. "Didn't you hear me fall?"

"Yes, I heard something. But that doesn't mean you should stop running and get killed by the guards' machine guns!"

"I'm sorry," Farhad apologized, "but I've hurt my knee very badly and can't move."

The two guides immediately slipped under his arms and helped him hop over to the rock where he hid with the rest. Farhad thought he was going to die from exhaustion and pain. *"Oh, what a bad start,"* he told himself! Then he wondered if he could survive the trip. What if the revolutionary guards got him? Why had he not continued living in his underground world? Wouldn't he have been safer there?

Suddenly a weak voice flickered from deep within, reprimanding him for being a coward and reminding him of how he had survived under much harsher conditions in the past. Yes, indeed, what had happened to him? Had the past difficult nine years made a coward out of him? Could it be that all his senses were confused because of stress and displacement?

The group stayed motionless, waiting quietly for the apparition of the patrol car on the dark road high above. The general was worried about the horses. *"What if they suddenly decided to neigh or move about noisily?"*

He became overwhelmed with fear. He could hear his loud and unruly heartbeat blasting in his ears. Blood gushed like crushing waves into his temples and he felt dizzy. It was amazing what a scared creature he had turned into!

"*What will I tell the pasdars about my nine years of hiding if I'm caught?*" Farhad asked himself. He could not give them the names of his benefactors. They would be put to death. Farhad had to think of some other story. Then he thought the best thing for him to do in case of being caught would be to try to run . . . in which case the *pasdars* would definitely shoot and kill him.

The roar of an engine filled the silent, black night. The road lit up like daytime and the air and the mountain started to vibrate under the heavy tires of a large vehicle. Suddenly one of the young guides with a squeaky voice called out, "Look, look everybody, it's only a tractor going from one village to the other!"

"Ah!" they all exclaimed in unison, but still stayed put until the tractor turned behind the other side of the mountain and darkness engulfed the sky and the environs again.

Holding on to the bridles of their horses, Farhad and the other fugitive began climbing back to the road, followed by the guides. As the general limped uphill, moaning with great pain, his mysterious companion said hello to him and introduced himself, "Sir, my name's Parviz."

"Glad to meet you, Parviz. I'm Farhad. It's so nice that we'll be traveling together," Farhad uttered. And then after a short pause, he asked the fellow without preamble, "Say, why are you running away?"

Farhad, for some reason, immediately felt some affinity with the stranger, who like himself was fleeing the Islamic regime.

Parviz sighed, "I was a *Mojahed*, working clandestinely against Khomeini's regime."

Farhad cut in, "The *Mojaheds*, in the first two years of the formation of the Islamic Republic, were causing great headache for Khomeini and his men."

Farhad stopped a second to take a breath and to rest his hurting knee. The horse protested with a shrill neigh, displeased to be stopping so abruptly. Soon he began jerking his head back, refusing to move on. Right away, one of the guards who was walking behind came to Farhad's rescue and together they managed to help the horse restart the climb.

The guard instructed Farhad politely, *"Agha,* you shouldn't stop so abruptly while going uphill. You throw the poor animal off balance."

Farhad exploded, "I know, it isn't the first time I've handled a horse!" *"There I go again,"* he told himself, *"losing my temper and acting like a spoiled kid!"*

"You know, with this painful knee it's impossible for me to go at a steady pace," Farhad apologized for the second time within a few short minutes. Then, turning to Parviz in the dark he said, "Yes, we were talking about the *Mojaheds* causing Khomeini and his men a headache. What happened? It seems like the members of your organization got dispersed and escaped to foreign countries."

"Yes, that's right," Parviz confirmed. "Unfortunately, I was not as lucky as my other colleagues who got out of Iran in time." Parviz sighed and continued, "I was arrested and imprisoned."

"I'm sorry! I'm sure they gave you a hard time at the prison," Farhad remarked, feeling guilty for having hidden like a scared mouse for nine years while others served prison terms.

Parviz did not respond. So the general carried on, "Tell me, how did you escape from the prison?"

"I didn't escape. After spending five years in prison, I was released on the basis of good conduct," he told Farhad. "But I had to sign a document, promising I would never engage in counter-Islamic Revolutionary activities."

"Otherwise?" Farhad inquired.

"Otherwise, they said I'd be arrested and executed without a trial. Also they put my name on the blacklist, forbidding me to leave Iran."

"Oh yes? That's terrible! My family members are also on the blacklist."

For a short while a total silence reigned over the mountainside and the only noise that could be heard was the clatter of the hooves in the black night. It looked as though everybody was musing over something or the other. Farhad could imagine how much Parviz must have suffered at the hands of the prison guards during the five years of his imprisonment. He wondered whether they had managed to break his spirits.

"So, did you really repent, or are you going to be active from outside Iran?"

"Well," Parviz paused a second and then carried on, "I don't know what to say. All I can tell you for the moment is that I want to get as far away from Iran as possible."

Farhad knew how disappointed Parviz must be in his country and the system that tortured and forced everyone to obey the Islamic rules. But then, the general wondered if it were any different during the Shah's reign, when he himself was one of the enforcers of His Majesty's rules. Farhad pushed that thought conveniently aside. *"It is not a simple question to be answered,"* he convinced himself, *"especially in my present confused condition."* But the truth of the matter was that in serving the Shah, he had done what was expected of him. Just the way Khomeini's men were trying to perform their duties by torturing and forcing people to obey Islamic rules. He knew that he was not innocent. Nevertheless, he had been a hero, he proudly thought. He had served Iran fearlessly and did not deserve to be hunted down like a dog.

From the polite tone of Parviz's voice and his manner of speaking, Farhad characterized him as a sophisticated person. It was a shame he could not see the fellow's face. In the total darkness, under a thick cloud-covered sky Farhad could barely make out his silhouette of medium height and frail frame.

"Did they torture and make you give the names of other *Mojaheds*?" the general persisted with his line of questioning.

Parviz heaved a sigh and responded grimly, "Yes, I was tortured, but I couldn't help them."

Parviz stamped his foot angrily on the rugged mountain surface, startling his horse, and carried on, "Khomeini's government had already crushed the *Mojahed* movement by the time I was arrested."

Farhad nodded, "Yes, you're right. The *Mojahed* movement didn't last long."

"That's why they finally decided to free me. They knew that a wingless bird could not fly," Parviz concluded, trying to kick a pebble blindly. Farhad thought that his companion must be very frustrated and hurt, from the way he kicked at the rugged mountain in the total darkness.

The *Mojaheds,* in the beginning, cooperated with Ayatollah Khomeini in overthrowing the Shah. Then, when Khomeini proclaimed himself as the ruler of Iran, they turned against him. Despite being a religious group, they did not approve of the mullahs' hold on the government. They favored freedom and a secular democratic republic with Islamic social norms and rules. In 1981, they started organizing demonstrations in the streets in opposition to Imam Khomeini. Of course, Khomeini and his government could not tolerate such hostilities. President Banisadr, who was democratically elected in 1980 and was a liberal-minded person, supported the *Mojahed* movement. His confrontations with the Imam in 1981 led to his impeachment by the new regime. Then he was forced to go underground and so did the *Mojaheds.* The *Mojaheds* also escaped to France and Iraq. For a while they tried to be active from abroad, but soon they realized that there was nothing they could do anymore. The Islamic regime was already well established. In the end, the *Mojahed* movement fizzled out.

Farhad wondered if a regime based on *Mojaheds'* principals wouldn't have been better for the Iranian people than the present regime! One thing was sure: It would have been a democratic system of government and people would have had freedom of speech.

The general's thoughts went back to Parviz. He thought that although the man was a fugitive like himself, his name was not on the most wanted list. Parviz chose to run away. They had freed him. He posed no threat to Imam Khomeini's government anymore, while the general was considered to be the *"enemy number one"* and was being hunted like a dangerous criminal.

"Do you have any idea where you're going to end up after Turkey?" the general demanded of his companion with whom he had already bonded. All the smugglers that Farhad had encountered during his short trip had had nothing in common with him. They had all been crude, provincial and rough. Parviz was more like himself. Even his tone of voice had a different ring to it. What's more, he appeared to be calm, gentle and friendly.

Turning his face toward the general in the darkness, Parviz responded, "Yes, I'll be going to Germany. I've got a brother there. He'll help me with becoming a political refugee."

"Good luck!" the general uttered earnestly.

"What about you? Do you know where you're headed?"

"No, I've no clue whatsoever. Nobody tells me anything," Farhad muttered, throwing his hands up in the air. "Everything seems to be so secretive when it comes to my case."

"Why is it? What were you doing before Khomeini came to power?"

Farhad sniggered, "Have you heard of General Shirazi?"

"Oh, yes, who hasn't?" Parviz said matter of factly.

"Well, that's who I am!" the general announced.

"Good gracious, are you?"

At this point everybody laughed. The guards who were quiet all the while began chattering among themselves and the friendly head guide said jokingly to Parviz, "Little did you know that fate would one day bring you face to face with a famous guy, of course, without being able to see his face!"

Again, the travelers roared with laughter as their voices magnified and ricocheted in the mountainous environment.

"Not so loud, guys," Farhad whispered, shuddering with fear. For a minute he felt like hundreds of pairs of *pasdars'* eyes with built-in projectors were zoomed on the fugitives. A cold tremor ran down his spine as he looked around in the quiet night, not being able to see who and what lurked around.

"Oh, boy!" the head guide exclaimed and then told them in a gentle, personable way. "He's right. From now on no more loud talking or laughing please, okay?" Then, immediately after having said that, he yawned aloud. "Oops!" he bit his lower lip. "And, of course, no yawning, either! But seriously fellows, jokes put aside, we have to climb faster now."

The general said despairingly, "I don't know how I can do that with this badly injured knee! Under normal circumstances I think this cut would need some stitches. My sock is wet with blood!"

"I'm sorry, sir, you have no other choice but to go faster. We have a set schedule. If we don't get to the next station on time, the guides taking over from us will move on without you two."

Besides, they absolutely had to arrive at their first station before daybreak. Otherwise, he said, the villagers would be awake.

"We've got to make sure that nobody sees you," the head guide said, putting a firm hand on Farhad's shoulder for his attention. "It could be very dangerous. If you're detected the villagers will definitely report you to the *pasdars*."

The general could see the outline of the guard's face but not his expression. But it was obvious that the fellow was serious and had no time to sympathize with Farhad and his problem. So he nodded obediently, "Even if I crawl, I'll somehow keep up with everybody."

"Good!" he said, sounding pleased.

Although the travelers could not see each other's faces and were not well acquainted, they seemed to be getting along well. Even Mahmood sounded friendly and cooperative.

The three guides had a good disposition and Farhad felt comfortable having them around. He already knew them in the darkness from the tone of their voices. The head guide had a deep masculine voice and the other guide spoke with a soft, singing tone. The third one had a thin voice for a man and a heavy *Azari* accent.

Farhad endeavored to take his mind off his painful knee by

trying to reel back the images of the past, but found such imagery more torturous than the agonizing pain of his knee. The climb was horrendous! Farhad advanced laboriously with a sharp, stabbing pain shooting down his leg with every step. The injured knee reminded him of the bullet wound in his arm, which he had received about twenty years before, in a tribal conflict in Lorestan. He was then younger and braver. It was amazing how little he had cared about his injury in the heat of the shootout.

Presently he was escaping, not fighting, and the wound not only was painful; it also annoyed him. He did not need an impediment that would slow down his flight.

Ignoring the pain, he tried to concentrate on the climb until finally they reached the paved road, mounted the horses, and set off for the summit.

The horses climbed with extreme care. It was clear that they had mounted that steep mountain several times before and knew exactly where they were headed.

Mahmood broke the deadly silence after about two hours of climbing and said, "We're near the summit. Soon, we'll get to a path that skirts around the mountain and descends to the valley below. That's the path that we're going to take." Then clicking his lighter a couple of times, he finally managed to light it, took a quick look at his watch, and declared, "It's midnight. We should arrive there in about four hours if we continue at this pace."

As the fugitives continued their climb, the winds became stronger and the lightning zigzagged across the sky. The rumbling of the thunder shook heaven and earth like an explosion of a bomb. In no time, the sky started dumping buckets of rain on the mountainside, soaking the travelers through and through in seconds.

The skittish horses sidled toward the edge of the mountain nervously instead of advancing. They jerked their heads back and tried to throw their riders off their backs.

"Hey, guys," yelled the head guide over the din of the storm, "you'll have to get off and lead the horses. Otherwise, they won't budge!"

Farhad and Parviz obeyed his order by carefully sliding off their horses. Then they dragged the beasts behind them with great difficulty as they fought their way uphill through the foul weather. A couple of times Farhad lost his footing, nearly stumbling down with horse and all. If not for the help of the guides in the back, Farhad and the horse would definitely have rolled down the mountain instantaneously.

As Farhad was struggling with his horse, the head guide came up to him. Placing a friendly hand on his shoulder, he joked, "See, since you didn't have a chance to take a shower in Tabriz, now you're taking one, free of charge."

"What a dangerous moment for joking," the general pondered and then grunted, not sounding very friendly, "As if I need one in this nasty weather and with this damn aching knee!"

Farhad sounded like a grumpy old man complaining about his knee and the weather. It was obvious to the guides that he was not taking the conditions of his escape kindly.

"Well sir," the guide said softly, "you don't seem very happy. I assure you that there is nothing any one of us can do to make this trip pleasant for you." He then laughed and went on, "But we do care about your safety!"

The rain stopped after an hour and the fugitives remounted. Farhad's teeth chattered vigorously as now an ice-cold wind gusted through his wet clothes. He thought he had never felt so cold in his entire life, and shivered uncontrollably.

After an hour of struggling uphill, they got to the path near the summit and started their descent toward the valley.

"Easy, easy," the friendly head guide urged the riders. "Don't let the horses go down too fast. Remember what I told you in the beginning of our trip?"

The general could not take it any longer. The cold wind was unbearable! "Let me get down and walk. It's too cold sitting up here," he pleaded with the guides.

One of the young guides eased Farhad down the left side of the horse and asked, "How's the knee? Can you walk?"

"It's not good at all. The pain is killing me but it's better to limp with difficulty than to freeze to death."

"He's right," said Parviz, with clattering teeth. "I think I'll get down too and walk."

Farhad lagged behind the group as he dragged his painful leg on the rough surface of the mountain. However, he no longer cared about the pain.

The head guide slowed his pace to let Farhad catch up with him. "Are you all right, sir?" he asked with his deep, soothing voice.

"Thank you, not too bad. But I would have felt much better if I were lying in a clean and warm bed, instead of going through this ordeal!" Farhad answered with his usual grumpiness.

The guide chuckled, "I know, I would love to be in a bed, too. Even a dirty one would do!"

The whole company laughed under their breath and the gloomy night took on a friendlier air.

The general turned to the head guide and asked, "By the way, all this time you haven't told us what your name is."

"Oh, yes, my name's Ahmad," he declared.

At that point one of the guides called out, "Hey guys. I'm going to go down this other path. It'll take me to the nearby village. I'm bushed and need to rest."

Soon after the guide left them, Ahmad let the group take a short break. Sitting on a rock, the general gazed at the starless indigo above. From high up, where he was seated, the real world seemed millions of miles away. Dark clouds hung in the sky and the universe looked vast and awe inspiring! Farhad looked to his right and then his left. There seemed to be nothing around them but total darkness and silence. The obscure atmosphere of the quiet night overwhelmed him and changed his gloomy mood. Suddenly he became conscious of God the almighty, the creator of that immense and mysterious universe. His might over man's destiny and the mere thought of Him filled Farhad with reverence. The general became aware that it was His hand that had guided them all up through the strenuous and dangerous climb to that scary height. And it was He who had protected them against the *pasdars*.

Ahmad's voice disrupted the general's thoughts. "Let's make a move, guys. Don't forget that we have to reach our destination before daybreak."

THE FIRST STOP

Farhad looked up at the black, somber sky covered with a thick blanket of clouds. There was no trace of stars, and the only light which softened the harshness of the night glowed faintly from somewhere down below.

"Where is that light coming from?" Farhad asked Ahmad anxiously.

"You'll soon see."

"Is that the village where Parviz and I will be hiding for the day?"

Ahmad laughed. "Have some patience, you'll soon find out."

The horses descended cautiously, clacking their hooves against the hard surface of the mountain. Farhad was the front rider and Parviz followed behind. Ahmad walked next to Farhad's horse, petting its neck occasionally and murmuring encouraging words in its ear. The second guide and Mahmood slogged behind like two floating ghosts.

Presently, the dusk began to wear off and faces and figures started taking shape. Farhad noticed that Ahmad, their pleasant head guide, was a stocky fellow with dark wiry hair. He seemed to be about thirty years old. Like most men that Farhad had seen during the trip, he was wearing a pair of old blue jeans, a black shirt and a tattered dark gray jacket.

Within an hour, the faint light below grew stronger and a stone-built building flooded with searchlights came into sight.

Ahmed looked up at Farhad and said with a broad smile on

his face, "Do you see that well-lit building at the foot of the mountain?"

"Yes," Farhad nodded, wondering why Ahmed looked so pleased. *"Does he think I'm stupid?"* he pondered. *"What else could it be but a pasdar station?"*

"That's a nest of wasps," he sniggered.

The second guide, who looked to be under twenty, laughed and blurted out, "Yes, and there are twenty revolutionary, armed *'wasps'* guarding the station and this area."

Farhad's stomach twisted with horror! Did that mean they were walking straight into the den of lions? He could not understand how those young guides could be so flippant about such a serious matter.

"We aren't going down there, are we?" Farhad grimaced.

"Yes sir, we are! And you two gentlemen will be resting in the nearby village for the day," Ahmed replied.

"What do you mean?" Farhad queried with great consternation. "You guys sometimes don't make any sense!"

Parviz, who had remained silent all that while, cut in anxiously, "He is right. Why don't you make it clear what exactly is going to happen?"

Ahmad said reassuringly, "Leave everything to me, and please, please trust us!"

Farhad could not do otherwise anyway, so he kept quiet and tried to forget about *"the nest of wasps"*. But the mere thought of the *pasdars* petrified him. For a moment it felt like he was completely surrounded by them and nobody could save him from their cruel clutches. Then, fear gave way to heartache. It pained him to think that those *pedar sags* were the ones who made him a fugitive and took over his beloved country. Farhad felt frustrated and jealous. Yes, he was jealous that they had power and his was gone.

Ahmad's deep voice brought Farhad to himself. "Hey there, General, I think we should move slightly faster."

The general gently spurred the horse, and as it quickened its pace, he got overwhelmed with his dark thoughts again. Soon he dismissed them saying to himself, *"Well, what the heck! Iran does not belong to me now."* He knew that he had no place in that country and that he should not get all worked up in leaving it to its new owners.

"Easy . . . easy," Ahmad grumbled. "I didn't mean that fast!"

Parviz decided to dismount and walk. It was not easy for him to ride on such a steep slope. But Farhad preferred to ride on. He was certain that walking downhill and putting pressure on his painful knee would make it even worse.

Farhad was surprised to see that the closer they got to the valley, the further to the left the *nest of wasps* moved, until it gradually disappeared from sight. The guides had skillfully managed to circumvent the *pasdars'* station.

Presently Farhad addressed Ahmad, "Now I understand why you were so relaxed about the *nest of wasps*."

"Yes, didn't I ask you to trust us?"

"I'm sorry, I should have known better!"

"We know exactly which roads to take to avoid the *pasdars*."

They finally reached the bottom of the mountain. The guides helped Farhad to slowly slide down the side of the horse. His knee was now completely stiff.

Mahmood and the young guide left, tagging the horses along. Farhad, Parviz and Ahmad walked on a bit further until they reached a green spot.

Ahmad said with a tired voice, "We are near the village where you two would be resting for the day. Why don't you guys hide behind these bushes, while I go and fetch your host."

Parviz inquired apprehensively, "Why can't we go with you?"

It seemed to Farhad that his companion was afraid of being abandoned in that forsaken wilderness. The general had exactly the same feeling. He felt unsafe for the two of them to be left all by themselves.

Ahmad explained, "I first have to make sure that the fellow was given the message and that he is around."

Farhad wondered why. *"Weren't the smugglers well organized, as they claimed to be?"* Ahmad explained to him that because most of the villagers did not own telephones, they had to send messengers to inform a trusted villager that he would be hosting fugitives in his house. Each time, the smugglers chose a different household in order not to attract attention and to minimize danger.

It was not quite light yet. A total silence reigned over the valley. Except for the tall, wild bushes with thorny purple flowers waving with the gentle breeze, and the gurgling sound of the small nearby creek, the valley appeared static and mute. Even the birds seemed to be asleep.

As soon as Ahmad left them, the general rested his fatigued body on the damp ground behind the bushes moistened by the early-morning dew. Parviz sat next to him hugging his legs. He was wearing a gray flannel suit and a white shirt. Farhad guessed him to be from the north—the Caspian Sea area—because of his fair complexion and blue eyes.

Ahmad's presence during their short trip had given Farhad a temporary sense of security. Now, with him gone, he felt lonesome and lost in that strange and forbidding wilderness. Presently, Farhad got overwhelmed with fear, *"What if Ahmad does not return? What if the pasdars patrol the area?"*

The general realized that he had turned into a coward. He told himself that if Leyla were around she would remind him that once he used to be a strong and fearless person. A person, who in battle, had had the willpower to survive under the toughest conditions. *"But then it was different,"* he thought, *"I had willed to stay alive because I had something to look forward to: getting back to my family. What do I have to look forward to now? Starting a new life in America!"* he decided. Farhad then looked up at the clear sky, allowed himself a weak smile and willed himself to survive.

After an hour, which seemed like an eternity, Ahmad returned with a short, round-faced, bald man. He was their host and his name was Akbar. Akbar, bowing politely, beckoned them to follow him.

Farhad, Parviz and Ahmad staggered listlessly behind Akbar, passing through green fields that had come alive with the early-morning chirping of the birds. As they pressed on, the road took a downhill curve, from where they could spot a village. From a distance, the little cottages looked like upside-down boxes arranged in a row amidst some trees. Soon they entered the village and walked along its deserted, uneven streets. The box-like huts were built of mud and bricks mixed with hay—*khesht*—with grass growing on their rooftops. Their green-blue-and-white dilapidated wooden doors were firmly shut, and no noise could be heard from within.

Farhad was sad to see Ahmad leave them for good when they reached a crossroad of four narrow paths. He had to go.

As they hurried through a labyrinth of dusty streets, spotted with old, small cottages and shuttered green grocery and food stores, Akbar seemed to become increasingly nervous. He kept glancing at the closed doors anxiously, as if expecting one of them to suddenly fly open.

At the end of a winding street, they came up to a walled-in compound, just as the roosters took turns in announcing the daybreak. This was where the two fugitives were to stay until nightfall.

Akbar turned to them and whispered, "It is now prayer time and everybody is awake, I can't take you in through the gate. You never know, somebody might already be out in the courtyard."

Akbar steered the two fugitives to the back of the walled-in house. Cupping the palms of his hands, he asked Farhad to place his left foot in it. He then swiftly hoisted him onto the top of the wall. Farhad landed in a large, densely wooded garden with tall poplar and sycamore trees. Next, Parviz and Akbar pounced into the garden and helped Farhad to his feet.

The host led Farhad and Parviz through the grove of trees

toward the courtyard at the far end of the garden. The yard was paved with yellow bricks. A small blue-tiled pool lay in the center, and a school of large and small goldfish swam in its greenish water. A few feet away, facing the pool, they could see several small low-built huts along a circular, raised, covered porch. Akbar's home was at the far end of the porch. Fortunately, all the hut doors were closed. They quietly sneaked past the shut doors of Akbar's neighbors and entered his hut. The main door opened directly into a large, scantily furnished room. Its once white walls and high cobweb-covered ceiling were completely smoked over.

Akbar's young wife, who was busy lighting the *tanoor*, greeted them with a nod and a shy smile. The bread oven was smack in the middle of the room, dug out in the ground. It had clay walls and was about six feet deep.

The hostess knelt on the floor by the *tanoor* and emptied two large basketfuls of charcoal into it. She then added some wood splinters and crumpled paper. As soon as she threw a lit match into the oven, the whole thing caught fire, shooting up smoke and leaping flames. In a short while, the flames died down, the charcoal became ruby red and the clay walls became searing hot. Meanwhile, the hostess worked the balls of dough, prepared the night before, into near paper-thin circular shapes. Very carefully, she placed a thin circle of dough on a large, round cushion with a wooden handle attached to its back. Holding onto the handle, she slapped the cushion onto the hot oven wall and removed it with one swift motion. The thin, round dough stuck to the hot wall. Then she smacked a second, third and fourth piece of dough against the oven wall.

Gradually, brown bubbles started forming on the circular, thin, white bread called *lavash* and the air became permeated with the aroma of delicious baked bread. The young woman then picked up a long wooden handle with a hook attached to its end and carefully removed the bread from the furnace wall. She then thrust the baked thin *lavashes* on a clean, large cloth, allowing them to cool.

On the floor, not too far from the *tanoor*, three small children slept in soiled beddings. An old oil hurricane lamp, with a cracked, smoked-out chimney gave off a dim light to the bare room. On the right side of the *tanoor* lay a large tribal carpet. Its off-white background covered with dark blue-and red-flowers and branches, somewhat enlivened the dark room. A steaming *samovar*, with a red-flowered china teapot placed on the top, brewed an aromatic tea. The pleasant odor of the freshly baked bread and the tea filled the air, making Farhad's mouth water.

Farhad eyed the hostess affectionately as she bustled around the *tanoor* and the *samovar* with a contented, smiling face. He knew how hard women worked, both at home and in the fields. Moreover, that poor lady not only had to do all those chores, she also had to entertain refugees like Parviz and himself. He wondered if, from time to time, she could enjoy some pleasurable things! But what was there for a woman to do in a dingy village other than bake bread, plow the fields and bear children?

As soon as the hostess served them tea and bread, Farhad felt as hot as a furnace. Parviz looked at him astounded and exclaimed, "Goodness, your face is all red. Are you okay?"

It was then that the general felt he was burning with fever. It looked as though he had caught a cold the night before on the mountain in the cold, rainy weather.

Akbar regarded him kindly and said, "A long rest will do you a world of good. Anyway, soon you two will have to move to the food storage room right there in the back." He motioned with his head to a gray wooden door at the back of the large room and went on, "You can sleep or rest all day long until dusk. By the way, you better use the toilet before retiring because you can't leave the storage room at all. The neighbors are all over the place and we don't want them to see you."

Farhad and Parviz took turns sneaking out onto the covered porch and used the toilet shack, with a hole in the ground, closest to Akbar's hut.

Before retreating to the storage room, the two fugitives washed their hands and faces using a brass pitcher and a small basin brought out by the hostess.

Parviz asked Akbar, "What's going to happen tonight?"

Akbar muttered, "Very late tonight, another group of guides will meet you at the foot of the mountain. From there until the next station they'll be in charge."

"But until then we'll have to be locked up like prisoners in a dark food storage room all day?" Parviz hissed fretfully.

Akbar responded, shifting uneasily from one crossed leg to the other, "Yes, sir, and you can't use the bathroom all day; you can't even talk to one another, in case somebody overhears you."

Akbar's wife cast her large, black eyes down timidly, as she served them more tea. She also served some more fresh bread and feta cheese. Farhad sweetened the tea with lump sugar, as he bit into the fresh bread and cheese wrap and washed it down with the delicious tea. It was so tasty! He had not had anything to eat since their departure from Tabriz. The sweet tea and the bread and cheese wrap reminded him of his breakfasts with Leyla and the children, making him homesick.

As soon as Farhad and Parviz entered the dark, humid, and foul-smelling storage room, Akbar closed the door from outside with a padlock.

Farhad suddenly felt claustrophobic in the dark, enclosed room. Rubbing his chest dismally, he protested, "Oh, God, I need fresh air! How can we spend the whole day locked up here? It's worse than the basements where I hid all those years."

A sarcastic smile parted Parviz's lips, as he looked at him reproachfully, "Be thankful that you have a safe place to stay."

Instead of feeling embarrassed, Farhad arched his eyebrows and said scornfully, "Look who's talking! Weren't you the one complaining about it just a while ago to Akbar?"

Parviz grinned and said, "No, honestly, do we have a choice?"

Farhad shook his head grudgingly and looked around the dark room with resignation.

"You seem like a difficult and spoiled person, general," Parviz joked.

"You're wrong. Maybe that was what I used to be in the past, but after spending nine miserable years in smelly basements, I am duly humbled. I'm just bad tempered these days."

"I'm joking, general, don't take me seriously," Parviz said, smiling warmly.

There were two sets of bedding arranged on the floor for them. It looked less soiled than the children's bedding near the bread oven.

Farhad took off his damp clothes and spread them on the burlap sacks of winter provisions of wheat, potatoes, rice, beans, chickpeas, onions and dried fruit. Then he lay down on one of the mattresses and pulled the quilt over his shivering body. It seemed like his fever was rising. To make things worse, he also had a terrible sore throat, not to mention his knee, which was throbbing like the regular ticking of a clock.

From the outside noises, Farhad could tell that the neighbors were up and going about their daily chores.

Both fugitives were very tired and sleepy. Before the weight of fatigue could shut their eyes completely, Farhad felt something long and smooth crawling over his face. He immediately grabbed and hurled it across the room, spitting out, "Snake!"

Parviz tried to choke his laughter in his pillow, as the wild scream of a cat filled the dark room.

"What do you know, it was merely a cat's tail!" Farhad said humorously, feeling sorry for the poor animal, which, in the pursuit of a mouse, had nearly sat on his face.

"It's a good thing it didn't relieve itself on my face!" he added, putting a hand on his mouth to stifle his laughter.

"Well, well, I didn't know you could be so good tempered and funny!" Parviz breathed.

In no time, the fugitives succumbed to a deep slumber and slept all day until just before midnight, when they woke with a start with the squeaking of the storage door, which Akbar flung open.

Akbar let Parviz and Farhad use the toilet, which they both so badly needed, and then they sat around a plastic tablecloth on the carpet. Akbar's wife sluggishly carried a steaming bowl of chicken soup with some shredded chicken and chunks of potatoes in it. It was obvious that a long day's hard work had sapped the energy out of the poor, quiet woman.

As Farhad sat by the tablecloth, an idea flashed in his head, "Tell me Akbar, for how much would you sell your plastic tablecloth?"

"Whatever for?" Akbar looked at him quizzically.

"You'll see," Farhad responded.

He grinned craftily, "Oh, I guess one hundred *toomans*."

"What? Are you joking? This old thing isn't worth even one *tooman*!" the general protested. He hated greedy people who were not even ashamed of taking advantage of desperate human beings.

"Take it or leave it," Akbar said, shrugging nonchalantly.

"Son of a gun!" the general grumbled to himself. *"I would strangle him if I had my way."*

"Okay, then bring me a pair of scissors," Farhad demanded.

After dinner, the general handed the hundred *tooman* bill to the greedy host and cut a hole in the middle of the tablecloth, big enough to pass it over his head. He was going to use it as a raincoat in case of need.

Akbar, looking happy over his clever transaction, beckoned, "Come on guys, it's time to leave."

Thanking their tired hostess for her hospitality, Farhad and Parviz cautiously crept out into the darkness of the quiet garden and walked behind Akbar through the tall shadowy trees to its end. The neighbors were all asleep, children, parents, dogs and cats . . .

Although nobody seemed to be around, Akbar did not want to risk anything by taking Farhad and Parviz out through the squeaky main gate. They had to get out the same way they came in—over the wall.

First, Parviz climbed the wall quietly and jumped down into

the street. Then Akbar helped the general climb onto the top of the wall and Parviz carefully eased Farhad down into the street. Then it was Akbar's turn. He climbed up the wall swiftly like a panther and leapt lightly down into the dark street.

They had hardly gone a block on the narrow, unpaved path through puddles of muddy water, when a dark figure with a flashlight started towards them.

The mysterious fellow flickered his strong flashlight from one person to the other, as his dark figure grew larger in the eyes of the scared fugitives.

"Don't panic!" murmured Akbar. "Let me handle this."

"Who is it?" Farhad whispered, crossing his arms and placing his palms under his armpits—he always did this whenever he felt scared.

"It's the night guard who patrols the streets," Akbar remarked casually.

"Goodness!" the general panicked, as Parviz slowed his pace to walk in the back to keep out of the guard's sight, just like a scared child trying to hide behind his parents. "We're finished!" Farhad whimpered.

As soon as the stocky, dark figure closed in on them, Akbar exclaimed, "Hey, Farshad *Agha*, is that you?"

The patrolman hesitated a second. It was obvious that he had not put a face to the voice, despite the flashlight.

"Yes, it's me. Who's this?" the guard demanded dryly.

Akbar laughed, trying hard to appear cool. "It's me, Akbar. Don't you recognize my voice? Didn't you see my face with that strong flashlight?"

The night guard shined his light directly at Akbar's face. Akbar protested, "You're blinding me, Farshad *Agha*, please!"

Farshad, who by then had recognized Akbar, exclaimed with a deep voice, "Oh, sorry, I didn't recognize you right away, Akbar *Agha*. What are you doing in the streets at this hour of the night?"

"Are we in trouble?" Farhad wondered, his throat as dry as the desert.

Akbar coughed nervously, trying to save time and to give

himself a chance to come up with a convincing story. Then he uttered with a controlled calm tone, "My cousins from Tehran are visiting us and my wife had prepared a feast in their honor. We ate so much that we couldn't sleep on heavy stomachs. We decided to go for a long walk to digest the food before going to bed. Besides, we have so much to talk about. Oh, by the way, I have a little gift for you."

"What . . . ? What did you say? A gift?" the guard asked eagerly.

"Oh," the general thought. *"Akbar was trying to grease the guard's palm!"*

"Yes, I said a gift," Akbar stressed. "Remember that potato deal in Tehran I told you about last month?"

The guard thought for a while and then exclaimed, "Oh, yes . . . yes, I remember. Did you get it?"

"Maybe he thinks he is going to receive fifty percent of the profit," the general sniggered within.

Akbar sidled closer to the guard. Putting on a gleeful voice, he said, "Yes, my cousins have brought me the good news. They say the deal is going through. And here's your little gift for bringing me good luck."

Akbar dipped his hand into his pocket and brought out a bill, slipping it into the guard's hand. The guard quickly put the money in his pocket and thanked Akbar for his generosity.

Farhad and Parviz were relieved, thanking God for their luck in having encountered an easygoing *pasdar*.

The guard then asked, "How long are your cousins going to stay here?"

"Not long. They're leaving for the next village early tomorrow morning. They need to attend to business there."

"What a good storyteller! He does come up with great tales," Farhad thought.

"Just keep on walking and don't look back," murmured Akbar, after the guard walked away. "Pretend you're strolling aimlessly."

The three men went through a few more muddy streets,

stumbling over stones and mounds of dirt, until they reached the outskirts of the village. Although Farhad could not see much, he could feel that they were now traversing a wide-open space with some thorny dried bushes, which from time to time caught on to their trousers and let go of them with a snap as they pulled away.

After fifteen minutes of trudging in silence, they noticed the road took on an uphill grade. They had reached the foot of a hill.

"Let's rest a while. My knee is killing me," Farhad implored Akbar.

"No sir, we can't. Unfortunately we have no time to spend on aches and pains," responded Akbar briskly.

Farhad's knee was throbbing even worse than before. Feeling overwhelmed with his problems, Farhad wished he could put his head down and rest forever. *"Oh, God, why do I have to suffer so much?"* he looked up at the black sky despairingly. *"I have already gone through hell for so many years . . . Damn the pasdars and their regime!"*

The general went on and on cultivating negative thoughts in his head, until he suddenly realized that he was again nagging and being ungrateful. Hadn't God saved him from execution? Hadn't his escape up to that point been a safe one? Akbar was right. There was no time for moaning and groaning. Farhad knew that he had to move on. He had to stop being weak and had to keep pushing forward, pain or no pain, until he could reach his final destination.

After a long, wearisome walk, the three of them finally arrived at a spot where two guides with fresh horses were waiting for them. It was as dark as the night before, with black clouds hanging overhead like a thick, black blanket. Farhad could see nothing but the silhouettes of the guides and the large beasts. He thought that soon they would all start recognizing one another by each other's voices. Knowing faces and characters did not matter much on this trip. Besides, based on Farhad's experience so far, by the time they got to know their guides, they had to say goodbye and meet another bunch.

IN TEHRAN

One rainy afternoon as Leyla, Parvin—her sister—and her mother sat dolefully in the kitchen sipping tea in silence, the doorbell rang. Leyla, who was in no mood to socialize, remained in the kitchen. Her mother and sister, Parvin immediately covered their heads and moved into the foyer to open the door and find out who the unexpected visitor was.

Two bearded men, wearing black collarless shirts, were standing behind the door.

"Hello, my name's Hooshang Afshan and this is my assistant, Faramarz Sobhani. Can we come in?" Hooshang asked, and stepped inside without waiting for an invitation. "We are from the Bureau of Security," he added, clasping his hands in front of him and twiddling his thumbs.

Parvin, who by then was quite used to such visits, closed the entrance door behind the security officers and led them into the sitting room. The revolutionary guards constantly bothered Parvin and her family in Tabriz.

The bearded men walked in front with Parvin following behind. Upon entering the room, Hooshang slumped his square body into the gray sofa, with his short legs spread out in front of him on the red-and-blue Persian carpet. His docile-looking assistant, Faramarz, meanwhile, stood behind a wooden chair across from him, waiting for Parvin to sit down first.

"Do sit down, please." Parvin urged Faramarz politely while keeping her head up, without looking into his eyes. She had on a long, brown skirt, a white scarf and a long-sleeved white blouse.

Parvin did resemble Leyla a bit, except her hair was straight, tied in a bun behind her head. Her skin, like Leyla's, was alabaster white and her eyes were large and jet black.

Parvin's old, stooped mother entered the room draped in a black *chador*. Faramarz abruptly sprang to his feet to greet her and Hooshang did the same reluctantly.

"Sit down . . . sit down, gentlemen. What can we do for you?" Mrs. Kazemi, Leyla's mother asked them briskly, knowing full well why they were there.

"Well, Mrs. Kazemi," said the man through thin, pale lips as he scratched his black, wiry beard, "the same usual, old question that you've been asked for so many years." He swallowed, "Where's your son-in-law? We've heard that he has recently escaped from Iran. Can you tell us where he is headed?"

Mrs. Kazemi's pale, old visage flushed with anger. She felt insulted to be taken for a fool.

"What! Do you think I'm so dumb as to tell you where he is headed even if I knew?" She frowned, adding more wrinkles to her dried up plum-like face.

The government agent's face fell. He was furious at the old lady for her insolence.

"It's for your own good that I'm asking you to cooperate with us," he retorted rigidly.

Leyla's mother leapt out of her seat with furious, rounded eyes, looked the agent straight in the eyes and screeched, wagging a thin, long finger at him, "What would you do to helpless women? Kill them . . . ? Torture them . . . ? Is this what you do nowadays?"

Hooshang, who found himself cornered by the clever old lady, scrambled to his feet impatiently, as his timid assistant also followed suit.

"I just thought you'd cooperate with us. Your son-in-law is a traitor, and I can't understand why you should be protecting such a person."

"To hell with him and all of you. What do I care anyway, my life is over, and I don't give a damn what happens to the whole world, including myself," she bluffed with a forced anger.

The frustrated government agent rolled his eyes, heaved a sigh and said, "Didn't you once tell a government agent who previously came here to question you that you were Imam Khomeini's follower?"

Leyla's mother looked perplexed. She shifted her weight clumsily from side to side and inquired, squinting her eyes, "What has that got to do with my son-in-law?"

The officer pressed, "A lot! Your son-in-law is Imam Khomeini's enemy, and you are protecting him."

The old lady snarled, "How do you know that? Did you ever have a chance to speak to him? Maybe he isn't. I'm sure that if you guys had given him a chance he would have been very valuable to your system."

Hooshang cut in, "Please, lady, give me a break! Do you think you're talking to a child? I know Farhad. I used to work with him." He shook his head disapprovingly and continued, "How could somebody who served the Shah wholeheartedly be of any use to us? Or, how would it be possible for him to change his allegiance so easily?"

Leyla's mother shrieked with anger, "Hey, mind what you're saying, Mister! Let me assure you that my son-in-law was a servant to nobody. All he cared about was his country."

The intelligence officer sneered as he said, "Yes . . . yes, I know! Well, thank you for your time. We'll now visit your daughter, the ex-general's wife. Maybe she'll have more sense than you."

The old lady's eyes widened as she barked, "No, you won't! She isn't living at her former house anymore. My daughter's right here with us. The poor woman has lost her mind thanks to you guys and your revolution, which destroyed her life and took her husband away from her!" she coughed, clearing her scratching throat from all her screeching. "And let me tell you this, Mister, my son-in-law didn't escape recently as you might like to believe. We think he was killed during the turmoil of the Revolution," she lied.

Leyla's mother, knowing very well that they would never harm an old woman, spoke freely and fearlessly. In addition, by saying those words, she hoped to create some doubt in their minds about the rumor that Farhad had recently escaped from Iran.

The intelligence officer kept shaking his head in disagreement with the old lady. He then beckoned his colleague to follow him out. From there they went straight to the office.

Hooshang turned to Faramarz and said, "You know what? We have to double the reward on the general's head. I have to get this man even if I lose my life over it!" Hooshang banged his fist on his desk, jolting the glass ashtray noisily on the solid wood and added, "Why don't you arrange with the National TV right away to broadcast his picture during the evening news for the coming two days?"

Faramarz bowed, with his forehead nearly touching his beltline. "Yes sir, that's a great idea. How much shall we say the reward is now?"

Hooshang arched his eyebrows, creating furrows of wrinkles on his narrow forehead. Pondering for a while, he grinned wryly and said, "Let's more than double it. Yes, let's assign fifty thousand *toomans* to this project." Then, bobbing his head like a horse he added. "I think that's a good sum of money for the villagers around the Tabriz and Khoy area. The reward can render someone who is trying to make ends meet very rich!"

Hooshang could not wait to capture Farhad. He was burning with desire to crush his long-time enemy under his feet. Besides, he wanted to show off his might and position to General Shirazi, who he thought was now running like a scared rat.

Hooshang believed that he could kill two birds with one stone. Not only would he eliminate his foe, but he would also become a national hero. He was absolutely certain that his scheme was going to work. The price he had put on Farhad's head was a good sum of money.

Hooshang rubbed his smallpox-scarred face with his hairy hand, satisfied at his own brilliance and snarled, "Hurry up, Faramarz, what are you waiting for? Call the National TV right away. I want this message out by tonight."

Faramarz sprang out of his chair and nodded, "Yes sir, I'll do it right away!"

THE REWARD

At midnight, when the village guard Farshad, returned home from his rounds, Shirin, his wife was waiting up for him in front of the TV. They were among the lucky villagers to own one. They also had a telephone, which was a necessity for Farshad's profession.

Farshad sat on the floor, carpeted with a thick, beige Bakhtiar rug. He leaned his tired back against the hard cushions placed along the wall, cupped his hands behind his head, and started watching television. They were broadcasting the last edition of the evening news. Shirin was nine months pregnant and bloated like a huge balloon. She moved uneasily in her place on the floor where she was sitting and placed a hand on her husband's arm. "Farshad, I think you'll have to prepare yourself to fetch the *mama* tonight. I'm not feeling so well." She groaned, straightening the white scarf over her brown hair.

"Hush, *zan*, let me see what they're saying!" he said, pushing her hand away unintentionally.

Shirin withdrew herself from Farshad and slumped back against the wall cushions uncomfortably. She felt hurt and somewhat insulted that her husband had called her "woman", instead of "darling", or simply Shirin.

"Who is this general they're talking about? Is he an important person?" Shirin asked Farshad, forgetting her grievance against him.

"He used to be, during the Shah's regime. He is the only one of the Shah's trusted officials not to have been captured after the

Revolution," Farshad explained. Then, suddenly, he jumped to his feet and burst out, "Wait a minute . . . wait a minute! What if one of those guys I saw tonight is that famous general who is on the run?" Biting his lower lip, Farshad pressed on, "Hey, the government is offering a generous reward for his capture, Shirin. You never know, we might have struck a gold mine!"

"I don't understand you. What are you talking about? Who are the guys you saw tonight?" Shirin demanded, appearing confused.

Farshad explained to his wife that, while patrolling the streets, he had come across Akbar with two men who were not dressed like villagers.

"I think Akbar *Agha* is up to something," Farshad said dryly. "He told me that those two guys were his cousins from Tehran."

"Maybe they were, and that's why they were not dressed like the villagers," Shirin argued, shifting uncomfortably in her place.

Farshad shook his head. "No. I don't think so. I think he was helping them to escape, because after saying goodbye to me they strolled toward the mountains."

Shirin looked baffled and Farshad looked annoyed with his wife's slow-wittedness. Furrowing his brow, Farshad uttered succinctly, "They announced on the news that they think the general escaped two days ago." He then squinted his eyes in contemplation, shook his index finger several times and glanced intently into his wife's eyes. "You know what?"

"What?"

"It would take two days for fugitives coming from Tehran to get here through mountainous routes."

"So what? Besides, you've got no proof that those guys were fugitives," Shirin said obstinately.

"Why do you always have to argue with me, *zan?*" Farshad raised his voice, as Shirin frowned, got to her feet with difficulty, and walked away to the kitchen.

Farshad mulled over his encounter with Akbar and the two men for a while as he paced up and down the room.

"Have you heard Akbar or his wife ever mention having any relatives in Tehran?" he called out to his wife.

"No." Shirin stuck her head out of the kitchen. "You're right. If they did, his wife, Nili, wouldn't have stopped boasting about it."

"There you go!" Farshad retorted with satisfaction. "Yes, I'm sure he was helping them to escape. Otherwise, tell me, why would they be going towards the mountains?"

Shirin could not understand what the mountains had to do with those men's escape. She was a young, innocent eighteen-year-old, who knew nothing about the geography of the area.

"The smugglers take the refugees to Turkey through mountainous routes where there are no checkpoints." Farshad explained patiently this time. He then instantly went to the telephone and rang the village patrol station. "Hello, hello," he shouted over the phone. It was a bad connection and he could hardly hear the guard on the other end of the line.

"Hello, is that you, Ghasem *Agha*?" Farshad shouted.

"Yes, it's me. Who is calling?" the other person shouted back.

"It's me, Farshad."

Farshad told his superior officer, Ghasem, about his encounter with Akbar and two strangers from Tehran. He went on, "Look, if I'm right, and if one of those men is the *famous* general, the officials in Tehran should know that I'm the one who has recognized him."

There was a brief silence.

"Hello, hello, are you still there?" Farshad yelled hoarsely.

"Yes of course. Tell me, what would my cut in this affair be?" he asked and then pressed, "why should I trouble myself for you?"

Farshad's face fell. In his excitement about collecting the reward, he had forgotten that nothing came free in Iran. You had to bribe almost everybody.

The voice from the other end of the line persisted, "So, what do you say?"

"Okay . . . okay, half and half," Farshad responded fretfully. "We'll split the money in half."

The voice echoed contentedly, "Now we're talking! I'll organize a search party, and dispatch it toward the Turkish border right away." He paused a little while and added, "In the meantime, what do we do about Akbar?"

Farshad, who had just received some cash from Akbar, did not wish to create any problems for him. Besides, he thought that Akbar had harmed nobody. He was a nice man and if ever he were helping the general escape, he most definitely was doing it for money. So Farshad urged, "Don't do anything about Akbar yet. Just leave him to me. You have enough on your hands to deal with."

"All right . . . all right, you have a point there. Hey, by the way, don't you think it would be better for you to head this search party?"

Farshad did not know what to say. He did not feel like getting out of his cozy house that late at night. He had hoped that other *pasdars* would be sent on that mission.

"I wouldn't mind doing it, but unfortunately I can't." Farshad sounded regretful.

Ghasem demanded sternly, "Why the hell not?"

Farshad gave out an audible sigh of disappointment and replied, "You see, sir, my wife's about to give birth."

"So? Haven't you got a mother or a sister?" the *pasdar* retorted sarcastically. "Helping women to give birth is a woman's job, not a *pasdar's* duty!"

Farshad frowned and swallowed angrily. "Yes . . . yes sir."

"Okay then." Ghasem now sounded kinder, "Bring them over to look after your wife, and you, yourself, get down here on the double."

Farshad cursed the greedy head of *pasdars* for outsmarting him, but there was nothing he could do about it. He had to obey his orders.

"All right, sir, I'll do that," agreed Farshad grudgingly. "And I'll get there as soon as I can."

"Hell," he told his wife, as he put his socks and shoes back on. "Why can't these greedy people leave us alone? They want to touch someone's blood money without having lifted a finger to capture him."

"I know," she moaned, massaging her belly gently and rocking her body from side to side. "But don't worry. Twenty-five thousand *toomans* of '*someone's blood money*' is not a small sum. Think of all the things we can do with it!"

For a second, Shirin's conscience started bothering her, but she immediately brushed all thoughts of righteousness aside. *"This is not the right time to think of morality,"* she thought. All she was concerned about at that point was money; with a child on the way, they needed so many things and had no money to afford them.

Farshad smiled contentedly and rubbed the palms of his hands together, "You're right. How would I ever lay my hands on this kind of money otherwise?"

"Exactly!" exclaimed Shirin and walked back to the kitchen to make herself a cup of tea.

"You know what? We can build ourselves a big house with probably ten thousand *toomans* and still have fifteen thousand left."

ALONE HIGH UP

ON THE MOUNTAIN

"Goodbye," called out Akbar, as Farhad and Parviz mounted the horses.

The general turned his head away and puffed at his cigarette. Pretty soon, he thought, he would be running out of them. Farhad still had a few left, which he had brought along from Tehran. He did not know how he was going to live without cigarettes. Through all those years of hiding in the basements while struggling with boredom and loneliness, Farhad's only comfort was smoking. For Farhad who had been a heavy smoker for years, quitting that bad habit was not going to be an easy task.

"Another friendly guy left behind," Farhad called out to Parviz, as the horses started to climb the high hill. *"Thank God for a nice road companion like Parviz,"* the general consoled himself. In the meantime, he wondered what was going on in that fellow's mind, as he watched his shadowy figure wobbling from side to side on the huge horse.

The thought of their encounter with the *pasdar* at the village kept bothering Farhad. *"What if he became suspicious?"* he wondered. *"What if he started having doubts about us being Akbar's cousins? What if it suddenly dawned on him that we are fugitives?"*

Farhad pulled onto the harness nervously and the horse jerked his head up and neighed, protesting against the harsh reining of its rider. Farhad could not help it; he was very anxious and his

153

mind was buzzing with scary thoughts. He did not believe that things would go as smoothly as they had so far. He was scared.

Farhad turned back and looked at the two shadowy figures of the guides staggering uphill behind the horses. The sight of their somber shapes and the effect of the tranquil and dark mountainside brought back to him the memory of a very special painting. The painting belonged to his sister and her husband when he was a small boy. He loved it and was mesmerized by the silhouettes of the two men leading their camels on foot in a moonlit desert. Sometimes, instead of playing with his friends, Farhad would just sit in front of the painting and lock his eyes on the figures of the two men dressed in Arab-style garb and flowing headdresses. He would imagine himself being one of them, slogging up a sand dune with his camel following behind. Gazing at the men enviously, Farhad would think that maybe one day he too could travel at night in a cool and peaceful desert. And now, here he was, a middle-aged man traveling through a dark, calm night on a treacherous and precipitous mountain.

The visualization of the scene of his favorite painting transported Farhad back to the safe world of his childhood and soothed his soul. It presently calmed his nerves and took his mind off his doubts and fears.

The group continued their journey at a slow pace in the dark until they came up to a spot with a narrow path winding downhill. The horses immediately turned into it without needing any guidance, carrying their riders down to the valley below. At the bottom of the hill, they traversed a flat stretch of land for about half a mile until the land sloped upward again. The caravan was now about to start their climb on a precipitous, rocky mountain.

The travelers climbed with great difficulty for two hours until, a few feet before reaching the summit, they came across a path leading downhill. The short, stocky guide broke the silence, "It's time we gave the horses some rest. Besides, we'll have to wait here for another group to join us."

The general felt apprehensive. Any change during their risky enterprise disturbed him.

As soon as they dismounted their steaming and heaving horses, Farhad crept closer to Parviz and muttered, "Do you feel like meeting a new bunch of people?"

"No," he replied indignantly. "God knows what kind of people they're going to be!"

Presently it started raining and a gusty wind chilled their bodies to the bone. Farhad pulled out the plastic tablecloth from the saddle bag and wore it like a Mexican poncho. It was the same tablecloth which he had bought from Akbar for one hundred *toomans*.

They waited for a long while but there was no sign of the new company. The short guide got to his feet and said, "It looks like these people are lost. My friend and I have to go looking for them."

The square-framed guide also got up, shaking his clothes like a wet dog and said softly, "You two don't move until we come back."

"What if you don't come back?" Parviz cried out frantically.

"Do you think we'll leave you by yourself on the top of this mountain?"

"We'll be back," the second guide reassured Parviz, and then they walked away, leaving the two desperate fugitives struggling with the unruly and spooked horses.

"Hold on tighter to the harness of your horse," Farhad yelled over the rumbling noise of the storm, "we should by no means lose these valuable beasts!"

He was right; without the horses they could not endure the severe conditions of the trip.

"I'm doing my best! Don't forget that I'm not as strong as you," Parviz hollered back.

"Look, I can't handle two horses, you better take care of yours," Farhad warned him.

Soon the horses calmed down and started sniffing the rough surface of the mountain for some dried grass.

The red gleaming lights of a revolutionary guards' post lingered beneath in the distance like a glowing volcano in the dark. Farhad felt like an unprotected, helpless animal preyed upon by a ferocious beast. *"Who is going to protect us now that we are left completely on our own?"* Farhad looked to Parviz for comfort, but to his great astonishment he found him crying quietly.

"Poor guy!" he told himself. *"I suppose he is as dismayed and fed up with life as I am."*

"What's the matter? Why are you crying?" the general inquired, placing a friendly hand on his shoulder. "Are you sick, or what? If it is of any consolation to you, I'm feeling miserable too." he added ruefully.

Parviz replied, still sobbing, "Yes, I feel very sick. But that's not why I'm crying."

Farhad fumbled in his pocket for his cigarette box. He now was down to three. He felt a genuine compassion for Parviz. He knew what he must be going through! At times he too felt like crying and if he were not embarrassed, he would have done so a hundred times.

"Then why are you crying?" he finally asked Parviz.

Parviz tried to regain his composure before answering, "I've heard that sometimes these smugglers abandon the refugees on top of the mountain and disappear. To tell you the truth, I'm scared. Look how long they've been gone. I don't think they're coming back."

Farhad frowned, admitting to himself, *"I think he's right."*

He could visualize the two of them wasting away on the precipitous mountain under harsh weather conditions, and from hunger and thirst. Like Parviz, Farhad had also heard about the guides abandoning the refugees. But then suddenly a thought flashed into his mind.

"You know what? If they had such an intention, they would not have left the horses with us. These animals cost a fortune. They are even more valuable to the smugglers than you and I."

Parviz chuckled, his hope picking up. "Do you really think so?"

"Absolutely!" the general assured him. "Besides, even if what you're saying was true, I know exactly what we could do."

Parviz wrapped his arms around his bent knees and seemed eager. "Oh yes? What?"

The general told Parviz that they could surrender themselves to the *pasdars*.

"That's ludicrous! Are you out of your mind? If that happens, they'll shoot us down like ducks!"

"No, they won't." Farhad's voice echoed in the desolate mountain, "They won't shoot us. They'll let us go if we each pay them one thousand *toomans*." He beamed. "Then we can sneak back to Tehran and hide again as before. I know for sure that this can be done. It has happened several times before!"

Parviz asked dubiously, "Are you sure of what you're talking about?"

No, he was not a hundred percent sure about anything! Moreover, he was starting to doubt the return of the guides himself. Yes, indeed, what if they never returned? How would they get back to Akbar's village? Neither Parviz nor Farhad knew the way back, even if they managed to descend the treacherous mountain without the help of the guides. However, he was not going to mention that to Parviz, who was near to having a nervous breakdown.

Parviz interrupted his thoughts. "You didn't answer my question."

"Oh, I'm sorry." Farhad expressed, "I personally don't know anybody to whom this has happened. Ahmad, the nice guide, told me that if we were ever caught, we could bribe the *pasdars* one thousand *toomans* per person and they'd let us go. He also mentioned that he personally knew of many such cases."

Parviz grunted, "Come on, why would the *pasdars* let fugitives go free for such a small sum of money?"

"You'd be surprised what these guys would do for even a small sum of money," Farhad said to him in a friendly tone. "You see, these poor guys are not well paid at all."

DEAD END

Farhad was overwhelmed with fatigue and illness, and Parviz's sullen mood was the last thing he needed to deal with. High fever had dehydrated him and his injured knee was extremely painful.

"Oh, how I'd give everything for a glass of water!" Farhad voiced loudly, grimacing as he shivered uncontrollably. "If only the Shah had shown an iron fist against Khomeini's followers, we wouldn't have to go through all this pain," he complained.

Parviz sniggered, shaking his head. "Come on, man, you don't mean it, do you?"

"I don't mean what?"

"That the Shah did not show an iron fist."

"Yes, I mean it."

"Oh, yes? How about those massacres?"

"What massacres?" Farhad barked harshly.

"What massacres? Does the phrase *Black Friday* sound familiar?" Parviz's sarcastic, loud voice echoed in the mountainous land.

Of course it did. Who hadn't heard about that horrible incident? On a Friday, right before the revolution, Iranians gathered at Jalleh Square in Tehran for peaceful demonstrations. The Shah's army opened fire on them, mercilessly massacring thousands of innocent people. The killings of the Jalleh Square, instead of acting as a deterrent, further kindled the fire of the rebellion.

The general consented, feeling embarrassed. He blamed

himself partly for not noticing certain signs of discontent among people. Perhaps he and other high-ranking officials should have been the Shah's ears and eyes and should have helped him realize that the country was in turmoil.

The general sighed, "I remember the *Black Friday*. That was a terrible incident!"

Parviz exploded, "Indeed it was! And how about setting fire to the movie hall, where hundreds of people were charred?"

Farhad did not wish to admit to himself that the Shah may have been the instigator of those horrible acts. Although he sometimes blamed the Shah for all his misfortunes, he still loved the deceased monarch. He had served the Shah wholeheartedly for a lifetime, finding him a symbol of perfection. The general had, in a way, worshipped him. He had killed for him, imprisoned the Shah's opponents, and fought bloody wars without fear for his own life. Through all those years he had had just one goal: to serve the Shah and his country with utmost devotion. However, regardless of how Farhad felt about the Shah, he could not believe that the Shah in person would have ordered the massacre of unarmed citizens. His feelings about the arson in the movie theater were the same; he did not want to accept that his ruler could have committed such an atrocious act.

Farhad responded glumly to Parviz, "If people's claims about those incidents are true, then . . ."

Parviz cut in angrily, "Of course it is true! We all know that the Shah ordered the Jalleh Square massacre, and that the malicious burning of the cinema was orchestrated by *SAVAK*." He breathed nervously and went on, "Afterwards, the cruel bastard spread the rumor that it was Ayatollah Khomeini's followers' work."

Farhad sighed. "I can't understand why he would do such a thing!"

Parviz answered succinctly, "Very simple! He wished to turn the people against Ayatollah Khomeini, whom they believed to be their savior." Parviz then rubbed his hands together to warm them and pressed on, "Yes sir, your *powerful* ruler, instead of

changing his despotic ways, which were the cause of the unrest
in the country, was using devious methods to stop the spread of
the revolution."

Farhad felt dismayed and immeasurably disappointed to think
that he had loved and served a person who had lacked
compassion for his own people and had committed such brutal
acts. He thought that he must have been blind not to realize what
sort of a person the Shah had really been. But then again, he
started doubting those rumors and hoped with all his heart that
they were not true, because Farhad could not understand how a
God-loving person could set fire to a place filled with his brothers
and sisters. *"The Shah was religious,"* he thought, *"he had gone
to Mecca, hadn't he?"*

"It surely was the work of the *SAVAK* without the Shah's
knowledge," Farhad told Parviz, and immediately scrambled to
his feet and started pacing the mountainous ground before Parviz
had a chance to respond. *"Stupid man,"* he berated himself, *"if
the Shah did not know what atrocities SAVAK was up to, then he
was not fit to rule!"*

While Farhad was busy wrestling with his thoughts, he heard
some noises in the dark. He dipped a shaky hand into the creased
pocket of his trousers for his cigarette box, but decided against
it. There were only two and a half cigarettes left now. Who knew
when he would lay his hands upon a fresh box again! He could
not even borrow any cigarettes; none of the travelers smoked.

The noise grew louder and Parviz panicked. "Oh, God, I
think it's the *pasdars!*"

"Oh, for goodness' sake, calm down. You're making me
nervous!" Farhad snapped at Parviz bitterly.

Parviz urged, "Aren't you afraid? It might really be the
pasdars!"

Farhad did not answer. He presently felt numb and had no
strength to deal with anything. The stress of self-doubt and
conflicting emotional upheavals had sapped his energy and left
his mind dazed. Besides, how could he console or be of any help
to Parviz when he could not take care of himself? Farhad had

turned into a defenseless and weak person, who needed others to protect him.

As Parviz grabbed Farhad's arm for support, a tired voice echoed from a distance, "We're back, fellows!"

Farhad freed himself from Parviz' grip and cried out: "It's the guides! Didn't I tell you that they'd come back for us?"

Parviz laughed nervously as the same guide who had spoken now approached them saying, "Hi guys, I must tell you that we had a hell of a hard time finding these people. They were totally lost."

The swaying dark figures of a group of people and their children on horses took shape and a discord of voices brought the gloomy, lifeless night to life. With all of them around, it suddenly became very difficult for the general to distinguish who was who. At first he panicked and felt lost, but soon he composed himself and got ready to leave with the crowd.

The group now set forth on their journey, leaving the last Iranian checkpoint behind, a light speck down below.

The horseback ride and the mountain climbing went on uneventfully. The rain had stopped and the night was peaceful, but extremely cold. No words were spoken among the sleepy travelers and the guides. Except for the clopping sound of the hooves of the horses against the rocky mountain, the night was mute.

Farhad was overwhelmed by a strange feeling. It felt as though he were riding with a group of solemn phantoms. For the first time in so many days, Farhad felt totally detached from the real world. Lost in reverie, he dreamed of verses depicting the beauty of the night. Immersed in the world of poetry, he envisioned Sadi riding by his side. Pretty soon Molavi and Hafez came to life, reciting verses of hopeful and soothing messages to him. Next, Leyla appeared with her drowsy eyes, whispering words of encouragement in his ear: "Go on my brave, don't give up. The future is bright!" Farhad wished he could live in his world of vision forever, where there was hope and beauty. Where there were no *pasdars* to haunt him, and where he needed nobody to shield him against the revolutionary regime.

At around two in the morning, the caravan arrived at a plateau not far from the Turkish border, where a group of sheepherders had set up a camp. The sleeping shepherds woke up as the group arrived, and came forth to greet them. They were such friendly mountain people, ready to help in any way they could. It looked like they were used to meeting fugitives passing through their camp. It must have brightened their lonely, isolated life every time they came across some travelers. One could see it from the broad smiles on their young faces, upon their encounter with the travelers.

"Could you give me some water? I'm dying of thirst," Farhad implored the friendly shepherd wearing a long sheepskin cloak and a rimless felt hat.

"But of course, *Arbab!*" replied the man amiably.

"How nice," Farhad thought, *"to be called 'boss' the old-fashioned way."* He then gulped down the water which tasted salty to his palate, making him feel sick.

Under the dim light of the lantern, the refugees' figures and faces were vaguely visible. The area around the tents was still dark and Farhad could see only his immediate surroundings. The three young shepherds looked alike. Their faces were unshaven and they wore the same kind of sheepskin cloaks and felt hats.

The tired guides looked to be in their mid-twenties. The general pitied the poor fellows. They had walked, God knows, for how many miles and indeed deserved the short break.

The travelers and their children had all dismounted and were stretching their stiff bodies. They were well dressed and looked like city folks. The general wondered about the reason why those people had become fugitives. *"Are they of the Bahai faith?"* he asked himself. The *Bahais* have always been one of the most persecuted religious groups in Iran. They are the followers of an Iranian self-proclaimed prophet, who lived in 1863. *Bahais* accept all the religions of the world and believe that Bahaullah, their prophet, was the embodiment or incarnation of all the other prophets.

There appeared to be about twenty-five to thirty people in the group. Farhad looked around, still perched on his horse, trying to locate Parviz among the travelers, but to no avail. He assumed that another guide might have met up with Parviz and taken him away separately when the caravan had arrived on the mountaintop. There was no point in worrying about Parviz. The smugglers arranged everything covertly. During the trip, the fugitives were hardly ever advised of what the next move would be.

After a short break, one of the guides called out, "Everybody, listen up. We have to cross the Turkish border before dawn. So pick up your children and mount your horses."

They immediately obeyed and the caravan headed out in a single file with each person looking at the wobbling buttocks of the front horse and the wiggling hips of its rider. But the moment the fugitives left the dimly lit shepherd's camp, a total darkness engulfed the universe with its mighty jaws, rendering Farhad fainthearted and depressed again. Such sudden mood swings had become a habit since the beginning of his hiding days. They had gotten even worse after Farhad turned into a fugitive. He was now a weak and scared creature who had long lost all the toughness of character that he possessed as a military man. Farhad, through the long years of hiding, had relied on his benefactors for protection and survival. And now he felt that he was a *nobody* without the presence of the guides.

Presently, the fear of being separated from the group began torturing him. *"How could I find my way in the dark night if my horse went astray?"* he wondered. Then he remembered that those were trained animals and knew exactly where they were headed.

He clamped his arms around the beast's neck and whispered in his ear, "Hey, buddy, you know, I'm starting to like you. Thank you for taking me safely up and down the steep mountains and hills!"

To Farhad, having turned into a dependent person who now needed the smugglers like a child needed a mother, even the horse appeared as a protector. Farhad relaxed, half-dozing as the gentle horse swayed him softly. The night was freezing but beautiful, and the passage through the mountainous terrain in the black night mesmerizing and awe inspiring.

The group rode on at a slow pace for four hours, while the guides followed behind the caravan. Being the last rider in the file, Farhad turned back several times during the journey and offered to share his horse with either one of them. They refused.

"Poor fellows, they must be worn out!" he told himself. But then he decided that this was their job and they were used to it.

The general was trying very hard not to fall asleep by busying his mind with millions of themes. At the moment he was toying with the prospect of his final destination of America. Of course, nobody had yet mentioned anything about it, but he wished with all his heart that he would eventually end up there. He had such empathy for that land and its people! Maybe later he could somehow help his lovely wife and children to also join him. Farhad smiled and stroked his horse's mane. He liked the idea of them all being together in America.

As the night gradually yielded itself to dawn, the weary, dust-covered travelers started yawning and stretching. At four thirty in the morning, the sky was pearl gray, and the air, crisp and chilly.

A droning sound of voices filled the air as each person looked at the back rider and greeted them.

"Good morning, everybody," the young voice of a guide resonated in the air. "We should be arriving at the Turkish border in about half an hour, where my two colleagues and I will part with you."

The way the guide announced the details of their arrival to the Turkish border sounded to Farhad like the announcements made by stewardesses and stewards aboard an aircraft.

The three guides, who had trailed along all night through, were approximately of the same medium height, but one was slightly shorter. The guides barely spoke to one another or addressed the fugitives. If they ever managed to open their mouths, it was for the purpose of yawning, announcing something, or giving instructions to the fugitives. They reminded Farhad of mechanical robots void of any emotions, programmed merely to perform a job.

After the guide's announcement, a man with curly, gray hair and a thick black mustache asked the guards, "What's going to happen to us at the Turkish border when you guys leave?"

The shorter guide, who sounded extremely fatigued, responded, "The Turkish guides will take over from that point onward."

As the group of riders and the three guides slowly descended the mountain, the weak rays of the early-morning sun started breathing some life into the dusk of the mountainside. Then gradually, the brightening sky cast light over the ragged range of mountains and the empty, dry land below.

Farhad shifted his glance from the magnificent sight of the high peaks of the gray, adjacent mountains to the valley down below. The land appeared vast and dry with a few scattered dark shapes here and there, which Farhad believed to be trees.

The general fixed his gaze below at the valley and saw a blurry silhouette of something. *"What could that possibly be?"* he thought to himself.

A scared voice broke the silence, "Goodness! Do you all see what's down there?"

"I see something, but I can't tell exactly what," Farhad responded, squinting to sharpen his focus. Then, to his horror, the picture took on a clearer shape. Farhad shook his head with disappointment and looked back at the guides who were now coming to the front of the line.

The children, who were riding with their mothers, soon woke up and started asking for something to eat. Then the men dismounted and helped their wives and the little ones slide down the horses. Farhad looked at the children and thought about how nice they had been all through the trip. He remembered his own children when they were small. Then his life rolled in front of his eyes like a film. He regretted the passage of time and wished that a mysterious hand could take him *"back in time"*. He told himself that he would marry the same girl, choose the same career and do the same things all over again. He had no qualms except that he had been naive in his outlook towards the Shah. That would be one point that he would wish to change. Although he did not know how!

Then Farhad told himself that if he were to go back in time, he would accept becoming Ambassador to England. The Shah had offered him that post a year before his downfall. Farhad had begged the Iranian monarch to allow him to refuse his kind offer, claiming he would not make a good diplomat. The Shah had granted him his wish. Farhad thought that if he had accepted the assignment, he and his family would have become political refugees in England and he would not have been forced to be torn apart from them.

"Well, what's done is done!" he told himself, *"For the moment it seems that we've got a bigger problem on our hands."*

Farhad rubbed his eyes to make sure that he was not dreaming. Alas, no, what stood there was as real as the moon and the sun in the sky. He froze with fear like a dazed animal, which gets blinded by the bright headlights of an oncoming car.

All hope of freedom vanished in him like a cloud of smoke in the wind. What was he supposed to do? Run away? But he was not alone. All the others were in danger too!

"Dammit!" he cursed loudly. "To come all this way to be captured right before entering Turkey!"

Millions of confusing thoughts bombarded his mind. He had no clue what was going to happen. All he knew was that he was petrified! He had such a horror of the *pasdars*. During his hiding days he often had nightmares about being carried to the prison yard by two sneering revolutionary guards and being tied to an execution post. Then, each time he would wake up with a start, with his heart racing madly and his body soaking in sweat right before being shot.

For a brief second, a deadly silence reigned over the mountainside. The crowd had become speechless and paralyzed with fear. Even the children seemed to realize the gravity of the situation. They clung on to their mothers and remained motionless, like little statues. Then, gradually the crowd came out of the reverie and a nervous chorus of voices filled the air.

Women were wailing as they held on firmly to their children and men were shaking their heads in disbelief and muttering something under their breaths.

"Well, ladies and gentlemen, this is it. Say your prayers!" A middle-aged man called out, as another fugitive dressed in black pants and shirt demanded firmly from the guides, "Do you have any idea what you're going to do? You're responsible for taking care of us and it's your duty to get us out of this mess!"

The three guides, who looked as pale as ghosts and who were whispering together, ignored the fellow's remarks. They went on talking for a while longer and then the one with the short, square figure finally said, "I don't see what we can do, except to stay put. Who knows, some miracle from heaven might save us."

"*Miracle?* That's ludicrous! What if they decide to shoot?" Farhad burst out, fumbling in his pocket for his cigarettes.

The guide looked at him angrily and hollered, "Do you have any better suggestions, Mister? If you do, then let's hear it!"

Farhad cast his eyes down and remained silent. He realized that they were merely simple guides, whose job was to lead the fugitives through complicated mountainous trails. If Gholi, the head smuggler were around, he surely would have found a way to handle the situation.

The same guide who had flared up at Farhad now added calmly, "Maybe they'll have mercy on women and children. I don't know, anything could happen!"

The refugees sat down on the cold, stone-strewn, dusty ground of the mountain slope. Men clustered together to one side, women opened their bags and started feeding their children, while the hungry horses desperately searched for some dried grass. Farhad believed that the women, for their children's sake, were trying to pretend that everything was all right. However, on second thought, he wondered if their motherly instincts had overridden their fears, or if they had, like typical fatalistic Iranians, succumbed to destiny. They were probably thinking: *harcheh bada bad*— whatever will be will be, and *Khoda Bozorgeh*—God is great! This is a great Iranian characteristic. They leave everything to God.

Farhad took a hungry puff from the saved cigarette, but put it carefully out, stored it gently back in the box and asked the guide, "What will happen with the Turkish guides? What time were we supposed to meet them?"

The short guide, who had snapped at him earlier, looked at his shoelaces, appeared somewhat embarrassed, and answered, "They'll wait until nine in the morning. If we don't show up by then, they'll leave." He then sighed, threw his hands up in the air and continued, "But it's only five o'clock now and lots of things can happen within four hours."

A DILEMMA

Farshad and his two companions, who had driven all night and arrived at the unmanned Turkish border at three in the morning, were facing a dilemma. They had not expected to see such a large crowd of fugitives. Farshad had thought that at the Turkish border they would encounter the general, another refugee and one or two guides. He had no idea what he was going to do with all those people. Especially when there were so many women and children among them!

Farshad made a fist, smacking his left palm with it angrily several times. One thing was clear to him. There was no way he was going to harm those women and children! For Iranian men, protecting the *zaifeh*—the weaker gender, as they like to call them—and children is a duty. Being gallant to women in society is considered a gracious behavior. For example, when people stand in line in bread bakeries with open furnaces, men almost always let women pass ahead of them. Also, in buses, if all the seats are taken and a woman walks in, the nearest man will get up and offer his seat. Of course, there are exceptions to this custom and not all men are gallant.

Farshad thought of his wife and hoped that everything had gone well with the birth. His heart leapt with joy at the thought of holding the baby in his arms upon his return. He hoped to be able to walk out of this situation as fast as he could and get back home to his family.

"Listen, guys, I want no shooting. Do you hear me?" Farshad ordered the two young guards, Ramin and Abolfarz, while the crowd on the mountain remained motionless, awaiting their fate. In the meantime, the pleasant early-morning sun spread over the surrounding mountainous landscape and a gentle breeze brushed against Farshad's young olive skin. He squinted in the early-morning sun and looked up at the crowd on the mountain and said, "This is it. I think it's time to make a move. Fellows, remember I want no shooting no matter what happens. We are here to arrest the general; that's all."

Abolfarz, who had never seen Farshad so softhearted before, wondered what was happening to that dedicated *pasdar*, whom he had known to be tough and unforgiving. They had been on several missions previously headed by Farshad and had even shot at some escaping fugitives. Abolfarz himself hated killing the miserable runaways, but like Farshad, being dedicated to the Islamic government, he believed that his duty to Ayatollah Khomeini took precedence over his feelings.

"What if there are some armed guys among the fugitives? Won't we be forced to shoot back if they decide to open fire?" Abolfarz asked, holding on firmly to his machine gun.

Ramin shook his head disapprovingly as he turned his lean sinewy body to face Abolfarz. "Nonsense! Do you think they're crazy?"

He then tucked his dark fringe of hair, which was getting into one eye, under his military cap, and carried on, "Don't they have eyes? Can't they see our powerful machine guns? Do you think they'll risk the lives of their wives and children?"

Ramin, like Abolfarz and Farshad, was a tough soldier and had, on certain occasions, fired at fugitives without any remorse. He was a calculating, cool-headed *pasdar*, who could, out of experience, tell if a fugitive was dangerous or not. Ramin had been in the police force a few years longer than Abolfarz.

Farshad nodded with consent. "That's true. But supposing you, Abolfarz, are right and a stupid fugitive decides to shoot. We'll return his shots only by firing in the air." Farshad pressed, "So I repeat. You're not to shoot at anybody, unless I order you to do so."

The two *pasdars* gave out a chorus of assent. Then Farshad, immersed in deep thought, casting his eyes at the rocky surface of the mountain, beckoned for the guards to start their uphill climb.

"How could I get out of this impasse without hurting anybody?" Farshad wondered and prayed to God for assistance. Somehow that morning he was in a charitable mood and wished he could let those people go. *"But how? What about the general and the reward? Besides, what would I tell Ghasem if I return home empty handed?"* He thought that first he should find out whether or not the general was among the crowd. In any case, he did not see the need for endangering the lives of all those people. Meanwhile, Farshad readjusted the machine gun on his shoulder and pushed it back to face the valley. *"Would the poor women and their children sense that I am going to them in peace?"* he mused. Farshad reminded himself again that he was interested only in capturing the general and that he had no intentions of hurting the *"weaker gender"* and their children.

The crowd, noticing the advancing *pasdars*, suddenly became jittery. Farhad lifted his dizzy, sleepy head to see what was going on and noticed with distress that the guards had started their ascent. "Dammit!" he cursed, stupefied with fear. His head began turning like a spinning wheel, he felt nauseous, and beads of sweat trickled down his face, despite the chill in the air.

The general staggering to his feet, gazed at the dismayed fugitives who were busy saying their prayers and begging God to have mercy on them and their children. Next, he looked to the guides' pale, scared faces for comfort, but they stared vacantly back at him. It was obvious that they had given up hope, possibly brewing the same kind of scary thoughts in their minds that Farhad had! Of course, they were in the same boat as the general. The guides would doubtlessly be executed for helping people to escape illegally.

The general wished to find a way to get them out of that muddle. He knew that acts of bravery would be futile against such heavily armed revolutionary guards. Suddenly, he remembered how Leyla had managed to come up with a convincing story that night in a dark side street in Tehran during their encounter with the *pasdar*. He too should think of something intelligent, but what?

Farhad knocked at his forehead with his knuckles several times as if trying to clear his mind, and remembered the saying that goes: *"Nothing is impossible under the blue sky"*. He told himself, *"True, nothing is impossible. I'm sure there is an answer to our problem."* For some reason he felt himself responsible for every man, woman and child on the mountain slope.

The general began pacing the length of the narrow area in front of the sitting crowd on the mountain, as he groped in the pocket of his creased gray pants for his last cigarette.

The gray-haired man, who had earlier questioned the guides, jumped to his feet eagerly and lit the general's cigarette. Being an observant person, he could tell from Farhad's pensive countenance that he was trying to come up with a plan.

The general took a few hungry puffs at his cigarette as though it were the sole existing pleasure in his life, which under the circumstances it indeed was. Soon he put it out carefully and stored it in his pocket. He had to use his last priceless *"jewel"* with thrift.

The brief smoking acted as tonic on his fragile nerves; it also helped clear his perplexed mind. He could think more clearly now. It was imperative for him to urgently come up with a solution!

Suddenly Ahmad's voice echoed in his head.

"Bingo!" the general rejoiced within. *"Why hadn't I thought about it in the first place?"* he wondered.

Farhad beckoned the fugitives to gather around him. "Listen up, ladies and gentlemen," he called out.

All voices of talking, praying and crying subsided right away, as people fixed their eyes on him.

"I have an idea about how to solve this problem, but it will require your cooperation," he announced, shifting his lanky body from foot to foot, as the faces of the fugitives lit up with enthusiasm and curiosity.

Farhad explained, "If you pay one thousand *toomans* per person, excluding the children, I can persuade the guards to let us go. Please hurry up and bring me the money before they get here."

All the screaming, talking, and arguing that followed told Farhad that some of them were unhappy about the sum they had to pay. The general thought that, even in danger, certain people's love of money took precedence over their sense of safety.

Then he heard the strong voice of the gray-haired man prevail over the din of the crowd, "For God's sake, hurry up and dig in your pockets. These are our lives we're talking about!"

A young, haggard-looking fellow with unshaven dark face responded, "The problem is that we don't have much money on us. The previous guides took most of it. Besides, what are we going to do when we reach Turkey with empty pockets?"

"Listen, brother, if we don't pay them we won't get to Turkey at all. It's as simple as that," Farhad prompted.

The gray-haired man insisted, "Come on guys, he is right!"

The men came forth grudgingly and handed Farhad their money. Farhad could understand their concern. Without money you could be a burden to whichever country you ended up in and there was a danger for you to be deported to Iran.

When the guards finally approached the group, Farhad had twenty-five thousand *toomans* stashed away in his jacket's pockets.

The general moved up and greeted the *pasdars* warmly, wearing a broad smile on his drawn, tired face. He acted like there was nothing wrong and as if he had come across his beloved *cousins*. It was amazing! He was behaving like his old self again: friendly, bold and decisive. What's more, his leadership qualities were starting to surface.

"We are a bunch of harmless people and are on our way to Turkey," Farhad uttered without preamble to the head guard, whose face looked somewhat familiar to him. *"Could he be the pasdar we had bumped into the night before?"* Farhad wanted to know. If he really were, then his consternation about that encounter all night through may not have been groundless. However, it was impossible to say. Farhad had seen the face of the night guard very briefly and in darkness.

The head guard scrutinized Farhad's face warily.

"That's it, he has recognized me!" the general told himself, being overwhelmed with fear all over again.

The head guard went on examining the general's visage a bit more. Then, he dug into his pocket and pulled out a folded-up flyer. Opening the leaflet gingerly, he studied it while squinting his eyes. Suddenly a crooked smile lit up his face. Yes, he was sure that the general was among the crowd. *"True, I have to split the reward money with my superior, but still,"* Farshad thought, *"I would be considered wealthy with twenty-five thousand toomans in my pocket."*

"Do you know this guy?" Farshad demanded sternly, shoving the flyer into Farhad's face.

As the guide stood there holding up the leaflet, he examined the general's face closely and suddenly uttered, "You look familiar. I must know you from somewhere."

Farhad clenched his hands nervously, digging his long fingernails into his palms. *"Yes that's it!"* He believed that the guard had recognized him and would soon put the shackles on him. *"What am I supposed to do?"* he mused. *"Could I put up a fight against arrest, or should I surrender with dignity?"*

The general took a deep breath in trying to compose himself. He had to think of something and find a way not to yield to the *pasdars*. It was imperative for him to come across as a relaxed and fearless person. He could not allow Khomeini's men to be the winners. Farhad and his friends had managed to confuse them for nine years. He had to go on tricking them a bit longer. There was no way Farhad would let them get the better of him, especially now that he was standing on the threshold of freedom!

Farhad ignored the guard's remark. Instead, he examined the flyer and was shocked to see his own picture staring back at him. The photo on the leaflet dated back to the days when he was the military governor of Khouzestan.

The general stepped back in bewilderment, with his stomach churning. *"Hooshang Afshan will hunt me down even on the highest peaks of the mountains,"* the general told himself. In the picture, he appeared tall and graceful in his glamorous general's uniform and the numerous medals decorating his broad chest. Above the picture it read, *"Help us capture the enemy of the Islamic republic, the ex-General Shirazi, and earn fifty thousand toomans."*

Although the general had suspected that the guards' presence there could be because of him, he had not been prepared to have his own wanted poster shoved into his face.

"Yes or no?" the guard bellowed harshly in Farhad's ear.

Farhad took on a serious demeanor, looked the guard straight in the eye and breathed, "I don't believe I do."

"You really don't?"

"What exactly did he mean by that question?" Farhad panicked within.

"No, I don't," the general responded.

The guard presently turned to the men who stood in the front row with their backs to their wives and children. Farhad knew he had changed radically since the taking of the picture on the flyer, especially during those last few days, with the agony of pain, fatigue and fever. He was at least thirty pounds lighter and appeared quite lanky. His ribs felt like sharp blades covered with a layer of skin. His hipbones protruded like two boomerangs and his feet appeared larger now that he was so much thinner. The guide had definitely not recognized him and, of all ironies, he was asking for Farhad's help in identifying the picture on the leaflet!

Just as the general had thought that Farshad had finished with him, he turned back to him and demanded briskly, "What's your name? Can I see your ID?"

Farhad fumbled absently in his soiled jacket's inner pocket.

"Yes," he answered, sounding annoyed with the guard as he handed him his fake passport.

"Ali Bagheri?" He looked at Farhad inquisitively and then back to the fake *sejel*.

"Yes sir, that's my name," Farhad responded, suddenly feeling apprehensive.

The general stood motionless, scared to even blink an eye.

He felt like a dazed mouse nailed in place with fear at the sight of a cat.

The guard kept on inspecting the fake *sejel*. *"When is the damned pasdar going to decide whether or not I'm the general?"* Farhad thought.

Still holding onto the false document, Farshad turned his back to the general, held the flier high in the air and yelled out to the crowd, "Does anybody know this guy?"

"Please help me, dear God!" Farhad implored the Almighty.

A cacophony of voices filled the air like the sounds inside a bazaar: haggling of merchants and customers, grunting and groaning of load bearers . . . In the meantime, Farhad waited fearfully as the members of the crowd scrutinized the picture on the flyer and passed it around.

"What is happening? Have they recognized me?" he wondered. For a second Farhad thought all eyes were fixed on him.

The general decided to prepare himself to run. He could not allow them to arrest him. Meanwhile, he was well aware that he had no chance against the powerful machine guns of the *pasdars*. *"What difference does it make?"* Farhad pondered. *"I'm going to be shot one way or the other."* Farhad decided that he would be a hundred times better off being dropped by a machine gun while running than at an execution post.

As he was contemplating his horrid end, suddenly all the voices subsided.

"That's it! They are going to denounce me," Farhad reasoned, while slowly sidling away into the crowd. Then he heard them call out in unison, "No. We don't know him."

"Oh, thank God!" he breathed a sigh of relief. The general had been spared. God had shielded him against the *pasdars*.

Regaining his composure, the general stepped forward, still shaking uncontrollably, and said, "Officer, we have a proposition to make."

Farshad grinned. He knew exactly what the *proposition* was going to be. Nevertheless he inquired, "What kind of a proposition?"

Farhad closed his eyes for a brief second, trying to calm his nerves, which had gone haywire under the duress of the situation. The general then placed his hands on his bulging pockets and declared, "We've put together twenty-five thousand *toomans*. It'll be yours if you let us go."

Farshad was overwhelmed with joy! He had not expected to get rich so fast and so effortlessly. He had expected to capture General Shirazi and claim the reward money. But not having found him among the fugitives, he had prepared himself to return home empty handed. Fortunately, now Farshad had the opportunity to pocket twenty-five thousand *toomans*. He thought that he would give five thousand to Ramin and Abolfarz and keep twenty thousand for himself. He would instruct the two guards not to breathe a word to a soul about their encounter with the fugitives and keep the question of the *anam* a secret. They would definitely obey him. The two guards respected and loved their chief. Besides, if anybody found out about their receiving any *anam*, they would have to give it to the head of the *pasdars*, or be punished.

The fugitives waited in utter silence. Some women held their children tightly in their arms while others squatted with their arms draped around their little ones. It was a pivotal moment for everybody. They were soon going to find out about their fate.

THE NEWS

It was nine o'clock in the morning and the chief *pasdar* of the Sar village had not yet heard from Farshad. Earlier he had called Tehran and informed Hooshang Afshan's office about the possibility of his men having located General Shirazi. Hooshang, in turn, had not wasted a second in reporting to the Tehran media the news of the alleged arrest of the general. He had to take advantage of every little opportunity to get his name out in public. It was also important for him to advertise his pivotal role in the arrest of General Shirazi.

Leyla, who had returned from her mother's home a few days earlier, turned the television on early in the morning after her son and daughter left for the university. The announcer, a young man with thick, dark, joined eyebrows, interrupted the report about the events in the *Majlis* and said, "We just got word from Mr. Afshan's bureau that they believe they have captured General Shirazi near the Turkish border. He was one of the Shah's important . . ."

Leyla could not hear the rest of his words. She had to sit down to avoid fainting. She felt nauseous and dizzy. Leyla held her head in her hands and rocked herself from side to side. She felt devastated and blamed herself for Farhad's arrest. *"I shouldn't have urged him to escape. The poor man hadn't wanted to leave,"* Leyla thought. But then suddenly a glimmer of hope flickered in her mind. *"The announcer did not say that Farhad was captured for certain,"* she mused, *"he used the words 'they believe they've captured . . .'"*

Leyla smiled, turned the TV off, and carried on with her daily chores. She knew that Farhad was capable of getting out of difficult situations. She told herself that even if her husband were arrested, he would surely find the way to solve that problem.

The loud ringing of the telephone startled Leyla out of her thoughts. "Hello, this is Leyla."

"Leyla, it's Simin. Did you hear the news?"

"Yes, I did."

"Are you okay? Shall I come over?"

"No, I'm fine. I don't believe they have him."

"I don't either, knowing Farhad."

Leyla went into her bright, sunny kitchen, sat by a vinyl brown table and started peeling some potatoes. Her mother and sister were going to come over for lunch and she had decided to prepare *abgoosht*. Putting the peeled and quartered potatoes in a bowl, she started trimming the thick layer of fat off the lamb meat. The dried beans and chickpeas were being soaked in a separate bowl on the countertop.

Leyla tried to visualize her husband somewhere near the Turkish border in the wilderness and wondered what exactly had happened. *Were the smugglers to blame for whatever might have happened?* she mused.

The fact of the matter was that nobody was to blame. It just happened to be a question of bad luck. However, on second thought, it couldn't even be considered as *bad luck*, for although Farhad and the rest of the fugitives had come face to face with the *pasdars*, Farshad, the head of the *pasdars*, fortunately had not recognized the general. He was merely debating with himself how to accept the *anam* that was being offered to him by a skinny, haggard-looking fugitive.

Farshad took the guards aside and started consulting with them. It was not clear what they were talking about. All Farhad could see in that huddle was the incessant nodding of heads. Then they walked back to Farhad.

Farshad said, "What we're about to do is highly irregular. However, since you're practically in Turkey and because of all the children and women, we'll let you go."

A loud cheer went up in the air as Farhad stood bewildered and stunned. He could not believe their luck! *"Is it real, or am I dreaming?"* he wondered. He had not expected things to go so smoothly. Farhad looked at the refugees. Women were hugging and kissing each other joyfully, and men were shaking hands. The children, seeing their parents so happy, were holding hands and turning round and round screaming happily.

"Thank you. Thank you so much, officer. You're very kind!" the general exclaimed gratefully.

Farshad faced the refugees and asked, "Do you all know what'll happen to you if we make you return to Tehran?"

"Yes, officer!" the crowd roared.

"I'm a God-fearing person and I don't like to have blood on my hands," the head guard claimed.

Farhad told himself, *"Strangely enough, the few pasdars that I have encountered have not been anything like the fearful beasts I thought they would be."* He smiled and went on, *"Or is it money talking?"*

The general approached Farshad and handed him the pile of the twenty-five thousand *toomans,* which he grabbed without any hesitation. Farshad then turned on his heels, with the guards tromping downhill behind him, holding on firmly to their impressive machine guns.

As the Jeep disappeared, leaving a cloud of dust behind, Farhad's companions screamed with exultation. They all gathered around him and shook his hand with gratitude. Farhad was also jubilant. A miracle had taken place. He closed his eyes for a second and thanked God for being so kind to them all. Farhad was also thankful that nobody had suspected that he was the wanted general. For once, the general was grateful for having fallen ill. He knew that it was because of his unshaven, sickly visage that people hadn't recognized him.

By the unmanned Turkish border, a group of Kurdish guides

awaited the fugitives. The guides were Turkish citizens who lived at the bordering villages of Turkey and Iran. Hence, from there on, the Kurds took over the expedition from the Iranians and the fugitives set off for the first village in Turkey, with each family being assigned to a separate guide. Farhad and his guide, a quiet young fellow with a tall, trim frame, left on horseback before the other fugitives.

The general could not believe it. He was on his way to freedom! He was actually in Turkey and Hooshang Afshan could no longer touch him!

Suddenly life took on a brighter edge and Farhad was filled with positive energy. Everything appeared beautiful and promising, even the boring, barren landscape, with its low, brown hills. He was in one of those optimistic moods which God knew how long would last.

Farhad's guide spoke Kurdish and Turkish but no Persian. He looked at the general, smiling with friendly eyes from time to time, but they did not exchange any words during the two-hour trip through dirt roads and hilly terrain. Farhad knew some broken Kurdish, but not enough to carry on a conversation. Instead, he sat limply on his horse, mulling over the recent amazing incident. Farhad could still not believe how lucky they all had been. Especially himself! If he had been identified, there was no way the head *pasdar* would have let him go. Not only would he receive the reward money, but he would also become a hero for capturing the wanted general.

The landscape at the bordering Turkish region was very much like the Iranian Azarbayjan. The distant high mountains snugly encircled the vast valley. The dried, golden, short bushes, which occasionally swayed about with the sporadic gusts of wind, and the pebbly dry land added to the monotony of the environment.

At seven thirty in the morning, Farhad and the guide rode into a partially green Turkish village where barefooted children ran about playing on unpaved sidewalks, littered with scraps of paper and household garbage. The general had never seen so many hungry stray dogs sniffing around nervously in search of food. As Farhad and his sleepy guide turned into a winding street with narrow sidewalks, flanked by some half-grown birch trees, his attention was drawn to the mud huts. Most of the huts had a single multipurpose room, with open doors facing the street. The family members in those huts were sitting cross-legged on the floor around their plastic tablecloths. The steaming *samovars* with brewing teapots placed on the *samovars'* tops stood on one side of the tablecloth. Round-faced women wearing white headscarves sat by the *samovars,* pouring tea for their husbands, while children slept on the floor next to the breakfast setting.

A small dog yapped at them as they dismounted in front of a closed green door, which swung open as soon as the guide pounded on it with its bronze hand-shaped knocker. A short, chubby man opened the door and exchanged greetings with the guide. The tall Kurdish guide then introduced Farhad to him and left. The new host had brown hair and small beady eyes with long eyelashes. He bowed politely to the general, beckoned him to enter and closed the massive wooden door behind them with a loud bang. Despite his looks and physical condition, Farhad entered and walked upright, like a free general, just the way he had during his glorious days. He felt like a hero again and was proud to have solved a dilemma a short while ago. In fact, all he thought about after that incident on the mountain slope was how he had saved his, and over twenty-five other people's, lives. Ever since the Shah's downfall, he had not felt this way. Hiding and being on the run had turned him into a bitter and frustrated person with lack of self-respect.

Farhad and the host passed through a narrow corridor. The inhabitants' rooms were located on the right-hand side of the corridor facing sheds of goats and sheep. Farhad held his hand over his mouth and nose to avoid inhaling the terrible odor of manure permeating the air. Soon they entered a large room with a bread oven in the middle, just like the *tanoor* in the Iranian village.

The four men who were sleeping around the furnace woke up as soon as Farhad entered the room, and bombarded him with questions in Turkish. Farhad stared at them like a mute and deaf person. Not only could he not understand what they were saying, but he also felt dazed from fatigue and the lack of sleep. It seemed like his brain was on fire.

Farhad tried to make his Turkish host understand that he was ill and needed some medication. Unfortunately the man could not understand him.

At the far end of the room, three brick steps led to a bedroom where a mother and her two children were sleeping. The host wobbled up the steps, entered the room and woke them up. He wanted Farhad to sleep there instead. The woman looked furious as she and her children staggered down the stairs. Farhad did not care a bit. All he wanted was to lie down and let sleep soothe his fatigue and pain. The only thing that mattered to him now was his own survival.

The general entered the smelly, untended room. The large mattress and the covers where the woman and her small children had been sleeping were filthy and the ceiling was black with thousands of flies. Farhad knew that they would attack him the moment he lay down. But he was too tired and had to sleep, flies or no flies. Even the dirty bedding couldn't deter his need for rest.

Farhad threw himself, fully dressed, on top of the soiled covers and closed his eyes. Just as he was about to doze off, the children's mother, wearing a grayish-white scarf, burst into the room noisily pretending she had forgotten something. She looked around and then at Farhad with shrewd, angry eyes. She left, slamming the door as hard as she could just to annoy him. Farhad had no energy to react to her rude behavior. Nothing mattered at that point. He just wanted to slip into a state of oblivion. The horse ride, lack of sleep and his high fever had sapped all his energy, rendering him weary beyond care.

Farhad had slept for only two hours when suddenly it felt like somebody was strangling him with a pair of strong hands. He thought it was a *pasdar* trying to kill him. Farhad woke up screaming hoarsely, "No . . . no, you cannot kill me. I'll break your neck and tear your heart out!"

Once fully awake, he realized that he was having a nightmare. But he still could not breathe. *"What's happening to me?"* he wondered. Farhad rubbed his eyes and sat up, looking around. The room was filled with such a thick smoke that he thought the house must be on fire.

Farhad rushed down the steps into the large room and found the hostess bending over the bread oven, trying to start a fresh fire. He could not understand how the poor woman could breathe in that room filled with heavy smoke. He stormed out of the room coughing violently and then, opening the gate, he dashed out into the street for some fresh air. Two women, wearing head scarves and long robes, rushed out from next door to find out what was going on. When they saw the general standing outside, they tried to push him back into the enclosed corridor saying, "No, no. Dangerous!" in Turkish.

"No, ladies, I'm not going in there. I can't breathe," Farhad argued.

"Okay, okay," the younger one, who smelled strongly of rosewater, nodded. "Come . . . Come."

She led the general into a nearby small cottage. Farhad could tell from their behavior that the neighbors knew about his being an Iranian fugitive and were concerned about his safety.

They entered a clean room with a bright-colored Turkish carpet and some large, white pillows placed alongside the clean, whitewashed walls.

The family members had taken their shoes off and left them by the door.

The petite, dark-complexioned hostess, with a pair of almond-shaped, startling black eyes, took Farhad to a clean bedroom. Her eyes reminded him of Leyla's. She smiled timidly at Farhad, bowed and sidled out. The room smelled fresh and the bedding was exceptionally clean. There, Farhad slept soundly, not having to worry about lice and grime.

Around twelve thirty, a young man woke Farhad and invited him to have lunch with the family members. Farhad stared at his new host's round face and dark, thick mustache with bewilderment, not remembering where he was for a short second.

The hostess was serving bean and potato stew from a large bowl. The four family members, father, mother, a ten-year-old son and a six-year-old daughter, sitting cross-legged on the floor around a white linen tablecloth, all helped themselves to the stew from the same bowl. They dipped pieces of bread into the bowl and scooped out some stew. Then, holding the morsels in their cupped palms, they shoved them into their mouths with the help of their thumbs.

Farhad could not bring himself to share the food with them. He was not used to eating food from the same pot as others. Luckily, he had a good excuse. When they offered him in Turkish *'Booyouriz,'* he responded, "No, thank you. I'm sick and have no appetite."

Although people around the general felt nervous about his safety, he himself felt more relaxed being on Turkish soil. He decided to shave off his beard and moustache and look normal again.

When Farhad gazed at his face in the mirror, he was flabbergasted! He looked like a starved prisoner of war with his bony face and bulging eyes. No wonder nobody had recognized him!

In the afternoon, the head of the Turkish smugglers, Osman, came to see Farhad. Osman at first appeared very serious in his neat gray trousers and white shirt, but he proved to be quite friendly and kind.

After greeting Farhad politely, he said, "Sir, your friend from the United States has asked us to do our best to make your passage to Istanbul pleasant."

"Oh, that's nice of him to think of me!" Farhad exclaimed, not really knowing who the friend was.

"Yes," he replied, "but the problem is that because of the political situation in the Kurdish region of Turkey, we can't offer you much comfort."

Farhad's face fell. He knew exactly what the fellow was about to tell him and was not going to accept it. He had had enough of horseback riding and had hoped that in Turkey he would be traveling by car.

Osman looked at his shoelaces docilely and carried on, "Well, you see sir, unfortunately, because of the Kurdish rebellion, the squad cars and soldiers constantly patrol the area. So we're forced to take you to the city of Van via the mountainous routes on horseback."

"Oh, no!" he protested. "I'm very ill and tired. I can't take another series of trips on horseback!"

"I apologize for this inconvenience," he uttered, "but you don't have proper documentation. The Turkish guards might arrest and deport you to Iran."

Farhad glared at him, "Who says I don't! I have a fake *sejel* that looks more real than an official one."

"Still, sir," he grimaced, "we can't take any risks. The Turkish police are not as friendly and flexible as the Iranian guards and we have to take all kinds of precautions with our travelers."

Osman sat cross-legged on the carpet quietly and stared at the opposite wall, while Farhad paced the length of the room feeling restless. Although he had crossed Iran without being caught, it seemed as though he was not yet safe, even in Turkey. His fate was still unknown and he had no choice but to let the Turkish smugglers guide him to wherever he was destined to go. At least for now Farhad knew that he was headed toward Istanbul. The rest was a total mystery to him. The Turkish smugglers also operated secretively. No matter how much the general asked them, they did not tell him where his final destination was supposed to be. *"Could it be Germany, where most Iranian fugitives end up?"* Farhad pondered.

The general looked at his skinny hands with his veins bulging like wavy, thick wires and wondered if there was any more flesh left on his body to be shed. He knew that the hardship was not over yet. In fact it could last even longer than it had during his passage through Iran.

Farhad had to leave the same night with a Turkish guide. Luckily, he was better prepared for traveling this time. Osman had kindly given him a pair of woolen socks, a warm hat, a pair of gloves and some pistachio nuts, in case he got hungry.

Farhad got to like Osman. He was very kind and patient! Knowing that Farhad's Kurdish language ability was rudimentary, he was careful to emphasize each word succinctly to help the general understand him.

Osman was right. The general had to be very careful. He told Farhad about an Iranian caravan of illegal travelers who had recently encountered a group of soldiers on their way to the city of Van. They had ordered the travelers to stop. Instead, the fugitives had panicked and run. The soldiers had opened fire, killing four of them. That is why the smugglers had chosen to take the Iranian fugitives via the remote and treacherous mountainous trails.

THE IRAQIS

In Turkey, Farhad became friends with two Iraqi refugees. They were both very dark, with thick eyebrows and wiry hair. Mohamed was stocky and fairly tall. He was good tempered and laughed after uttering each sentence. Abbas was of medium height and serious looking. He was not as talkative as Mohamed and appeared pensive. Farhad met them the night when the two guides went looking for a group of refugees and left him alone with Parviz on the mountaintop.

That night, after Farhad managed to overcome his worries about having too many people around, he heard two men speaking in Arabic. He could not comprehend what was going on! *"Arabic-speaking people among a group of Iranians?"* Farhad reined his horse closer and demanded of one of them, "Did I hear correctly? Were you two speaking Arabic?"

The guy laughed heartily, leaning forward on his horse, "It's strange, isn't it? We, the enemy!"

"You mean you're Iraqis?"

"Yes sir. My name's Mohamed and this here is my friend Abbas."

Farhad did not know how to handle the situation. Yes, Mohamed was right, they were the enemies. The poor Iranians had gone through so much because of the power-thirsty Saddam Hussein.

Farhad remembered how awful the bombs sounded and how devastated they all would get each time a rumbling bomb exploded somewhere in the ground, shaking the basement he was hiding in during the Iran-Iraq war.

Farhad asked Mohamed, "Honestly, I'm very curious to know how you two ended up here."

"Well," Mohamed responded good temperedly, "Abbas and I were fighting in the Iraqi army against the Iranian soldiers. To tell you the truth, I didn't believe in that pointless war and neither did my friend. So we deserted and surrendered ourselves to the Iranian army."

Farhad shook his head and laughed. "It's ridiculous! You sought asylum in Iran and are now escaping from there!"

"Yes, exactly," Mohamed nodded. "When we became refugees in Iran, we didn't know—as the saying goes—that we were stepping from the frying pan into the fire!"

Farhad thought that he would probably become a deserter too if he were an officer in Saddam's army. Especially if he were a witness to Saddam Hussein's inhumane warfare tactics such as using chemical weapons to annihilate a whole battalion of the Iranian army, as well as thousands of innocent Kurds. However, he pondered, *"I would have thought twice before surrendering myself to Khomeini's men."*

"Were you imprisoned when you surrendered to the Iranian Army?" the general asked, turning his head and looking intently in the dark night at Mohamed, whose head was bobbing rhythmically with the horse's regular stride.

"In the beginning, yes. After many sessions of interrogations, they realized that we were genuinely against Saddam Hussein," Mohamed breathed. "Then after a while we were released and given refugee status."

Abbas, who hardly ever spoke, now cut in, "We were so sorry to have exchanged one oppressive system for another. It was suffocating. There was no freedom."

Farhad now realized why the other guy was always quiet. He could tell that Abbas was unhappy and that their situation had hurt him more than it had Mohamed. Farhad could sympathize with the poor Iraqi.

"Yes, you're right." He finally affirmed with a sigh, "The Islamic Republic is as dictatorial as the Iraqi regime. But you could console yourselves by thinking that your lives were spared. Who knows? If you had gone on fighting you might've been killed in action. So at least you're alive!"

Abbas concurred with a nod, "True, but I'd have preferred to have surrendered myself to a democratic country such as Germany or England."

TRAVELING IN TURKEY

Late at night, after Osman left, a tall, olive-skinned Kurdish guide picked Farhad up. Bidding farewell to his kind host and timid hostess, he started another journey on horseback. In Turkey, Kurdish guides used to ride on the same horse as the fugitives. The guides would tie themselves and the fugitives—who rode behind the guides—with a long shawl. This prevented the back riders from slipping off the horseback and falling into the ravine.

Farhad and his guide traversed some rugged, steep mountainous routes with much difficulty, and after ten hours, arrived at their destination. Farhad was exhausted and thought he could not take it anymore! He told himself that dying must be easier than traveling the way they had done during the past few days. Worst of all, Farhad was still burning with fever and his knee was not any better.

The general and his guide descended to another shabby village. The guide led him to a house at the end of a dark alley. The house was built with dark gray rocks and resembled a renaissance building with its dark brown gate and high walls.

The gate opened with a neigh-like groan and they stepped into a bare, cobbled court and then into a clean, large, dimly lit room. It looked like a boarding school dormitory. Tens of beds were placed in the room and people were sleeping or resting on them.

Farhad headed straight for an empty bed and, as he was about to lie down, he heard a soft, familiar voice saying, "Hello, sir."

Farhad turned his head toward the direction of the voice in the dimly lit, quiet room. He could not believe his eyes! His newly acquired friend, Parviz, was sitting up in a bed. Farhad was elated with the pleasant encounter. Parviz had been in his thoughts all during the journey. He could not explain why he had formed such an affinity with that fellow within that short period of time. Maybe it was because he was the first fugitive Farhad had encountered. Or maybe because traveling brings people together, provided they can get along. He remembered his sister, Nazilla, once telling him that to really know an individual, one had to travel with that person. She was right. Parviz was indeed a good human being and passed the famous *travelers* test with flying colors.

The general, forgetting his fatigue, got to his feet and limped toward Parviz's bed. Sitting on its edge, Farhad shook Parviz's hand fervently and whispered "Parviz, I'm so happy to bump into you again! I thought I'd never see you!"

Having lost his beloved family, maybe for good, Farhad cherished Parviz's friendship. It gave him strength and a feeling of security as well as a sense of belonging in his state of homelessness and loneliness. Besides, together they had gone through a lot within a short period of time.

Parviz's blue eyes shone with joy, "I thought exactly the same thing about you. We must have separated from one another that dark night on the plateau surrounded by all those travelers."

"Yes, I'm sure that's exactly what must have happened," Farhad hissed, realizing there were still some people sleeping in different beds. "Anyway, I'm happy you went your separate way, otherwise you would have gone through a horrible ordeal."

Parviz's eyes widened with surprise. "What ordeal? What happened to you?"

Farhad crossed his leg, trying to make himself more comfortable sitting on the edge of Parviz's bed. He took a deep breath, looking green with exhaustion, and recounted the story of their encounter with the *pasdars* at the unmanned Turkish border. Then he walked over to his bed. The people in the room were now gradually waking up and chatting with one another. It was morning already, but it did not matter to Farhad. He had traveled all night and in a flash of a second, he succumbed to a deep sleep.

He must have slept for twelve hours before waking up with a start in the noisy room, to find Parviz and others ready to leave.

"Here we go again on our separate ways!"

"I know!" Farhad said groggily, yawning and scratching his head. "Who knows, our paths might cross again." He then sat up in his bed, smiling mischievously. "Have a good trip and don't fall off your horse!"

Parviz shook his head. He could not figure out Farhad. One minute he appeared short tempered and irksome. Next, he behaved idiotically and funny! Like that day in the food storage when he had mistaken the cat's tail creeping on his face for a snake.

Soon, the general's guide arrived and led him on foot to the outskirts of the village. A heavy-built man with a low, thick voice was waiting for them in the darkness with a horse. Farhad wondered why Parviz and he could not go together, since they were both headed to Istanbul. Then he guessed that it must be safer this way.

"Mount the horse," the husky guide ordered. "There's no time to waste."

"Tell me something new. There's never any time to waste!" Farhad grumbled, leaping on the horseback skillfully, despite his painful knee.

Then the guide mounted the horse, tied himself to the general with a shawl and they set off toward the steep mountainous trails. The night was dark with a few stars flickering weakly. Farhad had the impression that they were headed toward a black, bottomless pit where the world and all hope ended. When Parviz and the Iraqis were around, Farhad experienced a strange sense of belonging. With them gone, he felt desolate and abandoned.

As the horse rocked them steadily, Farhad's stomach churned, making him want to throw up. He tapped on the guide's shoulder and implored him, "Please, do shoot me and rid me of this misery. I know that you're carrying a revolver for safety. I don't really care what happens to me any more!"

The guide, who spoke some Farsi, turned back, trying to face Farhad and said, "Have some patience. This is the last night of your hardship. Tomorrow, when we arrive in the city of Van, you'll travel by truck to Istanbul."

At around two in the morning they entered a small village and rode up to a house. The guide told him, "You are going to rest here for a short while. Later a taxi will take you and the two Iraqi refugees to Van."

"Oh, the Iraqis are also there?" he inquired enthusiastically.

"Yes," he nodded. "Do you know them?"

The general nodded. "Yes, I met them a few days ago in the mountains while traveling in Iran."

In a small, disheveled hut, the general encountered the two Iraqis again. They were happy to see one another. Such encounters were quite beneficial as well as reassuring for the fugitives, as they did not completely give up hope.

The host offered Farhad some bread, cheese and tea, which he had to refuse. He was still too sick to swallow anything. Farhad stretched out on the damp-smelling carpet, while the host covered him with an old patched-up bedsheet. He rested there until nightfall, waiting for the taxi which never showed up.

Farhad's husky, broad-shouldered guide who had stayed in the house with him said, "I'm very sorry, but we can't wait here any longer. We'll have to leave on horseback again."

Farhad was furious and not willing to set his eyes on another horse! "How could this happen?" he bellowed. "You know what? This is becoming unbearable. You guys don't live up to your promises!"

The guide apologized again, "I'm really sorry. I don't understand why the driver isn't here yet. But don't worry, we might come across him in a short while."

That is exactly what happened.

The bright lights of the taxi on the dark road seemed like the most beautiful sight Farhad had laid his eyes on since his departure from Tehran. A weak smile brightened his glum face as he murmured contentedly, "Goodbye, horseback riding!"

The two Iraqis and the general dismounted and squeezed together in the back seat of the car. It felt so heavenly to be driven in a car after so many torturous days of horseback riding on hair-raising mountainous paths. Never mind that the driver drove like a maniac on unpaved secondary roads. The general felt like King Solomon riding a magic flying carpet.

He looked at Mohamed and Abbas. They too looked jovial. What a luxury!

Within two hours they arrived at the city of Van and drove straight to a nearby village. There they entered a house where, for a change, the proprietor owned a refrigerator and a few modern amenities.

A seventeen-year-old, docile-looking boy with light brown hair and well-built body greeted Farhad in Persian.

"Hello sir, my name's Farhad."

"Well, hello! Finally a Farsi-speaking young chap!" Farhad exclaimed boisterously. "It's so nice to meet you! My name's also Farhad. Farhad Shirazi."

The young fellow regarded the general quizzically and asked, "The General Shirazi, I assume?"

"Yes, son. The general himself," Farhad nodded.

"Oh, sir, it's such an honor to meet you!" he said, standing at attention like a soldier. "I'm so happy that they never captured you."

"Thanks," the general responded, looking at his hazel-colored, large eyes and tanned complexion. "I'm also honored to meet you, young lad!"

The young man reminded Farhad of his son, Jamshid, whom he missed badly. He also seemed to be a nice, polite kid.

The general asked the young man, "Why are you escaping from Iran? Are you scared of being sent to the Iraqi front?"

"Yes sir," he replied docilely. "I wouldn't want to be killed in a war which I don't believe in."

"I don't blame you," Farhad agreed and thought that it would be a pity to have such a young life wasted in a stupid war.

Luckily, they had not sought to enlist the general's son, because he was studying at the university. The country needed educated men, so the Iranian army left the university students alone.

"Where are you going from here?" the general demanded from the young Farhad.

"I'll be going to Sweden," he said, smiling broadly.

"Sweden? How come?"

"My brother escaped to that country a year ago and became a political refugee there," Farhad explained. "My friends from Istanbul are trying to help me join him."

"Good luck!" Farhad told the young man. Then, turning to their host, he tried to explain in his broken Kurdish, "I'm sick and am running a high fever."

"I have a good remedy for you," the Kurd replied and gave Farhad some herbal tea. It was amazing how fast the tea worked! Farhad's fever dropped in no time and his nausea stopped. For the first time in many days, he could drink plenty of water without throwing up. With his fast recovery, Farhad's mood picked up and life took on a pleasant form. He felt blessed to be amongst nice people. The young Farhad was delightful and the host and his wife were extremely friendly.

Farhad found the Kurdish people good looking and pleasant. They were mostly tall with regular features. They had light complexion, dark hair and grayish-green eyes.

The general stayed in his Kurdish host's house for three days. Then another youth from Tabriz joined them. On the third night, a different Kurdish guide arrived and took them all through dark streets to a garage where a six-wheeled truck was awaiting the Iranian fugitives.

As the three fugitives arrived, the driver and his assistant got off and instructed them before they got on the truck, "I want you guys to keep absolutely quiet whenever we come to a complete stop." The driver, crushing his cigarette butt under his shoe carried on, "Normally, this would mean that we are being inspected by the road gendarme."

"Yes," they all responded, happy to be heading towards Istanbul. Farhad had heard that Istanbul was a beautiful city. However, that was not the reason for his contentment. Istanbul, to Farhad, meant getting closer to freedom. He was sure that his fate would be decided in that city.

The driver's assistant reached into the cab of the truck and dropped the back of the passenger seat down. A round opening appeared behind it, giving way to its tarpaulin covered bed. He beckoned the refugees to crawl through the hole and hide against a row of wooden fruit crates, piled at the rear end of the truck. Any person looking from outside would have no reason to imagine that behind those fruit crates was an open space jammed with fugitives.

When the general's eyes got used to the darkness in the truck, he looked closely at the dark shape of a person sitting on the floor hugging his legs, and realized that the passenger was nobody else but Parviz.

"It's you again!" the general exclaimed. "It's so wonderful the way we keep bumping into each other."

For about three hours, they bounced along unpaved roads, going from village to village. In each village, the secret door would open and two to three more passengers would get in. After a while there were so many passengers in the back of the truck that they no longer were able to sit down. By the time they reached the paved highway, there were thirty-four standing bodies squashed together.

The travelers were all young boys, like the seventeen-year-old Farhad, who were escaping military service. From their mannerisms and behavior, Farhad could tell that they were mostly from good and prominent families.

Just before midnight, the truck stopped and the secret door opened. The driver peeped in with tired, bloodshot eyes and said in broken Farsi, "You guys can come out and relieve yourselves in the open air. We don't know if we'll be able to stop again before arriving in Istanbul."

The boys began grumbling. They did not like the idea of non-stop travel to Istanbul. How could they control themselves all the way to that city without using a toilet? The driver shook his head disapprovingly and said, "Hey, listen up guys, it's not my fault. It's dangerous and we should try to attract as little attention as possible."

He was right. It was not easy to find safe spots to stop and let the refuges relieve themselves. So everybody hurried out into the dark night and tried to make the best of their situation.

Farhad decided that traveling in a fast-moving truck while wobbling on shaky legs with thirty-four sweaty bodies pressing against one another was not any better than horseback riding.

Despite the cold weather outside, it was as hot as a sauna inside the truck, with hardly any air to breathe. All the body heat rising from thirty-odd energetic youths was enough to heat a huge hall, let alone the tiny space of their *fruit cage*.

Farhad turned to Parviz, who was sandwiched between him and another young man and commented, "God doesn't need to punish us in life after death, we are already paying for our sins right here!"

Parviz fixed his gaze on the general and nodded absently. He seemed to be millions of miles away. Farhad looked at him anxiously and wondered if he was all right.

"Anything the matter?" the general yelled over the din of the restless group and the noisy humming of the truck. "You seem very preoccupied."

"Huh? Oh, no . . . no. I'm fine," Parviz yelled back. "I'm just trying to think about different things to take my mind off the unbearable situation we're in."

"That's smart!" Farhad told himself and he too tried to think of better things.

Parviz, whose thoughts had been interrupted by the general's questioning, hollered, "That damned Shah!"

"The Shah?" the general inquired loudly, with his vocal chords hurting.

"Yes, the Shah," Parviz answered in a voice filled with rage. "If he had done his job properly, we wouldn't have to go through all this!"

Farhad's head bobbed involuntarily with the bumpy ride as if he were nodding his consent.

"You sound like me. That's normally what I say when I'm fed up," Farhad said, smiling broadly.

"Parviz was right," he thought. *"The Shah did indeed mess up the country and the lives of so many people."* In the beginning of his underground life, the general loathed admitting to the truth. As days and nights went by and he mused more and more over the Shah's system of government, it became clear to him that his ruler, in whom he had had such blind faith, had driven the Iranian people to rebellion. Presently he asked himself, *"If not for his autocratic regime, how else would the Islamic Republic have come about?"* After all, it was the Shah who forced the one-party rule, the rule of his *Rastakhiz* party. He did not tolerate opposition in the *Majlis*. "Opposition to whom? To me? I represent the people," he once told a reporter on national TV. Unfortunately, the *Majlis* deputies did not have the courage to stand up to him and to his secret police. As it concerned his corrupt officials, they drove the economy into the ground, while painting a rosy picture of national well-being for the gullible monarch.

"We practiced the fifteenth-century Russian *Potemkin* village trick," exclaimed one of his *basement hosts* when Farhad objected to an attack on his idol's character.

"*Potemkin* village trick, what's that?" Farhad grimaced.

"Oh, haven't you heard about General Potemkin? He was one of Catherine the Great's generals who thought of creating a prosperous mobile village with some happy people living in it. Whenever Catherine decided to travel in Russia, he would dispatch the village and its people to set it up along the route where Catherine passed."

"I see," Farhad nodded. "General Potemkin was trying to deceive Catherine into believing that Russian villages were all prosperous and its people happy."

"Exactly, while the Russian villages were nothing but ruins and its people a bunch of starving men, women and children."

Farhad knew where his host was coming from, nevertheless he asked, "Tell me how that relates to our situation during the Shah's rule."

"Remember when prices soared and staple food and produce became scarce?" answered his host. "The Shah, who did not believe the reports, decided to learn about the problem firsthand. So what do you think he did?"

Farhad sighed, looking glum. That sort of conversation always depressed him. His host pressed on, "Do you think he went to the south of Tehran, where people stood in lines for hours? No sir! His Majesty *Aria Mehr* went to an upscale supermarket a few blocks from the Niavaran Palace. Meanwhile, his court officials made sure that the shelves were well stocked and goods reasonably priced."

Farhad barked, "Oh, come on, I'm sure people have food shortages all over the world!"

"Yes, probably they do. But in civilized countries they handle these sort of problems differently."

"How?"

"That's a conversation for some other time. But listen to this. I used to know the supermarket manager. Apparently, the Shah asked him if it were true that people were having a hard time finding food and produce."

"Go on, what did he answer?" Farhad appeared more interested in the conversation now.

His host stood up, walked closer to Farhad and delivered the punch line, mimicking the humble tone of a loyal subject addressing his sovereign. "He said, 'No, Your Majesty, under your Imperial patronage all is plentiful!'"

Farhad looked at his host, arching an eyebrow. "What would you have said to the Shah if you were in the manager's shoes?"

"There you go. You have answered the question unintentionally."

"What question?"

"The question that there was so much wrong with the Shah's system." Farhad's host shook his head and carried on, "Of course, I wouldn't dare to answer his question any differently! If I had, I would be killed the next day." And then he added, "Did we have any freedom of speech?"

Farhad had nothing to say. His host had convinced him. What's more, he already knew that the court officials were a bunch of self-interested and devious people. They purposefully kept the Shah in the dark about the problems in the country. They were extremely corrupt and powerful. All they thought about was their own well-being, and not that of the country and the people.

ISTANBUL

The boys started arguing with one another over opening a corner of the tarpaulin to get some fresh air. Some were screaming with discomfort that they could not breathe, and others were saying that it paid to suffer.

Farhad, the young chap whom the general had recently met in the last Turkish village, waved his arms above the crowd to get their attention and yelled, "Look, guys, if the Turkish gendarmes arrest us we will all be detained in a camp for two years until they decide what to do with us." Then fixing his green eyes on the general he carried on, "Besides, if by any chance there is an important political figure among us, he'll be instantly handed over to the Iranian authorities."

Everybody became quiet. It seemed Farhad had managed to convince them. The general thought that the boys must have decided that it was far better to suffer than to be caught by the Turkish gendarmes. The Turkish military and police are not known to be the kindest creatures on earth!

The general looked at young Farhad with admiration. He wished he could tell him how thankful he was for his thoughtfulness.

"Parviz was right. The best way to take one's mind off an unbearable situation was to either mull over something interesting or maybe even to sing!" the general concluded.

Farhad tried to think about the past. He tried to picture Leyla's face. He tried to remember their life together.

"No." Farhad told himself. *"There is no point. It is too painful!"*

The general convinced himself that he should put the past behind him temporarily. Now that he had started a different life, he was obliged to keep sane. Farhad reminded himself that if he kept bringing the painful past back, he would certainly go crazy. He decided that he had to concentrate on building a new life. God had given him a second chance in life and he should make the best of it.

Farhad opted for singing. "Let's sing quietly. Yes, let's sing *'Ey Iran'*!"

The general had hardly uttered these words when the harmonious soft chanting of young voices filled the air. After finishing *"Ey Iran"*, they kept on singing one patriotic song after the other. Nobody was concerned about being overheard outside; they knew that the strong noise of the engine stifled all voices.

Singing helped. They all forgot about hunger, sleep, the need for bathroom and the terrible discomfort they were in. What's more, by leading them in song, Farhad had unwittingly acted as a leader. That was one strong quality he used to have in the old days. Farhad beamed, for it felt good to be in charge again.

From that moment on, the young men started looking up to him as somebody to respect and who was fun to be with; a middle-aged man who, rather than ordering them to keep quiet, had managed to change an unbearable situation into a pleasurable one.

Finally, in the late hours of the afternoon, after having driven about two hundred miles, the driver stopped at an isolated garage on the European side of Istanbul. The driver and his assistant got out of the truck, locked the doors, and went away without saying a word. The panic-stricken passengers listened with dismay to the sound of their footsteps gradually disappearing in the distance.

"Dear God!" one young fellow whispered, "they're abandoning us!"

The fugitives gasped for breath. The air in the back of the truck was excruciatingly hot and stuffy.

"Is anybody going to come and save us from this hell?" Farhad wondered, while almost suffocating. Again an argument broke out over opening a corner of the tarpaulin cover of the truck. They absolutely needed some fresh air, but most of them decided against it.

For two whole hours, the unfortunate bunch suffered from thirst and heat. To make things worse, the need to relieve themselves was becoming painfully unbearable for everybody. Parviz helped the general to take off his shirt. Farhad felt extremely tired and weak. He tried to slowly slide down to sit on the floor for a moment, while the others stood tightly packed overhead. The general could not breathe anymore and passed out.

The next thing Farhad knew, he was being dragged toward the secret door, which was now open. When they put him down on the floor, he felt dizzy. People's voices echoed weakly in his ears and their faces appeared distant and dim. Gradually Farhad regained his strength and took in deep breaths. *"Thank God for fresh air!"* he thought. He looked around to see if he could locate Parviz and young Farhad among the throng of refuges, but to no avail. A guide must have taken them away while he was unconscious. How sad it felt to find his gentle and kind trip companions gone! Presently he saw Osman, the Turkish head guide, bending over him. "Do you feel better now?" he asked apprehensively.

The general nodded and sat up, feeling the world turning around him. Unfortunately, Osman left in a hurry, not giving Farhad a chance to ask him for some cash. The Iranian smugglers, when taking Farhad's money from him back in Tabriz, had promised that the Turkish head smuggler would give him some cash at his arrival in Istanbul.

Farhad got to his feet and leaned his body against the rugged garage wall. He was lost and penniless! He also needed to smoke badly. Soon, Osman reappeared at the garage entrance with a skinny man and showed him Farhad from afar, and then disappeared again. The man came up to Farhad, shook his hand, and asked Farhad curtly in Farsi to follow him. Farhad was happy that his guide was now an Iranian and wished he knew his name. By then the general had learned that he should not question the smugglers about anything. He just had to follow their orders. Normally they were in no mood to talk or be sociable. They had orders from their heads in the network to do a job and that was what they did well. In the beginning Farhad had a hard time with it, but soon he realized that he should trust them and just do as he was told.

The general walked silently behind the Iranian fellow and observed the surroundings. Istanbul was an attractive city with wide streets and sidewalks shaded by large elm trees. Some Moorish-styled buildings with stucco facades and occasional blue-domed mosques gave a special oriental charm to the city. From time to time, they would come across an Armenian Gregorian or other church, which looked like any ordinary small building with no crosses on top. Farhad was aware that the Turkish government did not allow steeples or crosses on the churches.

The general and his caretaker passed through streets with heavy traffic. The strong smell of smoke, gas from exhaust pipes and burning charcoal hung heavily in the air. People, mostly dressed in western-style attire, scurried about; a few jaywalked, zigzagging through the heavy traffic and barely escaping being hit by the fast-moving cars. A number of women wearing long gray or brown Islamic robes and headscarves mingled with the rest of the crowd.

The sky was gray, and the evening air was quite nippy. Farhad was shivering in his light clothing. Luckily, his companion was walking very fast. Farhad quickened his steps, caught up with him, and asked, "How much farther do we have to go?"

"Ten more minutes," he replied.

Farhad arched his eyebrows and mused, *"What do you know, the man can talk!"*

They walked through a maze of side streets with walled-in

mansions. Most of them had iron grille gates through which one could see beautiful gardens with tall evergreen trees and colorful flowerbeds.

The Iranian stopped in front of a three-story building and unlocked the door.

All of a sudden he appeared friendlier. *"Befarmaid*—after you."

Farhad had expected the fellow to walk ahead with him following behind, just the way they had done before. But he stood back politely, with a slight bow and beckoned for him to enter the hall, which led to the staircase.

A narrow, winding stairwell led the way to the second floor and to a sparsely furnished two-bedroom apartment, with its French windows overlooking the garden of the house across from theirs.

As the Iranian turned the lights on, he carefully examined Farhad and grimaced, "Do I know you?"

Farhad shook his head. "I don't think so, because I don't know you."

He narrowed his eyes in contemplation for a second and suddenly snapped his fingers and blurted out, "But of course! You are General Shirazi. Nobody told me I was supposed to pick up the *'famous general'* from the bus station." He swallowed. "I thought you were a regular refugee and I was in no mood for one of them." He smiled good temperedly and continued. "We get so many refugees these days and I must confess that I'm not very comfortable dealing with strangers. Besides, the smugglers don't pay me well for taking care of them."

"How do you know me?" Farhad finally asked.

He beamed. "Don't you remember me?"

Farhad scratched his head. His gray hair felt like a coarse doormat from all the dust and sweating in the enclosed, stuffy truck.

"Sorry!" he answered flatly. Farhad did not have the faintest idea who the guy was.

"I worked for you in the Ministry of Defense. I must say that you have changed a lot. I didn't recognize you back there in the garage. You used to be a husky, muscular fellow."

The general racked his brain in vain to remember the guy from the past. He used to have tons of people under his command during those days, some of whom the general did not even know. Besides, his host must have looked completely different then.

Farhad scrutinized the Iranian carefully. He was thin, of medium height with lines running down the sides of his face. He was pale and had a yellow stain above his upper lip. It was obvious to Farhad that the man was a heavy and long-time smoker like himself. The thought of cigarettes made him yearn for one badly. During the last few days he had to content himself with only three cigarettes.

"May I bother you for a cigarette?" Farhad pleaded bashfully. "I assume you smoke, don't you?"

"Oh, yes, and how!" he responded, groping in his jacket's pocket for a pack and offering one to Farhad. He then clicked open his silver Dupont lighter, and a yellow flame flickered against the general's tired, drawn face. Farhad took a long, deep drag at his cigarette, drawing the smoke into the depths of his lungs.

"In which department were you working?" Farhad asked, after his host also lit a cigarette for himself and mixed two Scotch on the rocks for them.

To Farhad, the cigarette and the Scotch tasted better than any he had ever had in his life. He lay back comfortably in the paisley-patterned armchair and closed his eyes for a minute, still trying to see if he could remember his host.

"I used to work at the Department of Finance of the War Office."

The general sprang to his feet, pointed a finger at the direction of the Iranian and exclaimed, "Of course, I remember now. You're Abdi, aren't you?"

"You got it man," Abdi also sprang to his feet and this time they shook hands like two friends.

How much the man has changed! Farhad thought. He remembered Abdi as a young fellow who took care of everybody's

L

salaries. "You were the most important person to either a lieutenant or a general!" Farhad blurted out with excitement.

Abdi turned out to be a kind and hospitable person. Unfortunately, he was not going to be Farhad's host for long. The general was supposed to live in the house of a fellow called Javad, also a former Iranian army officer. Javad was being paid by Farhad's friends in the United States for his board. The fellow, for the moment, was spending time with his family in Paris. He was due back in Istanbul in a month.

After a week, Abdi took the general to Javad's apartment and lent him $150 for his food expenses.

Javad's apartment stood on a hilltop in a nice area; its large picture windows showed a view over a green valley that housed luxurious, contemporary villas. The two white sofas, the mahogany coffee table, navy blue elaborately designed carpet, and two art deco bright-colored landscape paintings matched nicely with the modern look of the apartment.

Farhad had to be very careful with how he spent his borrowed money and almost starved himself until a month later when Javad arrived. However, his arrival did not change things much. When Farhad complained about the meagerness of the food, Javad explained, "You see, sir, I can't afford to be a spendthrift. I'm responsible for the expenses of my family in Paris as well. Besides, life is very expensive in both Turkey and France."

The general gazed indignantly at Javad's pimple-scarred face and dark eyes. His charcoal-black tight curls and short, square forehead reminded him of the nasty Hooshang Afshan.

"Aren't the people from the States who have arranged my escape paying for my keep?" Farhad asked, holding his coffee mug between his cold hands.

"Yes," he said, "but not enough."

To make things worse, Javad was also economizing on heating. The general did not own warm clothing and shivered all the time with cold. To stay warm, he tried to spend most of his time in bed. Then he learned from Javad that his mysterious Iranian friend from Washington was going to call him soon. Farhad could not wait to find out who the *Iranian friend* was. He kept wondering if he was one of the men he used to know. Farhad speculated that *the friend from America* could be Ali, his second in command. He had no idea what had become of Ali during the revolution.

One cold, gloomy day, *the friend* finally called from Washington and introduced himself. "This is Sohrab. How are you, Farhad? Do you remember me?"

Yes, he did remember him. Sohrab used to be an important general serving in the Shah's army, stationed in Tehran. He was lucky to have left Iran with his whole family right before the Shah's fall. Sohrab was a U.S.-trained officer and it seemed that he had good connections there.

"So, it was he all along arranging everything," the general thought. During his risky voyage, he had often wondered how things had been arranged so skillfully. Of course, Sohrab alone could not have devised and planned every detail without the help of other powerful people.

Farhad was dying to find out what he was up to in America. He tried to find out about his work, but Sohrab dismissed the subject and started talking about other topics. Farhad felt that Sohrab did not wish to discuss the subject of his role in Farhad's freedom from bondage in Iran. Nor did he want to talk about what he was doing in America. Thus, the general dropped the matter temporarily. Besides, there were other important things to worry about. Farhad could still be in danger. His stay in Turkey was illegal and if ever he was caught, he would be deported to Iran without a shred of doubt.

Farhad, despite Sohrab's unwillingness to answer any questions concerning his escape, asked, "Sohrab, how did you find out about me, and why did you decide to help me?"

The line went silent for a moment before Sohrab finally spoke, "You have so many friends in the United States Special Forces. They're the ones who right from the beginning had set their minds on getting you out of Iran."

The general smiled, remembering all the nice friends he had made during his two military trainings in the States. They were really nice people!

Farhad wanted to know how long he was going to stay in Turkey, to which Sohrab answered, "Farhad, be happy that you're free and alive. Enjoy yourself for the moment and be patient. I'm busy arranging things."

"Still arranging things! What things?" Farhad asked again, "Where am I going to go from here?"

His heart suddenly started racing madly in the anticipation of Sohrab's answer. It felt exactly like the same situation when, at the Academy, he would stand in front of a board with the lists of names of the students who had passed their finals. His heart would go haywire looking for his name on the list and then when he would finally manage to find it, blood would rush like a stream to his face and temples.

Sohrab mulled it over a second and pressed, "Where would you like to go?"

"Where would I like to go? Do I have a choice?"

"Well, to a certain extent. For example, you can choose Germany or . . ."

"Oh, no. Not Germany," the general cut in, sounding disappointed. All during his arduous travel, the only thing that had given him courage to move on had been the idea of ending up in the States.

Farhad shrugged and whined, "Tell me what I would do in that country all by myself. I don't even know the language."

Sohrab spoke softly, "You are a clever man. You'll learn German in no time. Besides, I remember you being a very personable fellow. You'll attract the Germans to you like moths to a candle."

Farhad breathed an audible sigh of disappointment. "Sohrab, I'm not the same person you used to know. I'm not even courageous anymore!" Tears gathered in his eyes as he said those words and his windpipe narrowed with a crushing pain.

Sohrab threw in, "I don't believe it. You'll get back to your normal self once you take up a regular course of life."

"Sohrab, you haven't gone through what I have. I've changed. You haven't been humiliated or hunted down like a criminal the way I have. You haven't hidden like a scared rat in dark basements . . ."

"Well, you're right!" said Sohrab as the line went dead for a second and then he suddenly uttered, "How about the States, then? Would you be happy here? That's the only other country I'll have the ability to arrange for you."

Farhad's heart leapt with joy! *Would he be happy there? He knew the language, he was used to U.S. culture, and he had friends there.*

"Yes!" he yelled cheerily, jumping at the offer. His dark brown eyes glowed radiantly for the first time after many years and a glimmer of hope rekindled in his heart.

America it was! Sohrab agreed, and promised Farhad to start working at it more diligently.

The following week Sohrab sent the general $450, and a few weeks later, another $250. Farhad did not spend any of his money to buy himself warm clothes. He decided that he had to be careful with the way he spent it. Farhad had no inkling about how much longer he was going to stay in Istanbul! He had already been there for a month.

Abdi called the general one day and said, "Farhad, Mr. and Mrs. Alavi from Tehran will be coming to Istanbul next week. Why don't you call your family and ask them to send you warm clothing with the Alavis?"

"Thank you so much for thinking about me. I'll do exactly as you say."

Farhad allowed himself a faint smile of satisfaction. The Alavis' trip to Istanbul could not have happened at a better time when he indeed needed warm clothing. Things were starting to look brighter for him now and Farhad started feeling happier.

The general, of course, could not call his family directly. It would be very dangerous both for them and for him. He asked

Javad to get in touch with Simin and ask her to inform Leyla about sending some winter clothing with the Alavis.

Farhad felt like dancing with joy. *"As of next week,"* he thought, *"I will no longer be a prisoner at home."* Then the very moment that he received a pair of warm shoes, warm socks, a pair of brown corduroy pants and two pullovers, he left the house like a bird out of a cage. It was such a relief to get away from Javad for a few hours each day. Javad was so unfriendly that Farhad hated his company. Moreover, his host was starting to become impatient with Farhad. It was so unpleasant for the general to live under the same roof as somebody whom he knew did not want him around. Unfortunately, Farhad had no choice. His destiny was in the hands of other people. He had to act according to the instructions given by the *"guys"* from Washington.

The general had barely returned from one of his long walks when the telephone rang. Javad called out from the kitchen, "It's for you."

"Hello, Farhad," Sohrab's voice echoed from the other end of the line, "did you know that you need a passport?"

"No, how would I know? I have been waiting for orders from you," he said with a sarcastic tone.

Sohrab chuckled good temperedly and instructed Farhad to go to Ozloo Street the next day, to house number 40. "The man there knows everything about you. He will take your picture and provide you with a false Iranian passport," Sohrab added.

"Yes, Sohrab, I'll do that first thing in the morning. Tell me, what do I have to tell the guy?"

"Absolutely nothing," he asserted, "just tell him who you are. He knows exactly what to do. You don't even have to worry about any payments to him."

"How come? Does he run a charitable organization for Iranian refugees?" Farhad joked. By now the ice had broken between the two of them.

Farhad felt safe knowing Sohrab was taking care of him. He

felt like a privileged child dealing with a father who spoiled and provided him with everything. *"What have I done to deserve it?"* he wondered.

Sohrab laughed at Farhad's sarcastic remark. He seemed to be a fun fellow. He never lost his temper with Farhad when he appeared impatient about his stay in Turkey.

"I assure you that there is no charity involved! We have paid the guy $3,000."

Farhad dipped his hand into the pocket of his brown corduroy pants, leaned his shoulder against the cold kitchen wall and exclaimed, "I really don't know how to thank you!" Then after saying goodbye to his benefactor, he hastily trotted out of the kitchen without looking at Javad. He was well aware that the man did not wish to be bothered with him. All he wanted, it seemed, was to make money on him. Otherwise he did not care whether Farhad lived or died.

The general's fake Iranian passport, carrying the fake name: Ali Bagheri, looked amazingly real. Sohrab called him once he received the passport and instructed him to apply for a U.S. visa on the coming Monday.

"Good luck!" Javad smiled wryly and called out after Farhad as he walked out of the kitchen, "I'll be very surprised if you get a U.S. visa."

"Thank you for your good wishes," Farhad thought. *"I could do with some positive, friendly words!"* He looked disapprovingly at the hawkish profile of his host and wondered what sort of a dour experience in his childhood had made him into the nasty creature that he was.

Farhad took the pack of cigarettes from his pants' pocket. He pulled one out but did not light it. Instead he walked right back into the kitchen and confronted Javad sternly, "What are you talking about?"

"Well, brother, every day hundreds of Iranians line up in front of the U.S. Embassy from dawn till late in the evening, only to be refused by suspicious vice consuls." He then sighed and carried on, "They hate the Iranians and do everything in their power to block their entry into the United States."

"Surely there must be some American Consulate staff who can think objectively and not put all Iranians in the same basket." Farhad pressed, and then told himself, *"I wouldn't blame them for not wanting to issue visas for Iranians like yourself!"*

Javad sniggered, "Well, as I said before, good luck to you!"

Early Monday morning, the general went to the American Consulate. The visa line for the Iranians started at the bottom of the steps, not too far from the outdoor visa booth and coiled around into the side street. A Turkish employee of the American Consulate came out and handed the Iranians visa application forms. The Iranians started filling out the forms, one helping the other. Farhad thought that embassies and consulates all around the world normally treat their applicants with more respect and dignity. They allow people to form lines inside consulates. In addition, they provide the applicants with high desks on which they can fill out the forms. This, however, was a different case. These applicants were a bunch of wretched, no-good Iranians dealing with the all-powerful Americans who were wronged by Khomeini. Iranians did not deserve to be treated as decent human beings! *"Ironically,"* Farhad recollected, *"Khomeini is the same person whom the U.S. government had helped to come to power."* And, if it were not for Khomeini, those unfortunate people would not have become homeless and forced to stand in long lines outside American consulates filling out forms. Yes, if not for him they would not have to suffer such humiliations.

A cruel, cold wind rustled the leaves of the large oak trees that towered over the heads of the applicants. Women wrapped their coats and shawls firmly around their bodies. Men rubbed their hands together and stamped their feet to keep warm. Farhad shivered in his pullover and thought that his turn would never come. He had been standing in line for four hours and it had not advanced much. The daylight was already waning and the street lamps were gradually lighting up. A young woman with brown wavy hair and a warm smile, who was standing in front of the general, turned back and complained, "I'm sure pretty soon they'll close the window and send us home. This happens all the time. They don't give a damn about us Iranians. In fact they hate us."

Having lived a hermit's life for the past nine years and being cut off from the reality of the world, the general could not comprehend why the Americans should hate all the Iranians alike. He knew that during the Iranian Revolution, the angry crowd had taken American Embassy staff hostage. Farhad personally hated that act, but in a rebellious situation, furious mobs do not act logically. Besides, Farhad thought that the majority of the Iranians were not pro-revolutionary and anti-American. Take Farhad. He always believed himself to be a friend of America. He had many friends among the U.S. officers. Besides, Farhad remembered that when thousands of American families lived in Iran, they were respected and well treated as guests.

Farhad soon gave up standing in line in the cold, drafty street and decided to return very early the following day.

"Are you giving up?" asked the pleasant young woman.

Farhad smiled at her affectionately and uttered, "I'm not a young person like you and am really feeling tired. Besides, I need to put something in my stomach. I haven't eaten all day."

The general waved at her and headed down the street toward the beginning of the line. At the head of the queue stood an old, bent woman whose turn had come. As soon as she saw Farhad she asked him with a weary voice, "May God bless you, sir, could you help me up the steps and take me to the visa window?"

"With pleasure, *mother*," he exclaimed, holding her frail arm and helping her up the four broad steps.

As they stood in front of the booth, the clerk stretched his hand out of the small window and took the documents of the old lady. "Come back in fifteen days," the clerk said.

Farhad translated for the old woman what that person had said and turned round, holding on to the old woman's arm, ready to help her down the steps. Right then the clerk stuck his hand out again. "What are you waiting for? Hurry up and hand me your documents," he barked at the general.

"But . . . but . . ." Farhad mumbled, feeling shocked, not knowing how to react. He did not want the people who had stood in line for hours to think that he had jumped the queue. The general had merely wanted to help the poor, tired, old lady.

The man yelled impatiently, "I said hand me your passport and forms!"

Farhad tried to explain that it was not his turn yet. But the unfriendly clerk was in no mood to listen to any explanation. He simply grabbed the forms and ordered him to come back in fifteen days for an answer.

SURPRISE

The general could not wait to find out whether they had granted him the U.S. visa. The minutes and hours were passing by at a snail's pace and Javad was becoming more and more intolerant of his presence. Farhad did not feel welcome at his house. Javad was very short tempered and did everything to avoid talking to him. It was an uneasy situation. But what was there to do? Did he have a choice? Sohrab had told him not to make a move without his consent. During their last telephone conversation, Farhad told Sohrab that he would like to leave Turkey as soon as he received his U.S. visa.

"Not without me telling you to do so," Sohrab insisted.

The general was very disappointed! Why couldn't he leave immediately after obtaining his U.S. visa? He wished he could somehow make Sohrab understand that staying with Javad was torture. Moreover, if only Sohrab knew how much Javad hated having Farhad around, he would surely expedite his trip to the United States. Besides, Farhad yearned to get to the United States as soon as he could and start a new life. He hated his homelessness and dependence on that mean-spirited person!

The more Farhad let his mind wonder about such issues, the angrier he became with his people for turning against the Shah and destroying the stability of Iran under the influence of foreign powers. The general demanded of himself why they would not leave his country alone and why couldn't the Iranians decide their own fate? *"It is our oil which attracts them, just like bright light does to night flies and insects,"* he concluded.

Farhad remembered how, on the first night of his arrival in Istanbul, he and Abdi had held a conversation about foreign intervention in Iran. At one point during that discussion, Abdi took a sip from his Scotch and exclaimed, "I'm so proud that we ousted the British from our land in the '50s, and nationalized the oil industry."

"You're right," responded Farhad, while agreeing that nationalizing the Persian oil was the right move. The British had control over the Iranian oil from the beginning of the century until the '50s. Prime Minister Mosadegh, backed by the Iranian people, succeeded in nationalizing the oil industry. He created the movement of *Pan-Iranism* and the Shah was forced to flee to Rome with his second wife, Queen Soraya.

"I wonder how our destiny would have been shaped if the era of *Pan-Iranism* had lasted longer?" Abdi said, rubbing his chin pensively.

"We'll never know," Farhad answered, pouring himself another drink. "One thing's certain. We threw out the British and inherited the Americans."

Abdi consented with a nod. "And on the 28th of *Mordad*, the United States brought back the Shah."

The memory of that day was vivid in Farhad's mind. He was then a junior cadet. On that warm August morning, it seemed as if all of Tehran had risen against Mosadegh. *"Javid Shah,"* and "Death to Mosadegh," shouted mobs as they ransacked government buildings and wealthy homes. Mosadegh was accused of making a pact with the *"Red Devil"*—the Communist *Tudeh* party.

"When the Shah returned triumphantly, nobody in Iran knew that everything was engineered by Kermit Roosevelt, the senior CIA operative in Iran," Abdi uttered, shaking his head disapprovingly.

"That's right. And then, when the U.S. government didn't need the Shah anymore, they dropped him like a rag doll!" Farhad grimaced. No matter how much he liked the Americans, he could not forgive them for that.

In the thirty years since the Shah's return, and with the expansion of American presence and influence in Iran, the Iranian people adopted the Americans as friends. But friendship gradually gave way to hatred as the Shah's autocratic rule and the atrocities of his secret police stifled freedom. Iranians were convinced that the Shah derived his power from the United States. That is the major reason they turned against the Americans.

As Farhad recalled those conversations with Abdi and the past events, he felt even more depressed and whined, *"What's the point, the British and the Americans are out of Iran, but it is Khomeini now who has the oil! Who suffers as a result? Homeless people like myself!"*

Farhad sat on the edge of his bed, feeling disgusted with himself. He suddenly realized that he had become a bitter and self-centered character. Instead of being thankful for his successful escape, he kept fretting and cultivating negative thoughts in his head. Of course, no one could deny that his happy days were long gone and that the revolution had destroyed his, and millions of others', livelihoods. However, the mass population of Iran was satisfied with their situation. Those people held that finally they had regained their national dignity and prestige. For them, freedom did not have the same meaning as it did for the general. *"Were they free during the Shah's reign?"* Farhad pondered, and then berated himself that he had to stop blaming others and the foreign powers for his failed past. *"Such is life and I was not the only person in the world who suffered,"* he finally deduced.

Two days after he applied for the U.S. visa, at six o'clock in the evening, as the general was busy reading a book in bed and trying to stay out of Javad's hair, the telephone rang.

"Telephone for you," Javad called out.

Farhad sprang out of bed like an agile cat and rushed to the phone, thinking it was his friend Sohrab. Talking with Sohrab was the only pleasure he had those days.

"Farhad Shirazi?" a man's voice with an American dialect inquired.

"Speaking," Farhad answered heedlessly, wondering who would be calling him with that accent! He did not know any Americans in Istanbul.

"Why haven't you come to the consulate to pick up your visa?" he demanded.

"Visa? But sir," Farhad interjected, "I was told to return in fifteen days. It has been only two days since . . ."

The mysterious caller cut in, "Never mind that! Your visa is ready."

Farhad said politely, "May I ask, sir, with whom I have the pleasure of speaking?"

"Come to the consulate tomorrow at two in the afternoon; then we shall meet," he pressed on.

The general protested, "How can I just walk into the consulate and ask for my visa? Being an Iranian, nobody will let me in without a prior appointment."

The caller reassured Farhad with a soft tone, "Just give them your real name at the gate and they'll let you in." Farhad was perplexed. He could not understand how the caller knew that he was traveling under a fake name.

The general slipped in and out of sleep all through the night, and each time that he woke up, he was filled with a pleasant sensation. It was so elating to think that his trip to America was not a dream anymore. *"What a joy! I will soon be free for good,"* he muttered to himself as his heart leapt and danced to its rhythmic drum-like beating. In the meantime, hundreds of obscure questions buzzed in his head. *"What is this all about? Why are they calling me just two days after I applied for a visa? Are they making an exception in my case, while they give other Iranians a hard time?"* He had been very lucky with the visa right from the beginning, first with the incident at the visa booth, and then with the telephone call of that night. Farhad suddenly realized that God had been kind to him all along. The fact that he was still alive and the fact that the impossible was happening was nothing but a sign that He loved him. Farhad's eldest sister used to say that God acted as father to all fatherless children and that He always looked after them even after they became adults. It seemed as if He had indeed taken care of Farhad ever since his childhood. He recollected how miraculously he was saved from death at the age of seven.

Farhad and his friends used to collect apricot pits, crack the shells open, and boil the nuts to get rid of the bitterness. Then they would have great fun eating them!

One day Hooshy, Hormoz and Farhad went to Hooshy's house and started boiling the cracked pits on the small oil burner in the kitchen. There was nobody at home. They made a lot of noise and played, chasing each other around the burner. Suddenly, Hormoz lost his balance and nearly fell over the burner. Farhad, who happened to be on the other side of it, was not as lucky as Hormoz. The pot on the oil burner overturned, and the boiling water and the hot pits spilled out on his thigh.

Farhad screamed. The pain was excruciating and there was no adult around to help. The poor boy burst out into the street and dashed home, still screaming, and found nobody there either. He suffered for over an hour with the unbearable burning pain. Finally his sister returned from the neighbor's house and applied a home remedy to his burned skin which had, by then, developed into a third-degree burn. After a while the burning stopped. A few days later, large blisters formed on his thigh. In their neighborhood there were neither hospitals nor proper doctors. They had some healers, like the African medicine men, who were called *hakims*. Farhad's sister, seeing the sorry condition of her little brother's leg, brought a *hakim* to have a look at his burn. He gave Farhad's sister a homemade ointment to be applied to the blisters. Unfortunately, the ointment did nothing for the poor boy and the burn got worse. Gradually his flesh started to rot away, to a point where his thighbone was exposed. Farhad was dying. Everybody was sadly waiting for his life to end.

It was summertime and they were all sleeping outside in the garden at night. Early one morning, when Farhad was asleep in the yard, a burning sensation in the back of his neck and spine woke him up. Farhad was so weak that he did not even have the strength to call out for his sister. Finally, when it was prayer time and everybody was up, Nazilla came to check on her sick brother. Farhad made her understand that there was something wrong with the back of his neck. When Nazilla turned him over gently, she saw a large black scorpion in Farhad's bed. She quickly killed it with her shoe, and rubbed the smashed insect on his burning flesh. The scorpion had stung Farhad's back and the cure for it was the fluids from its crushed body. After a few days, not only had Farhad recovered from the sting of the scorpion, but his high fever also dropped. Then gradually the little boy's thigh muscles, which had been eaten away by infection, began rebuilding themselves.

What was the cause of his recovery, if not a miracle from heaven? Farhad wondered if it was the venom from the scorpion that had cured him. Who knows? Whatever it was, Farhad's sister believed that it was God's work. According to her, He was acting as a protecting father for a fatherless child. She believed that it had been God's will for the scorpion to sting Farhad and remain in his bed so that it could be crushed and used as a remedy.

THE VISA

The following day, the general set off towards the American Consulate. His legs carried him through the crowded streets of Istanbul like light floating clouds. Farhad was filled with positive energy. Buildings, trees, people, mosques and even ugly, bashed-up cars appeared attractive and pleasant beneath the velvety blue sky of the city. For the first time in nine years, he felt like singing and dancing.

"I can't believe this is happening to me!" the general murmured as he took giant steps on the crowded sidewalks of Ozloo Street.

He thought that finally his bondage was going to be over. He was going to go to the United States, where people lived freely and where there was no oppression. Amazingly, for him it felt like going home. He thought that America had always been like a second home to him. Farhad was sure that if Leyla were to hear him speaking in that manner, she would get very upset, but he could not help feeling the way he did. Then he wondered if things had changed in the U.S. since his last visit twenty-three years ago. *"Would I see my friends when I go to America?"* he asked himself.

The general began walking faster to get to the consulate on time, nudging his way through the throng of men, women and children.

He arrived at the foot of the impressive, gigantic consulate building feeling hot and breathless. Passing by the queue of frustrated Iranians, he climbed the long and wide marble steps confidently this time and rang the doorbell on the huge, elaborately carved oak gate.

A Marine guard let him in as soon as the general mentioned his name. He asked Farhad, "Could you wait a second, while I finish my telephone call?"

Certainly, he could!

As the general waited while the Marine guard carried on with his call, Farhad noticed his name written in large letters on a sheet of paper on the guard's desk.

When the Marine finished, he asked Farhad to go through a metal detector before letting him enter into a large, high-ceilinged hall supported by Corinthian pillars. A large and colorful Turkish carpet gave the place a merry atmosphere. Except for the neon tubes on the ceiling and scattered desks, one could think that it were some sort of a reception hall in a palace.

A beefy, bearded man with fair complexion and smiling face looked at Farhad as he stood there, not knowing what to do. The fellow approached him and demanded, "What's your name?"

"Farhad, sir. Farhad Shirazi."

"Oh, I know who you are. Follow me. I'll take you to the right person," the friendly man exclaimed and ushered the general into a bright room with beige curtains.

Farhad was shocked! He did not expect such a warm reception! He clamped his hands and shifted his body from one foot to the other.

Minutes seemed like eternity as the general stood humbly and patiently in front of a desk, waiting for the American official to look up at him. The general looked at the American flag on a long post behind the man, and at the smiling picture of President Reagan on the white, shining wall. Farhad suspected that the young official sitting in the black, leather high-backed chair was the consul. He was busy writing away and Farhad did not want to interrupt him. Suddenly becoming aware of Farhad's presence, the consul looked up inquisitively at the general.

"Sir, my name's Farhad Shirazi. I was told . . ."

"Oh, yes," he cut in, smiling broadly and exposing white regular teeth. "Sit down. Sit down please." He beckoned the general to a soft leather armchair and extended his hand toward him, "My name's Jim Taylor. I'm the person who spoke to you on the phone last night." Then without any preamble he asked, "Was the escape a rough one?"

"Yes, sir, quite rough and very tiring," the general said sullenly, wondering how Mr. Taylor knew about his escape.

Jim Taylor straightened his dark, short hair with his fingers, shifted his lanky body in his chair and commented, "I'm very happy to see that you're out of danger now."

He scribbled something on a yellow pad and carried on, "You served your country well during the Shah and didn't deserve such a harsh life after his fall."

The thought of those dreary days moistened Farhad's eyes with tears. He sighed and uttered, "True, but I'm thankful to be alive. Most of my colleagues were not as lucky as I."

It had been a while since anybody had spoken in such a dignified manner and used such a respectful tone with the general. It felt good to be commended! Especially when Mr. Taylor had shown appreciation for his past services to his country. Farhad had forgotten all about that. He had become accustomed to being considered a traitor during Khomeini's regime.

Farhad deduced that Jim Taylor's file on him must be complete, because he did not have to go through any interrogations that other Iranians would normally be subjected to.

Mr. Taylor stamped the visa into Farhad's passport and declared jovially in perfect Persian, "*Mobarak bashad agha.* Yes indeed, congratulations are in order! You are a political refugee from this moment on and can go to the United States immediately if you so wish."

It was amazing! Not only was he extremely friendly, but he also spoke excellent Farsi. It was obvious that he had served in the American Embassy in Tehran during the Shah. No wonder he knew so much about Farhad.

The general grabbed his hand with both of his, shook it fervently and asserted with a trembling voice, "Mr. Taylor, I don't know how to thank you!"

A HASTY DECISION

When Sohrab called that night, Farhad told him that he had obtained his visa and pleaded with him to expedite his departure to the United States.

"Farhad, I assure you that I'll let you know when the right time comes. For the moment please stay put and don't make any rash decisions."

Farhad gazed at the dizzying black-and-white design of the kitchen tiles and uttered with a disappointed tone, "With my luck the right time might never come."

"Your luck? How much more can you ask for? Hasn't everything worked out just perfectly?"

"Yes, you're right," Farhad regretted having spoken so mindlessly. "It's just that I can't wait to get out of here," Farhad uttered without minding Javad's presence. Javad, in turn, sneered with satisfaction and rolled his eyes, as if to say, *"They don't want you there, just the way I don't want you in my house."*

Javad was a nuisance. He always stayed in the kitchen during Sohrab and Farhad's telephone calls. He would always pry, pretending to do something or other. The general never volunteered any information to him. In fact, he hardly ever spoke to Javad. Perhaps if he had shown only a bit of compassion, things would have been different and Farhad would not have been in such a rush to leave his house. As it was, the walls of Javad's house were bearing down on him and he was becoming desperately impatient to get millions of miles away from that unfriendly place. Oh, how he wished he could start a new life with Leyla in the United States! *Could she escape, the way he had?* Farhad mused. *"Would I ever see her again?"* he asked himself for the millionth time.

When the general had met with the American consul at the U.S. Consulate, he had told the consul that his passport was fake.

Jim Taylor had said, "You're not the first refugee to have false documents!"

Farhad asked, "What if the Turkish officials at the airport discover that my passport is fake? Will the American Consulate help me?"

Taylor sighed and threw his hands up in the air, "All I can do is to wish you good luck and hope that you do not get caught."

Which meant *"no"*, Farhad assumed.

"What about my Turkish visa?"

"Your Turkish visa?"

"Yes. It expired in October and this is December."

Jim Taylor got to his feet and led Farhad politely to the door, saying, "General, all I can do is issue you a U.S. visa. You'll need to talk to your friends about the Turkish visa."

That evening during dinner, Javad announced that in a few days he would be leaving for Paris to spend the New Year with his family.

"Make sure to lock up my apartment properly and leave the keys with Abdi, in case you leave for the States before my return," Javad commanded.

"Okay," the general swallowed, "I'll do that if I leave, but at the moment my fake passport is loaded with problems." Farhad stated, "My Turkish visa is expired."

"Don't let that bother you," Javad said. "On the day of your departure, put a $100 bill between the pages where the Turkish visa is stamped."

"What for?" Farhad queried.

He sniggered, "Have you never heard of bribing?"

"Come on, what you're suggesting is very dangerous."

"No it isn't!" Javad arched his thick eyebrows, "If the immigration officer is on the take, he'll quietly put the money in his pocket and let you go."

"And if he isn't?"

"Well, then you'll tell him that you're willing to pay a fine for overstaying."

"Son of a gun," Farhad told himself, *"what a shrewd person!"*

Even though the general hated bribing, he found Javad's idea clever. Everything he had done so far had been illegal anyway. It was a matter of life, death and survival for him. At that point, it did not matter whether he was an honest person or not. His life was in danger, and to save it he had to try everything possible.

On the 30th of December, the general went to the Pan American Airlines office and checked to see if they had a ticket for him.

"No, sir," the clerk answered. "Rest assured that the moment we receive orders from our New York office to issue you a ticket, we'll immediately call you."

Farhad stood there mulling over his uncertain situation. He really did not want to live in that unfriendly apartment anymore. Although Javad had already left for Paris, Farhad hated that place. It reminded him of the bad times he had spent in Javad's presence. But, even more, he was impatient to move on and start a new life in the States.

Farhad was well aware that he was being irrational and impatient. This was a weakness that he had never gotten rid of. His impatience had often created problems for him in life, and here he was again, making the same mistake.

Smiling roguishly, Farhad asked the clerk, "Tell me, would you have a seat available to Washington tomorrow?"

The clerk rubbed his broad chin, shook his head, and said remorsefully, "I'm afraid that would be impossible at this time of the holiday season!"

The general insisted, "Could you check your computer before giving me a negative answer, please?"

"All right, but I'm sure it's a waste of time."

"Thank you very much for giving a little of your time to me!" Farhad said with a sarcastic tone.

The clerk had hardly begun checking the next day's Istanbul-Washington passenger list when his colleague at the next counter interrupted him. They talked for a while, ignoring Farhad completely. Their reticent disposition angered the general. He coughed to get the clerks' attention, but they continued ignoring him.

Farhad began tapping his right foot nervously on the floor. He expected a bit of courtesy from the PAN AM employees.

Finally the fellow decided to return to his computer screen, while humming a melodramatic Turkish tune and picking at the pimples on his face. Suddenly he winced, looked closer at the screen and announced with embarrassment, "Oh, yes, there is a cancellation. If you wish . . ."

Farhad cut in brashly, "I'll take it! Please issue me a ticket right away." The general could not believe his luck! He was happy that he had not given up easily.

The general paid a one-way fare to Washington and grabbed the ticket like an eagle snatching at his prey.

A ripple of joy filled his heart as he thought of his departure to the United States. He mumbled to himself proudly, "There, I did it at last. I'm on my way to freedom!"

Farhad was back to normal and in control of his life. He had taken a major step without seeking help from others, just like in the old days. *"Leyla would have approved,"* he thought.

That night Farhad called Sohrab, informed him of his decision to leave Istanbul and gave him his flight details.

Sohrab sounded irritated, "Didn't I tell you to wait for my instructions?"

"Yes sir, you sure did," he responded awkwardly. "You see, the expired visa on the fake passport will cause me trouble. I don't think it's wise to prolong my stay in this country."

Silence. Clank . . . clank. Then a buzzing sound. "Hello . . . Hello, are you still there, Sohrab?"

"Yes, I am," Sohrab's glum voice came back.

"Oh, dear," the general told himself. *"What have I done? He's upset with me."*

Farhad felt like a schoolboy who had angered his teacher by being disobedient. He knew that he had been hasty and that he should have heeded Sohrab's warnings, but what was done was done.

Sohrab added, "Well, you see, Farhad, we were well aware of the visa problem and were trying to find a cooperative Turkish Immigrations officer."

"I wish you would sometimes explain things to me. Why do I always have to be kept in the dark about the plans concerning my life? Not knowing what is going to happen to me drives me crazy!" Farhad burst out and continued, "If you had told me that you were working on the visa problem, do you think I would have done what I did?"

"Well, I'm sorry if I kept quiet about it. You see, I did not want to give you false hopes."

"False hopes . . . ? Even false hopes are sometimes helpful for a devastated fugitive like myself!" Farhad spat out the words like fire shooting out of the mouth of a dragon. Then he told himself, *"Oh, I feel so much better now that I've poured everything off my chest!"*

Farhad soon regained his composure and said softly, "I'm sorry, I shouldn't have lost my temper, especially with a person like you who has done so much for me!" Then he told Sohrab about the $100 bribing scheme.

Sohrab expressed in bewilderment, "But Farhad, this sounds so risky! I hope you won't face any difficulties!"

"I'm sure if that happens, I can deal with it," Farhad said confidently.

"I hope so!" Sohrab heaved an audible sigh.

After talking with Sohrab, the general called Abdi. "Good news! I'm leaving for the United States early tomorrow morning."

Abdi blurted out joyfully, "Finally! I'm so happy for you!"

The general was overcome with joy and could not believe that his dream was really coming true! Of course, he was somewhat embarrassed for ignoring Sohrab's advice, but he could not help it. The urge for freedom was too strong to be ignored. Farhad knew that he had acted like a child. *"But then,"* he reasoned, *"the child in people stays alive no matter at what age."* He was convinced that the reason human beings went on living and enjoyed excitement, even under duress and rough times, was because the *child* in them never died.

The following morning, the general arrived two hours before the departure time at a deserted airport. The two adjoining waiting rooms in Terminal 2 were empty, except for a few passengers sleeping, curled up on the seats and benches. The departure time was at seven o'clock. The flight was via Switzerland with an hour's layover in Zurich.

Farhad sat in a black chair, not too far from the check-in counter, and waited impatiently with a dizzy head and burning eyes caused by a sleepless night. When the PAN AM gate opened, he was the first person in line to check in his luggage.

The attendant was a friendly, young American woman who looked very attractive in her smart sky blue uniform and matching blue eyes. Handing Farhad the boarding pass she said, "Have a good trip to Washington, sir."

"You bet I will!" Farhad exclaimed flirtatiously and headed towards the departure gates.

At the Immigration desk, a skinny, wrinkle-faced officer with salt-and-pepper hair and narrow, brown lips looked at the general grimly through his bespectacled, cold eyes. The officer did not appear to be friendly. Farhad could tell it for sure from the way the fellow sized him up and ignored his polite greeting.

"Hello sir," Farhad repeated a little louder, thinking the officer had not heard him the first time.

Still no answer. Farhad sensed trouble in the air. Suddenly he lost his composure and fear overtook him. Blood rushed to his head, hammering forcefully at his temples and his heart raced ahead. *"No, the guy is not going to be cooperative,"* the general realized. There were two other passport control lines, but it was too late. Farhad was already standing at the first desk with others queuing behind him. He handed his passport to the officer with great consternation.

The officer examined all the pages of the fake passport carefully. He then came across the $100 bill and held it up. The officer gazed at Farhad with squinted, pensive eyes. Shaking the bill at his face, he asked frigidly, "What's this money for?"

"Almighty God help me!" the general pleaded. *"The fellow does not like to be bribed."*

At that point there was nothing else for the general to do but to play his trump card. *"But, what if he doesn't buy the second scenario, either?"* Farhad thought with despair.

"Go on, tell me why have you put a $100 bill in your passport," he barked, as people in the queue looked on.

Farhad stammered docilely, "It . . . it's to pay the fine for my expired visa."

The skinny, ill-tempered Immigrations officer frowned at the general, adding more wrinkles to his forehead, and then squinted again. He looked extremely upset, *"probably insulted,"* Farhad thought, as he clasped his hands together tensely. He could not remember if he had ever felt so mortified and disgraced.

"Stand aside," the officer ordered acidly, as he carried on checking the passports of four passengers standing behind Farhad.

After a while he took the general's passport in his skinny hands again and went through its pages once more. Looking at Farhad forbiddingly, he shook his head and snapped at him, as Farhad slowly edged his way back to where he was standing before. "No, don't come back yet. Stay where you are!"

After stamping all the passengers' passports, he made a telephone call and talked with somebody for a while. Within ten minutes, a police officer arrived. The Immigrations officer handed the passport and the money to the police and pointed to Farhad. The officer approached him and said frigidly in Turkish, "Come with me."

A cold sweat covered the general's entire body and he felt stupefied, thinking, *"Now what, dear God?"*

Farhad thought of running away and getting lost among the airport crowd. The policeman, as if reading his mind, suddenly decided to grab his arm. Holding firmly to his sleeve, he dragged him along through a narrow, dimly lit corridor. At the end of the suffocating hallway, they reached the office of the airport police chief.

Besides being scared to death, Farhad was concerned about missing his flight. But what was the point in worrying about his flight when he was not sure whether he could free himself of the muddle that he had created. No, on second thought, the general did not agree that he was the instigator of that problem. *Yes, it was that damned host of his.* He believed that Javad had suggested the $100 bribing scheme on purpose, knowing quite well that it would not work. Whatever, he had to find a way to resolve the crisis. He had survived worse situations before and was not willing to give up hope yet.

The gray-uniformed policeman gave a brisk military salute to his superior, who was sitting like a blob behind a desk in a musty, windowless office. He then handed Farhad's passport and the money to the airport police chief, who, in turn, went through each page meticulously. Every time the latter looked at a page in the passport, he peered at the general with a pair of small, blue, piercing eyes and raised his bushy eyebrows.

The general felt a tremor of fear going up his legs, traversing his whole body. The minutes felt like hours as Farhad stood there helplessly. Then, suddenly, he felt enraged from within. *"All right,"* he imagined himself telling the officer. *"Do what you have to do and relieve me of this misery. If you have to deport me, do so. If not, take the bloody money and let me go!"*

The general hated the officer's intimidating glances and could not comprehend why he should stand there and suffer like a fool. During the Shah's time, this bureaucrat would have stood at attention in his presence. *"I'm the same respectful person,"* Farhad told him in his mind and then decided to pull himself together. He decided that he was not going to reveal any signs of remorse, nor fear. Thus he stood straight, holding his head up and sticking his chest out. The general knew that a scared or guilty look gave one's opponent power over his victim, while a confident appearance worked in one's favor. Farhad remembered reading a book which described positive and negative energy fields encircling people. Those with positive rays around them had more power than those with a negative energy field.

The square-framed officer sank deeper in his high-backed armchair, waved the policeman out of the room and beckoned Farhad to sit down in the metallic, gray visitors' chair.

Farhad sat there for a few minutes longer while the officer went on examining his passport. His reticent disposition drove the general mad and made him wonder what the next few minutes had in store for him.

The officer removed his wide, round-topped cap, raked his fingers through his fair, wiry hair and finally spoke in distinct English, "Why did you stay the extra two months in Istanbul after the expiration date of your visa?"

"Good question," the general told himself. *"What do I tell him now?"* Farhad racked his brain for an answer as the officer stared on.

"I was sick and could not leave." No!

"I was waiting to receive some money from Iran." No!

Farhad finally said, "I had to wait for a friend to arrive from Iran so we could go to the States together. Unfortunately, his arrival was delayed. So I decided not to wait any longer."

"Why? Were you scared to go alone?" the officer smirked.

The general retorted nonchalantly, "You might say so."

He laughed at Farhad's remark and carried on, "Do you know that the fine for overstaying that long is $50?"

His deep voice sounded like the most melodious tune to Farhad's ears! *$50!* He was not at all ready for such a nice surprise.

"Sir, no, I didn't know the exact sum of the fine, that's why I attached a $100 bill to my passport."

"I see," he said. "Unfortunately, I cannot change your $100 bill."

Farhad felt relieved that, contrary to his expectations, the airport police chief was not as harsh as the Immigrations officer.

"Here, sir, I have three $20 bills. Why don't you return my $100?" Farhad exhorted.

The officer returned the $100 bill and snatched the three twenties brusquely, stashing them in his drawer. It was obvious that the officer was not going to report Farhad's expired visa to the authorities. Nor was he going to hand the money to the Immigrations office.

"How about a receipt?" Farhad asked.

"You don't need one," the officer affirmed as he stamped the exit visa in his passport.

"Thank God," the general breathed. *"I'm off the hook!"*

It was exhilarating to think that he was no longer illegal and was about to formally immigrate to a non-dictatorial land of freedom. Farhad was happy that another problem was solved and that the danger of deportation to Iran was out of the way.

"Go . . . go," the police chief ordered.

The general was convinced that the officer had gained more than his week's salary that morning. He wondered why the guy had not even offered to return the $10 to him. But why did Farhad care? Wasn't he the same person who had been willing to pay $100 in the first place? Why should he fret over $10 in change now that he was free to go?

NO END TO TROUBLES

As the general sank back, relaxing in his seat in the aircraft and ready to have his breakfast, he rejoiced, thinking that his troubles were finally over. Farhad rubbed his hands together joyfully and thought that a glass of champagne before breakfast would feel heavenly! Besides, he needed to celebrate his freedom. The only problem he had now was not having his beloved wife sitting by his side.

An Iranian fellow occupying the seat next to Farhad introduced himself. "My name's Iraj Vakili."

"Glad to meet you. I'm Farhad Shirazi," the general replied, shaking hands with him.

Iraj Vakili looked at Farhad with arched eyebrows and said, "I hope you have a Swiss visa."

Iraj, who obviously had not recognized the general, took a sip from his soda and pressed, "Lots of Iranians take this trip without knowing that they need a visa for Switzerland."

The general declared ruefully, "I'm afraid that I'm one of those Iranians!"

"Oh, no!" he exclaimed. "The Swiss authorities will return you to Turkey. They're very strict and take no nonsense. I know of a person who was returned to Istanbul."

It was like somebody had poured a bucket of boiling water over Farhad's head. He felt disappointed and disgusted with his luck. There was no way Farhad could return to Turkey. Without having a Turkish visa, the Turkish airport police would definitely deport him to Iran.

Although the general was starving before hearing that awful news, he completely lost his appetite as well as his desire for the champagne. Anyway, what was there to celebrate now? He was definitely going to be deported. Farhad thought that he was not a lucky man. There was no end to his troubles. As soon as one problem was solved, a new one surfaced.

The man, noticing his sad demeanor, said sympathetically, "I'm sorry that I had to break the bad news to you."

"It's not your fault," Farhad responded and then asked, "But why do we need a Swiss visa? Aren't we going to go through the transit section of the airport?"

Farhad wondered why the PAN AM clerk had not mentioned anything about the Swiss visa when he had purchased the ticket. Then he concluded that even if he had, there would not have been enough time to apply for one. But he thought that if he had known, he might not have bought the ticket and would have waited.

Iraj Vakili interrupted the general's train of thought, "About the layover at Zurich airport . . ."

Farhad interrupted, "Yes, don't we have to go through transit in Zurich?"

"No sir, we have to get to a different terminal. This means that we have to clear Swiss Customs." Iraj then shook his head. "How come nobody told you when you bought the ticket, or when you were checking in? I'm sure that, unlike most Iranians, you speak good English."

Farhad did not answer. He was confused and felt very inadequate. He just sat there and prayed for a miracle. Switzerland was not the Middle East and people lived only by laws and regulations. There was no way he could solve this difficulty as he had the previous ones.

The general tried to look out of the window but, being winter, it was still dark at seven thirty in the morning. Instead, what he saw was his own sad reflection in the glass with his gray hair, protruding forehead and deep furrows between his eyebrows. He gave his reflection a sad smile, and asked himself, *"Will my agony ever end?*" Then he fell asleep and dreamt that he had been deported to Iran. In his dream, the revolutionary guards handcuffed him. One of them slapped the general and bellowed, "Liars . . . liars! Your wife and that old mother of hers said that you were dead. Now you're really going to die. And so are they."

Farhad begged them, "Oh, no . . . oh, no. Please leave them alone. It's not their fault. I'm the one to blame."

The general felt ashamed. He did not want the *pasdars* to think that his honorable wife and mother-in-law were liars. They were noble people. He was the one who was the real culprit. He found himself to be selfish, cowardly and weak. He remembered how he hid under his wife's *chador* the first night of his escape in Tehran. Then he consoled himself, thinking that if he had not, both Leyla and the driver would have been arrested and maybe put to death for helping a *criminal*. In reality, there had been times when he had not been afraid for his own life. Unfortunately, there were so many others involved with him. They would have all been hunted down and arrested.

The captain's voice on the loudspeaker saved Farhad from that horrible nightmare. He looked at his watch and realized that he had slept for a whole hour.

"I'm sorry," the captain said, "to disappoint those passengers who had the intentions of shopping at the Zurich duty-free shops. Because of bad weather conditions, our arrival in Zurich will be delayed by half an hour." The captain sounded very apologetic. "Our late arrival won't leave the passengers enough time to go through the passport control. The Zurich airport is very busy at this time of the year and there are long lines at the Immigration control desks. We have contacted the airport authorities and informed them of our problem. They are going to change the departure gate so that you can make your connection to Washington in time. So, ladies and gentlemen, you won't have to leave the transit section."

"What?" Farhad turned to Iraj in disbelief. "Am I dreaming?"

The captain went on after a brief pause, "We really apologize to those passengers who needed to buy Swiss watches or some good Swiss chocolates!"

"To hell with Swiss watches and chocolates!" Farhad exclaimed.

Iraj smiled at Farhad, "Lucky guy, God loves you!"

Indeed God loved him! How many times had He saved him from disastrous situations?

The general called the flight attendant and ordered a glass of champagne for Iraj and another one for himself.

Raising his glass, the general said, "Here's to You, dear God, and thanks!"

Iraj laughed, looking genuinely happy for his trip companion. "Miracles such as this don't happen very often."

"You bet they don't," Farhad affirmed.

The general leaned back comfortably in his seat, feeling like a *pasha*. Turning to his reflection in the window, he smiled at it triumphantly this time, *"Hey man, end of troubles! I'm free at last. Yes, free like a bird and on my way to America!"*

0619